"Fire!" Mageta called as he rose once more from the trenches, holding a launcher. The general discharged a war bolt that vanished into the milling crowd of the enemy. Barrin couldn't tell if anyone fell, but the infantry in the trenches began firing in a sporadic barrage. There was a serious shortage of launchers and war-bolts, but the fire was a light rain on a pile of sand. The Keldons were dissolving away under the attack. Barrin could see the League technicians loading the weapons modules of the mantises and crabs. For a moment the wizard hoped the enemy might break, but then warlords in fantastic armor forced their way to stand in front of the Keldon lines. Barrin could hear their shouts as they exhorted the warriors.

"Do you think victory and glory are free?" an armored giant of a man bellowed. "A great people are known by the strength of their enemies! Kill for the glory of Keld! The final days are upon us! Kill the thieves, kill them . . ."

EXPERIENCE THE MAGIC™

ARTIFACTS CYCLE

The Brothers' War
Jeff Grubb
Planeswalker
Lynn Abby
Time Streams
J. Robert King
Bloodlines
Loren Coleman

INVASION CYCLE

The Thran (A Prequel)
J. Robert King
Invasion
J. Robert King
Planeshift
J. Robert King
Apocalypse
J. Robert King

ODYSSEY CYCLE

Odyssey
Vance Moore
Chainer's Torment
Scott McGough
Judgment
Will McDermott

ANTHOLOGIES

Rath and Storm
The Colors of Magic
The Myths of Magic
The Dragons of Magic
The Secrets of Magic

PROPHECY

MASQUERADE CYCLE • BOOK III

Vance Moore

PROPHECY

Masquerade Cycle

Distributed in the United States by Holtzbrinck Publishing. Distributed in Canada by Fenn Ltd.

Distributed to the hobby, toy, and comic trade in the United States and Canada by regional distributors.

Distributed worldwide by Wizards of the Coast, Inc. and regional distributors.

Printed in the U.S.A.

Cover art by Brom and R.K. Post
First Printing: June 2000
Library of Congress Catalog Card Number: 99-69352

9 8 7 6 5 4 3 2

US ISBN: 0-7869-1570-6
620-21570-001-EN

U.S., CANADA,
ASIA, PACIFIC, & LATIN AMERICA
Wizards of the Coast, Inc.
P.O. Box 707
Renton, WA 98057-0707
+1-800-324-6496

EUROPEAN HEADQUARTERS
Wizards of the Coast, Belgium
T Hofveld 6d
1702 Groot-Bijgaarden
Belgium
+322 467 3360

Visit our web site at **www.wizards.com**

Dedication

For Mother,
who never stopped pushing me to realize my dreams.

Acknowledgement

I would like to acknowledge the Tillamook Air Museum, my family for their care and support, and my editor for his suggestions which made this a better book.

CHAPTER 1

"Where in the nine hells is everyone?" Haddad muttered as the small group of men and wagons tramped through the night. "Are we lost again?" His feet disturbed a mound of stones collected at the bottom of the crumbling hillside.

The land seemed dead. Successive seasons of cold and heat had shattered rock and piled scree everywhere. The road was deep and cut wide, but the rock faces sloughed debris every day and covered the road or ate at its base. It was too cold for insects, and the column of marching men cut sharp shadows in the moonlight. Within hours the sun would rise and sear everything. It was a land of no good seasons.

"Quiet, Haddad!" Natal murmured. "I'm sure the sergeant knows where he's going." Natal stamped his feet to warm them in the night air. "Anyway, the last thing he wants to hear is you."

Both men were soldiers in the Jamuraan Kipamu League of Armies. The League had been named after Lord Kipamu, a legendary figure who was credited with many important military victories on the old-time frontiers of Jamuraa. Dead for centuries, if not millennia, the lord's name still commanded respect all over the continent.

Haddad nodded and shivered as he hugged his coat more tightly. He was wearing most of the clothing he owned. Haddad tried to tuck his hands into his sleeves but flailed his arms for balance on the uncertain footing. The noise of others stumbling over rock was overpowered by the sound of the wagon wheels crunching and sliding over the broken roadway. Sergeant Atul signaled a halt, and Haddad relayed the order down the line.

The chill breeze heralding the dawn cut through the men. None of the soldiers spoke, though chattering teeth sounded. Many moved closer to the wagons, holding their hands against the warm sides of the oxen. Natal edged closer to the animals, and Haddad shifted to give his comrade room. The friends were several yards away from Sergeant Atul as he conferred with the more experienced soldiers. False dawn began to reveal details of the landscape.

"I wonder if they know where we are?" Haddad questioned again. The sergeant's ears were sharper than anyone had suspected.

"You two quiet down. Check the oxen and wagons now." Sergeant Atul spoke with no perceptible malice, but the pair instantly started inspecting the condition of the draft beasts and the wagons. Haddad and Natal split and went down opposite sides of the line, checking the cargo and the beasts. They peered uncertainly into the dim light, hoping no problems would be found.

The sergeant continued to converse with the other veteran soldiers. Bad luck and poor communications had delayed the unit's departure far longer than anyone planned. Unsure of the road, the technical unit had set out into the wilderness. The combat troops were far ahead, and most of the unit wondered if they could find them.

The Kipamu League's punitive strike had left at its best speed in response to rumors of a Keldon raiding party. The barbarians were supposedly encamped only miles away, resting their beasts before returning to their base across the desolate plain. The Keldons were warriors and slave takers. They had swept over the world in ages past, though it had been decades since any League city had suffered a serious attack. Now the Keldons were once again raiding Jamuraa, and the League was eager to test its strength. Friendly forces had failed to catch the raiders during the past three incursions. The lack of success against raiders was a source of embarrassment to the army and the League leaders. Some civilians said that the army was scared to attack figures from childhood nightmares. The news that a target might still be within striking distance of the Kipamu barrack provoked an immediate response. A force of war machines and mounted infantry was dispatched. The mechanical forces were steel ants, the weakest and most common element in the Kipamu arsenal. However, the high speed of the waist-high metal insectoids made them the quickest force the army could field. Besides, the commanders said the low quality of their foes presented no real challenge to the League, just Keldon trash raiding small farms.

Haddad wondered if bravado ruled the army now. Seeking to crush their own fears, the combat troops had raced out into the field. The need for speed left the support troops exposed and without escort as they followed, chivvying their plodding oxen into the cold darkness. The support troopers carried supplies and maintenance equipment, but as noncombat troops they had none of the rashness burning in the commanders who raced to fight. The veterans looked for machines or cavalry for protection, but they found none. Sergeant Atul had said if he had a choice between shivering naked with a proper column of security or maintaining the current situation, he would risk frostbite.

"Natal!" Atul called, "come here."

Haddad followed his friend forward as the sergeant sent two veterans to the rear of the column. Haddad noticed each of them looked more calm and ready than he felt. Perhaps it was only his youth making him so nervous. Things couldn't be as bad as he feared. Haddad slung his launcher off his shoulder where he usually carried it. The sling was too short to quickly shrug off, and whenever he was nervous he carried it ready to fire.

The sergeant looked at the friends but did not comment on Haddad trailing along. There were several other men gathered around, looking like they were awaiting orders.

"Natal, you and Corporal Vanosh will advance ahead of the group until you find the combat troops or some sign of the enemy. If you catch the rear guard, ask for a security detail to return with you. If you find the enemy, fall back to here. Natal, you're on point. Advance rapidly but with care. Vanosh, trail Natal at a distance, and if necessary, fall back with news." The sergeant looked into Natal's face and looked satisfied at the young man's expression of determination and anxiety. "Just remember that returning with information is more important than being a hero. What are you carrying?" Atul gestured to the launcher Natal was carrying.

"Web round, Sergeant." Many men carried heavy weapons in addition to their military short swords, leaving their shields on the wagons. These wilderness lands were said to hold the parea, giant carnivorous birds that commonly attacked men. The birds were land bound but swifter than horses, which they could chase down and dismember. The launcher Natal carried had originally been developed to allow infantry to stand off lesser war machines. The web round would ensnare a steel ant and could stop a charging bird with ease, especially with the wide arc a web round covered.

"Haddad, what are you carrying?" Sergeant Atul looked pensive and fingered the hilt of his sword unconsciously.

"War rocket, Sergeant," Haddad replied. The rocket could cripple medium machines if used with skill and reflected Haddad's confidence in his marksmanship.

"Switch with Natal." Haddad slowly handed over his weapon and accepted Natal's. His friend looked even more apprehensive as he exchanged weapons. The sergeant waved Natal and the corporal forward and then turned around. Atul looked at the wagons stacked with parts for machines that might need repair after the Keldon raiders were defeated.

"Haddad, I want you to find reloads for the men with launchers and tell the drivers to keep their personal weapons ready for dismount. We'll pull out in five minutes." The sergeant pulled a sack of wine from his belt and took a shallow draft before handing it to Haddad. The wine tasted terrible but still cut through the cold dust coating Haddad's tongue.

Natal and the corporal disappeared from sight as he handed back the wine. Haddad wondered what else might be lurking ahead.

"Natal hasn't trained much with rockets, Sergeant." Fear and concern for his friend made him talkative.

"Natal's purpose is to find the combat troops or warn us of the enemy. If he has to fire he is most likely going to die. With the rocket he will at least die loudly and warn the rest of us," Atul said without looking at Haddad. "Find the reloads," he continued, "I'll speak to the drivers myself."

Haddad turned numbly as he watched Atul speaking to the drivers. The wind was cold, but Atul's words were colder. Natal might die, and Atul only wanted it to be noisy—a few minutes' warning at best. Haddad started back to check the wagons as Atul instructed. He wondered what his own life was worth in the sergeant's estimation. The column advanced once again. Haddad went quickly from wagon to wagon, quizzing the drivers and searching the cargo for heavy-weapon reloads. He found none.

The machines making up the strike force were the lightest in the League arsenal. The commanders had not loaded the ants' direct fire weapons. The League was still largely made up of mercenaries from the city wars ended only a few years before. Each city of the League had seen to its own defense and conducted small, stylized wars with other cities over resources, trade, or even honor. The wars depended heavily on paid mercenaries who fought according to a code of strictly limited warfare. Damaged machines and dead men were viewed as too costly. Heavy weapons were rarely used due to their fairly substantial costs, the damage they did to enemies who might be future allies, and the destruction of loot on the battlefield. Heavy weapons such as war rockets, toxic web rounds, and penetrating bolts were rarely used without desperation on the part of opposing forces. The current League commander did not consider a battle with the Keldon raiders as desperate. There were no reloads to be found in the wagons, just logistical supplies for infantry and modular repair parts for the steel ants.

Natal and Corporal Vanosh returned as Haddad looked through the last wagon; it had taken longer than he planned due to the poor light. The sun finished rising over the hillside as he hurried forward to report to the sergeant. He arrived in time to hear Corporal Vanosh speak.

"We found the rear guard, Sergeant. It's about forty minutes ahead with these oxen. The main attack has already commenced. The officer in charge said to advance with best speed to the main party. He was staying there to pull down stragglers fleeing the fight. He couldn't guarantee we wouldn't see warriors that eluded him. We observed three Keldon outliers pulled down before we hurried back here." Vanosh was calm as he spoke, but Natal was flushed and looked slightly nauseated.

The sergeant was silent and only turned to Haddad for his report.

"No reloads for personal launchers, Sergeant. I did find a few light crossbow bolts," Haddad stated. Sergeant Atul took only a few seconds to finish thinking.

"All wagons will advance at maximum speed. Keep your eyes open for Keldons trying to escape. If a large group is spotted, be prepared to stop and get into fighting formation. Spread it down the line," Atul ordered, and he waved the unit forward as Vanosh went back to spread the word. Haddad and Natal came together as the unit advanced at best speed.

"What did you see?" Haddad asked quietly.

"We walked maybe thirty minutes before we found the rear guard. Vanosh trailed me far enough back that I couldn't see him most of the time. Besides, he ordered me not to look back. I almost wept with joy when we finally spotted our forces." Natal paused and continued in a more controlled tone. "Vanosh hurried up, and we reported. When the first Keldon got pulled down, I thought I'd vomit. I've never seen a man killed by a steel ant before." Natal was too young to remember even the stylized fighting the League had practiced as unification occurred. "The Keldon was mounted on a camel and trying to circle around the force when he was spotted. The commander of the detachment sent out a pair of ants to stop him. They ran down the camel in seconds. The Keldon tried to run up the side of a hill, but it was unstable, and he made little headway." Natal became lost in remembrance of the scene and spoke more intently. "The ants rushed up with their legs churning out a stream of soil and small rocks. One of them pulled down the camel by shearing off a leg. The camel fell instantly, and the ant was at its neck as soon as it hit the ground. The Keldon kicked out of the saddle in time, and he was on his feet when the second ant hit him. He was trying to draw a sword, and you could see the ant take the arm off. He screamed and threw himself down the slope. The ant followed and caught him before he fell very far. It stabbed him with its legs and started dismembering him before they stopped sliding. You could see parts separating as they were ripped off. I never want to see anything like that again." Natal was shaking as he finished.

"It looks like any future fighting is going to be against the Keldons, Natal. The age of machines fighting machines has ended. The enemy is men only now. More of the fighting is going to be men against men. The Keldons raid too widely, and there are only so many machines." Haddad echoed the words of the pessimistic veterans. "You chose better than you knew when you went into the technical service. The infantry and cavalry are going to be fighting in the field, not sitting in garrison. When the real battles begin, we'll be in camp most of the time." His words were not those of a hero, but the earlier mercenary view of combat still was prevalent in the army. Combat was something you prepared for, but fighting was too dangerous and expensive to be eagerly sought. New recruits and new battles were changing the military, and Haddad knew he would be increasingly out of step with the mutable army.

"Hey, Haddad," Natal called, jarring his friend from his thoughts. "We've arrived."

The bodies of Keldons slain by the rear guard were clearly visible on the sides of the hills. Haddad thought there were less than ten killed, but it was hard to be sure. The Keldons had been dismembered and scattered by steel ants, and he closed his eyes several times as he tried to get an accurate count. Sergeant Atul motioned the wagons to stay put, and he collected an advance party. The column was surrounded by rises just steep enough to block the men's sight and limit mobility. Haddad could see the trail of disturbance the League assault forces left as they scrambled over the loose ground. He could hear what might be combat in the distance. It sounded as if there was fighting over the short rise before them. But noise could carry a long distance, and Sergeant Atul wanted a look before advancing blindly. Everyone climbed very slowly up the slope.

The sergeant crouched as he reached the crest, and the others did as well. The scene before them was so unexpected that they looked for several seconds in confusion. Slowly they began to realise what had happened. The

League assault forces, so confidently thrown against the foe, had been defeated.

The steel ants, so deadly under Natal's eyes, were scattered pieces, dismembered as crudely and sloppily as the Keldons Haddad had tried to count minutes before.

Still stunned, Haddad voiced his first thought, "We'll never fix everything with what we brought."

Natal nodded dumbly as Corporal Vanosh crabbed quickly over and whispered in Haddad's ear. "Shut your mouth, or I'll open your throat." The corporal had a knife in his hand, and Haddad realized the stupidity of saying anything aloud.

Soldiers picked over the battlefield, and Haddad realized he was seeing the enemy for the first time. From this distance, and with the sun behind them, it was difficult to make out details. The soldiers seemed very large compared to the League bodies scattered over the field, but perhaps the dead looked smaller when compared to the living. The figures were odd in proportions, and he could hear their voices, deep and guttural as they turned over and searched the pockets and wallets of the dead. Haddad grasped his launcher more tightly and wished he had the longer ranged war rocket load instead of Natal's web round. He looked to the sergeant for orders, but Atul stared beyond the debris below and farther on. Haddad followed Atul's gaze and saw the raiders' camp. Even from this distance, he could see League prisoners gathered under Keldon guard. There were huge machines of some type and only a few men with mounts of horses or camels. There were far fewer men than Haddad would have thought possible to overcome the League men and machines. Atul motioned everyone to withdraw. They slid down the slope, each trying to be silent and cringing at the odd word or oxen low from the supply group.

The sergeant whispered instructions even as Corporal Vanosh raced back up the line of wagons to start the retreat.

"The Keldons must be out looking for other League forces—there are just too few otherwise." He turned and addressed Haddad and Natal. "When we withdraw you two will keep your attention to the rear. Be prepared to sound the alarm, but stay quiet unless you clearly spot the enemy and he spots you. No unnecessary noise." Sergeant Atul gestured emphatically even as his voice remained at a whisper. But even as he attempted to salvage the situation, a loud cry of alarm sounded up the line.

"Raiders, Sergeant!" The corporal was coming back from the rear at a run. Drivers were on the ground and preparing for battle.

Sergeant Atul cursed. "Come on men! We'll see them off!" He grabbed two drivers. "Get water bags and blankets," he whispered. "We'll run if we can." The drivers dived into the rear of the wagons and began slinging out water bottles for after the fight. Haddad and Natal followed Atul as he reached the last wagon. They followed someone who knew what he was doing even as they left one point of the column exposed to attack. The corporal was up in a driver's seat, moving the wagon to the side to start a wall. One other driver was also moving his team, but the Keldons were advancing, a troop on camels closing fast.

The attackers seemed giants as they deployed. Each was larger than anyone in Haddad's company, and their heavy armor and decorations made them larger still. At this close range, the Keldons were even more fearsome looking, and their skin was ashen and faded. Each was yelling, and the sound seemed loud enough for thousands instead of the company that Haddad saw. Haddad's heart pounded, and he was short of breath as he neared the back of the column. He wanted to run, and determined not to be a coward, he ran toward the enemy. Each step brought the Keldons closer, and each Keldon shout made him more afraid. The mounted warriors brandished swords and axes, and now their shouts were one voice, battering at his morale and the morale of the supply column.

"Shoot when you can," Atul cried as he grabbed a shield from the back of a wagon. The League soldiers formed into clumps, and swords sprouted like weeds as each man cursed his luck. Natal danced around an ox and looked for a target. His launcher rose to his shoulder, and he fired the war rocket Haddad had given him.

It flew in a flat arc and hit the shoulder of a camel. The rocket's charge shattered the animal's side and removed the gray-skinned raider's leg in a bright flash. Haddad could hear the sudden amputee cursing as he and the camel separated, breaking up the Keldon line. As if Natal had ordered it, men with launchers let loose other rockets and darts. The Keldon charge was a mass of screaming animals and men, but the warriors swung wide and up the slopes on either side of the wagons. The deaths disrupted the Keldon battle cries, but every warrior was roaring. The League soldiers sent up a few cries of their own, but fear rather than rage sounded from the men around the wagons. Haddad and a few others had not fired, the web rounds being point-blank weapons. The enemy jockeyed for position to sweep down over the League. Many Keldons dismounted and gripped axes and shields. Behind Haddad, on the other side of the wagons, he could hear shouts. He glanced over his shoulder and saw the biggest of the raiders calling and signaling. This Keldon must have been near seven feet tall, cursing and yelling in a pall of smoke. Haddad barely had time to wonder where the fire was when the split Keldon forces descended upon the column.

Haddad spun on the nearest Keldon raider and fired his launcher. The round webbed the rider to his camel. Haddad could hear curses that rose to a shout as the camel went down heavily, whipping the rider into the ground. Gear shot off the body, and the Keldon's helmet skipped down the slope, finally hitting a wagon. The struggling animal and its attached corpse slid down the gentle slope to snare another Keldon mount. The rider of the second animal jumped free in time to avoid being trapped. The now standing Keldon wasted no time. He ran at Haddad, screaming a war cry, a long sword in his left hand. Haddad threw the launcher at the man hard. The raider batted it away but stumbled in mid-charge. Haddad drew his short sword, knowing the warrior would bowl him over.

Then Natal stepped forward, and Haddad remembered he wasn't alone in this fight. His friend picked up a shield and tried to push the Keldon away. The barbarian overtopped Natal by at least a foot and was in full armor, spikes, and studs of metal. The taller warrior swung his sword up and hammered it down. The blade screamed as it tore through Natal's metal shield and sank deep into his torso. His eyes rolled and blood flowed from his mouth as he tried to speak. The Keldon's blow had been too powerful, and his blade was now stuck inside Haddad's friend.

The Keldon swore as he tried to haul his blade free from Natal, his eyes wild and inhuman against the ashy skin. Haddad swung his sword at that face, committing everything to this one strike. His blade rang as it hit an armored shoulder and then skidded under the rim of the man's helmet, sinking into his neck. Even mortally wounded by the blow, the Keldon turned and struck Haddad with a gauntleted fist, the studs tearing a line of agony across the League soldier's scalp, right over the eyes. Blood poured down, and the pain and shock took him off his feet. Haddad could still hear the cries of other soldiers around him as he worked the blade free of the Keldon's neck and tried vainly to clear his eyes, to rejoin the battle. He pushed himself off the bodies of his friend and his friend's killer. The shouts of his comrades were falling silent as he struggled to stand.

The Keldons held the field, and the fighting revolved around one wagon, squatting under the heavy load of supplies it carried. The oxen lay dead in their traces. Atul's voice was falsetto against the cries of the Keldons as he and a few others fought on. Spears licked out from under the wagon as the last League soldiers fought like animals trapped in a den. The Keldons laughed now and threw rocks under the wagon. Another gray warrior cut heads from corpses and hurled them at the trapped defenders.

Haddad saw it all as if very far away as he picked up a shield and carefully pulled a sword free from a dead Keldon's back. He staggered into a charge at a Keldon who ignored him as unworthy sport. The discharge of the launcher must have been accidental, Haddad later decided. Or perhaps Atul had decided better to kill oneself than be dug out like a rat. The charge thumped into the bottom of the overloaded wagon and ignited hidden rockets buried there.

Accidentally or on purpose, the blast killed the defenders, and Haddad was knocked spinning as a piece of someone smacked into his shield. The Keldons close to the wagon screamed in rage at their injuries and at being robbed of their victory. Supplies that had been hurled into the air from the blast soon fell, mostly striking the wounded gasping on the ground. Haddad swayed drunkenly, turning to face the largest group of Keldons. He hoped to die fighting, but his eyes wouldn't focus, and he saw only blurs and shadows. A hand swept his helmet off, and then there was only pain and darkness as he fell.

CHAPTER 2

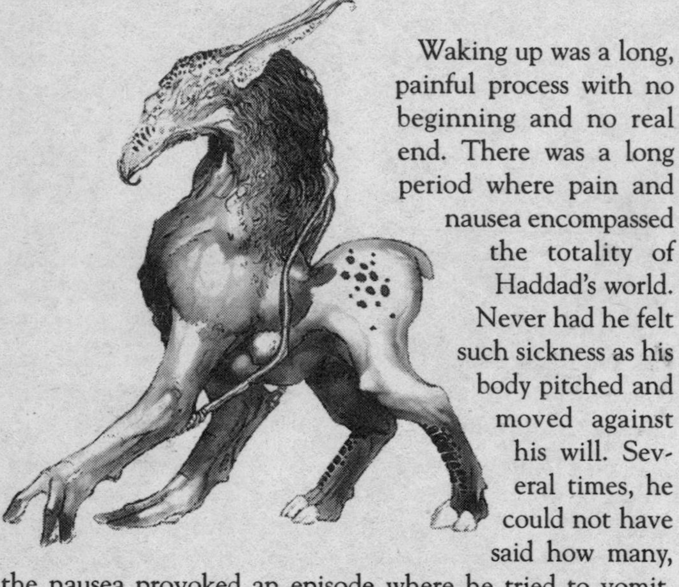

Waking up was a long, painful process with no beginning and no real end. There was a long period where pain and nausea encompassed the totality of Haddad's world. Never had he felt such sickness as his body pitched and moved against his will. Several times, he could not have said how many, the nausea provoked an episode where he tried to vomit. Haddad never did, but each bout wiped out any progress he made toward reaching normalcy, and pain blotted out his sense of time. Finally he mastered his illness and tried to call for help. His eyes were gummy, and his mouth and throat were dry. It was only after he was sitting up and looking at the moving landscape that he remembered the Keldon attack, the moment he went down. Commands in voices he had never heard brought him fully into the present.

"Slave, that one is too ill for the purpose. Find another to use." The voice was gravelly but quiet and with a feminine tone. The voice spoke in Haddad's native tongue, but the words sounded foreign, as if whoever was speaking them hadn't known the language for very long. He turned his head slowly to see the speaker. It was a Keldon, but this one was different from the warriors he had seen charging the line. She was a woman, six feet tall and dressed in dyed leathers. The red and orange tones were bright and jarring to his eyes. Her features were coarse, and her gray skin was wet ash in the shadows of the vehicle. She turned and looked at him with eyes rimmed with kohl. A hand shoved his head, and his vision clouded at the fresh pain. The cursing he heard became shouts of anger behind him. A struggle was occurring, and he turned to see what was happening. He found a man of his own nation crouched by him. The poor state of his clothes and the resignation in his body were obvious even to Haddad's still blurry vision. This was a man who had been with the Keldons far longer than Haddad cared to imagine.

"Don't look at them directly, boy," the man said as he looked off to the left of Haddad's face. Haddad tried to see what was happening as the sounds of struggle died down. The brightly clad woman was standing in front of a League officer restrained by two men. His mouth was bleeding, and he bared his teeth in challenge. The Keldon smashed his face with her gloves, which were heavy and studded. He fell to his knees, and the two men kept his head bowed as he began cursing in broken, incoherent mutterings.

"He challenged her with his eyes. Never meet their eyes.

Now she'll make him suffer." All this was delivered by the crouching man in a low voice that Haddad strained to hear as he looked around.

He must be in one of the large vehicles he had seen on the battlefield, Haddad thought. He was on a long deck that stretched maybe sixty feet from end to end. One side of the vehicle opened to the outside through several large doors, which allowed light inside. The landscape flowed by at a fair clip, and Haddad realized motion sickness contributed to his nausea. The vehicle he was in was packed with League prisoners. The captives were lying down, and only a few were not obviously injured or dazed. There was only a small group of what must be Keldon servants—all raggedly dressed men. They seemed rather stoic at the Keldon victory, and Haddad wondered what their status really was. Loud horns sounded outside the vehicle, and Haddad felt a moment of hope as he imagined it signaling the arrival of League forces.

"Hold his hand still," the alien woman said. Both servants rammed the officer's hand to the deck, and Haddad wanted to protest, but he couldn't drag a single sound from his parched throat. The woman drew back her metal-shod stave and then slammed it down on the man's fingers. The officer inhaled to scream, and he reared his head up, staring into her eyes. Before he could voice his pain, the stave rose and crushed his other hand. He did not scream but seemed to dissolve into the wooden deck. When the woman spoke she didn't even sound angry.

"Over the side with him." She gestured to an opening, and the body was flung clear. "Walking speed and a wide circle," she called, and the command was relayed by others, presumably carrying it to the driver of the craft. The passage of landscape slowed, and Haddad became more aware of the craft's curious gait. He could see other vehicles moving into his line of sight as the craft began to turn. The image that sprang to mind was of hermit crabs using toy boats as shells. The vehicles were overturned hulls in shape with wide doors and windows showing. He could see the gray faces of Keldons, in contrast with the captives, looking out. The land vehicles were balanced on dozens of legs, and the rhythmical sight of them made his motion sickness worse as the female Keldon spoke.

"I am Latulla, and you will obey," she said loudly but without any particular emphasis. "I will not be questioned or challenged. All other Keldons will receive the same obedience and respect, or you will be punished." Haddad watched other men being thrown from what he decided to call land barges. Some were limp and did not rise. Others got up and started collecting themselves.

"Some of you might be thinking of escape. Try and you will be punished, as I punished the slave without respect. Even if you should succeed, you will only find death." As she finished, Haddad could see groups of something breaking into the large circle of moving land barges. The timing was too perfect, and he realized he was seeing a planned performance and not some impromptu expression of rage or cruelty. This was carefully staged, and only his weakness and passivity had saved him from a similar fate.

The land birds of the wastes were now only a legend in the civilized cities of the League where Haddad had grown up. They had been relegated to the status of monsters of fairy tales, spoken of only to scare children. But in the wilds of the east, they were the primary danger faced by League patrols before the Keldons began raiding. They hunted in pairs or small groups, and their presence in a district meant panic. All that Haddad knew of the parea, called the running death by some, flowed through his mind. Then the beasts spread out and fell onto the men stumbling on the ground.

The birds overtook their victims, and when they reached the running men, they knocked them down with what appeared playful nudges of their beaks. Full-grown men fell and tumbled head over heels as a result of those love taps. Other birds snapped at flailing limbs and dismembered men as neatly and quickly as slaughtered chickens in the mess hall. More parea darted in, and Haddad wondered where they had all come from. At more than five hundred pounds apiece, the surrounding landscape couldn't support many of the vicious birds. He coughed and spit several times before he could make a sound.

"It's like a flock of sparrows hunting a field," Haddad said. The juxtaposition of that homey memory against the hellish scene was grotesque. "Where are they all coming from?" He was talking to himself, but the crouching slave—that was what he must be—answered him.

"Every trip they dispose of the troublemakers or the dead here. The parea can sprint past a galloping horse and run for hours. They come from miles around whenever the Keldons enter the wastes. Latulla takes advantage of the birds' hunger to shatter the spirits of the captives. I'd curse them all if I didn't know I'd end up out there."

The birds that straggled in found no moving prey and fell upon the bodies of the League officers and slaves. The unconscious victims mercifully died without seeing their devourers. The birds leaped and tore in a territorial display to keep other gorging birds away. Keldon warriors handled barbed lances to drive away birds that might come too near the barges. Another round of horns sounded.

"The lesson is over. Let it never be forgotten," Latulla

intoned. Haddad knew he would always remember and swore vengeance, but he swore it silently and with eyes cast down in apparent submission.

"Into traveling column and trail speed," she called and was once again echoed to wherever the control or helm was located. The barge straightened out, and Haddad's last view of the bloody scene was of the parea snatching meat from each other's kills.

* * * * *

Haddad sat morosely against the cavern wall, idly turning his mess kit in his hands as he dreamed of the next meal. The cave was shallow and dry, the wind blowing continuously into its mouth. One of many against a granite cliffside, it was stuffed with League soldiers and civilians captured by raiders.

How long had he been in captivity, Haddad wondered. Like his distant slave ancestors, Haddad was cut off from time. Each day was the same. It started with sunrise and stopped with sunset. Haddad wondered how his forebears dealt with the total lack of control. He had no idea what would happen to him or when things might change.

Latulla's barges had stopped within hours of the parea feeding. Haddad had stepped into a desolate valley ringed by sloping cliffs. The area served as a central collection and training point for the Keldons. Each load of humanity was dumped into this sewer and into slavery. The task of the overseers was to instruct new servants in the Keldon language. The turnover among prisoners and their teachers was constant. Haddad was sure it was to prevent escapes. It was impossible to plan anything or trust anyone as people appeared and disappeared without apparent reason. There was only one constant—the distribution of the food. A slave might have many instructors and sleep in many caves, but only one person would issue a captive's rations. The chit that Haddad carried continually locked in his fist was the only source of food besides the weeds growing in the arid soil. Twice a day he reported for food and spoke a few words of Keldon. If he showed no improvement in speaking, he received nothing. Some slaves starved to death as the world looked on—either for failure to learn or because they irritated the distributor of the food. Haddad had tried sharing rations, but the desperate stole what they could, and soon everyone bolted their food as soon as possible to avoid theft.

Goblins, elves, and League soldiers were all thrown together, locked in a desperate struggle to learn their captors' language. Each day was the same as bewildered captives arrived and apathetic slaves left. Haddad wondered if all of Jamuraa would be swallowed by similar camps.

"Food call," came a voice from outside the cave.

The issue of rations motivated all the captives, and they rushed out of the caves where they talked with Keldon-speaking slaves. Piles of food were set up, and Haddad hurried to get into the nearest line.

"I am very hungry, and I need food so I might serve Keld," Haddad said as he reached the head of the line. The slave passing out the food nodded and handed him bread.

"You have learned very quickly," the man said, "but continue to concentrate on speaking clearly." Haddad thought the threat of starvation centered the mind more surely than the slave's compliment. He retreated higher up and squatted to eat his ration. Most of the camp was congregated around the food, and guards moved in to keep order. Haddad could see a clump of new prisoners nearing the head of the line. The last load of captives had come from the south and brought lizard men and goblins to the camp. They were not yet broken by the turnover inside the prison. They still had their identities.

The roar of the lizard men as they fell on the guards shocked the camp. Warriors began to retreat as more and more prisoners joined in the rush. Keldons rushed from throughout the camp as the captives turned on the captors. Spear tips tore into the prisoners, but like a stampede, the pressure of the ones behind pushed the dying forward, tangling weapons.

"Come on!" cried an elf, and he began running toward the camp corrals. "We'll steal mounts and be gone before the bastards can put down the riot."

Haddad followed. The corrals held a few mounts for scouts and were at the mouth of the valley. A slim chance is enough in this hell, he thought as he ran for the horses. A few other prisoners fell in behind him, but most of the population was converging on the clumps of embattled guards. The corrals grew closer and closer. Then the elf leading the run slowed, and Haddad crashed into him, both prisoners spilling to the ground. Haddad cursed his bleeding scrapes as he started to help his companion rise. The elf only shuddered, blood pouring from the arrow wound in his chest. Guards stood in front of the corrals, one with a bow in hand. The archer and his companions must have come from the feed sheds to the side of the corral. Haddad watched him pick off one of the prisoners who stumbled to a halt as the Keldon guards unsheathed their swords.

Haddad turned and slowly walked away. He headed up toward the caves. If the riot pulled more warriors away from their stations, a guard post might be abandoned at the top of the cliffs. But even as Haddad walked the back slope, he could see the attack dying down. The fighting retreat of the

Keldons stopped with the guards pinned back against the sheds. The buildings stored gear for the raiding parties. Suddenly new figures entered the fight. Axes and swords cut through walls to fall upon prisoners. The new defenders were red, and the riot began dying, literally. Swords sheared men into pieces, and instead of the new fighters being buried under bodies, they mounted piles of corpses. Crazed captives lost their footing on the blood-soaked ground. Insane charges momentarily hid the scarlet fighters, but steel cleared away the curtain of flesh to reveal them anew. Now the prisoners broke and ran for the caves. The guards paused to bind up their wounds, and their allies all stopped.

Like machines, Haddad thought, and then the fleeing tide of captives was upon him. He ran toward the cliff side with the rest. The riot had failed, and who knew what the Keldons would do. Haddad moved into the cave and crawled onto a high ledge right by the entrance. More people poured in, and Haddad wondered if some might die of the crush in the back. Finally, the stream of people stopped. Haddad slowly got down and looked out the entrance. Keldon warriors were spreading out as land barges came from outside the camp. Guards began clearing out the caves and herding prisoners into the waiting transportation. The few supervising slaves that had been caught up in the riot called out.

"What's happening? We're innocent!" The language teachers were lost among the rioters. Haddad wondered if they would share the fate of their rebellious students.

"The camp is being cleared out to the main colony," a guard called back, blood clotting on his armor.

Everything was being loaded aboard the barges, Haddad realized. As if the bloody riot had been a graduation ceremony, the Keldons were shipping the prisoners onward.

Haddad stepped out of the cave, wondering if it was all a trap, if the guards were lulling them forward to take their vengeance. But their blows were no different from their usual brutality, and Haddad stumbled forward with a ringing head and the hope that he was headed somewhere better.

CHAPTER 3

Haddad slipped in and out of consciousness. The rocking movement of the land barge became hypnotic in its lulling power. The guards had distributed food and water only minutes after the prisoners boarded. Most were still in shock after the riot and had to be forced to eat and drink. Haddad tried to have as little as possible, not trusting such kindness after so many died. However, the barge slaves were old hands in a game Haddad was just learning, and they forced food down his throat.

The provisions must have contained some sort of sedative, for Haddad sat and dozed dumbly. By the time he was more aware, the main Keldon camp was appearing on the horizon. The convoy had traveled through the night and swung toward the coast. Haddad looked down to the sea and saw a large town, not a temporary camp. There were docks and piers stretching out into a bay. There were large ships waiting in the sheltered waters for a chance to unload. Small boats and rafts were also moored there, and sacks of cargo were being unloaded.

The heavy beat of a pile driver dragged his eyes to the construction of a new pier and warehouses. The Keldons were here to stay, the construction said. The town was much more incomplete. There were houses and what appeared to be workshops, but tents and small campsites spread in all directions. Systems of pens and feed yards put out an odor that fought with the smell of a working port. The convoy turned and headed into town. As they advanced, land barges peeled off to stop at campsites. Haddad could hear shouts from the front as a path was cleared. The slaves working outside spared only quick glances at the prisoners as they continued their tasks. Each slave slumped a little more as the convoy advanced at a walk.

"A full load of slaves for construction and mining!" bellowed a Keldon crewmember to the warriors outside. "Their army fell, and we raid their villages at our leisure! We're back because we could carry no more!"

Envy and jealousy colored the angry muttering outside, and Haddad memorized the rude gestures directed at the boastful warrior. The barge captain walked down to talk to Latulla in a forward compartment. He grunted at the shouting crewman to shut him up. The cuff as he passed was firm but not injurious, just a reminder there was work to be done and discipline to be enforced. Latulla left her compartment before the captain could reach it. Her clothes were visibly finer in quality. She was clad in leathers and fabrics of dark red and purple with fur trimming. Haddad smothered a laugh. Her color scheme reminded him of his favorite clown from childhood, but as she watched the slaves and hammered the deck with her cane, Haddad no longer found her humorous.

"Ready the slaves for processing, Captain." Behind her, servants were carrying out her possessions. "Save this one for me."

Haddad cried out in pain. Latulla's cane hit him before he even noticed her arm move. His face seemed to shatter as the flesh screamed in pain.

"I've marked him for you. Bring him to my house when you're finished here." Haddad could barely see, but her colors stood out against the bleak background, and he watched her exit the craft.

Haddad lay on his side, his face burning. Even the Keldons seemed to pity him, though it may have been a pain-inspired delusion. The crew sorted through equipment and supplies for unloading. Haddad recognized most of the supplies as having been produced by the Kipamu League. Arms and armor were inspected and thrown aside with disdain. There was more interest in the food and blankets. The barge slaves picked at the discard pile, not even looking at the weapons as they snatched pieces of gear.

The barge lurched forward several times then stopped. Keldon crew began throwing equipment to the warriors and slaves outside with instrucions of where to take it. The captain observed it all but only stopped the appropriation of a few items. Haddad grabbed a skin of water from a human passing by. The skin was almost completely empty, but each drop that fell on his face stung and then numbed the pain. Haddad wondered what he looked like. Where water touched, he could feel unbroken skin, but pain swallowed every other sensation when he touched dry skin.

The sides of the barge dropped, forming ramps. Kicks and punches from the crew drove the League prisoners down and through a gate. At the captain's direction, two slaves dragged Haddad out to stand off to the side. The barge rested before a walled compound. A crowd of men milled within. Prisoners, slaves, and warriors were organizing themselves into groups. In the background were barracks, but only a few people moved toward the buildings. Most prisoners were being questioned only briefly and marched out through other gates.

A man with a bucket of water walked past to the Keldons standing guard around the gate. The sun was high in the sky, and it beat down on Haddad and the slaves holding him. Haddad reached vainly for the ladle in the bucket as the man stepped around him.

"Wait!" said one of the slaves holding Haddad. The bucket carrier turned around.

The slave holding Haddad's left arm waved the man back. Haddad's escort had been just a blur off to his side, but now he recognized the rough clothes that had been a League uniform. There were patches and repairs where insignia were torn off. His face was . . .

"Face forward, prisoner," said the man in the tattered uniform, and he pushed Haddad's head around with his free hand.

"Give him some water, boy, and throw some on that bruise," said the other slave holding Haddad up on the right.

The water carrier took a good look at Haddad and gasped. "Is he alive? The whole side of his head is blue-black! Was he trampled by a barge?" The man's tone showed interest in the grisly details of Haddad's injury, but he made no move to provide water. "You know only the new master is to provide the first water or food. Do you want me to get into trouble?"

Now the slave on Haddad's right took a step forward and

gripped the water carrier's arm. Haddad was held up by the first barge crewman, and his head hung down.

"He's already been marked for an artificer." The words were low and gravelly, with rage evident in every tone. "He needs the water now, and you will do as my friend says." There were the sounds of a scuffle and a gasp of pain from the water carrier as two sets of feet came into Haddad's field of view. The dipper cast water into his face, and the numbing splash was as shocking as a blow. He staggered and crouched even lower. He could see the ladle dipping into the bucket as each of his companions drank in turn. He was jerked upright, and the water carrier was holding the dipper for him. His whole world was that small pool of water. Haddad tried for a moment to see his own face in a reflection, but a sound of impatience from his right prompted a long swallow. It was life and surcease that poured down his throat, and he felt human.

"Next time a barge man calls, you come," ground out the right man. The bucket carrier turned and walked toward the Keldon guards, shaking his arm and shoulder as if they had fallen asleep.

"Now don't look at us and don't talk." It was the man on his right, and Haddad could hear the tension in his words.

Haddad stood on his two feet and was careful to face forward. He brushed his face with his hand in a silent attempt to elicit more information.

"Your face was marked by an artificer, boy." Haddad dubbed the man Gravel as he considered the man's words. "One side of your face is a bruise with her sigil—purple and red in a field of black. It will heal very quickly, but there is no denying who your new master is until it clears."

"What's happening?" Haddad dropped his head and tried to whisper without moving his lips.

"No talking." Gravel's tones were light, but his grip was

creating another bruise. The other man, Army now in Haddad's mind, spoke.

"I'm talking to my friend here and not a new slave." Army squeezed his arm in emphasis. "Everyone knows a new slave cannot receive aid, comfort, or information from us until he is inducted into a house or crew." Haddad still kept his head low but dropped his hand from his mouth and looked into the yard. The slaves were slowly dragging him back to the side of the barge so he had a better view and they were sure of their backs.

"Look at the poor bastards," Gravel drawled. "Most of them working in construction and mining crews till they drop dead of exhaustion."

"Not like this boy here," Army answered. "Inducted into an important household. With any luck he could be stuck in the back rooms and only have to deal with other slaves instead of a Keldon overseer. If he had any skills, he might even receive special status." There was a pause as if Gravel and Army were considering his situation.

"Of course, he could never become a barge crewman," Army continued.

"Absolutely. Why, only a trusted slave can get barge duty with its freedom of movement, the chance for escape or sabotage on long patrol," replied Gravel. "A barge man could possibly even murder a Keldon warrior, if he was fast enough."

"Only a 'good' record would give a slave such a chance," Army answered. "Plotting any act of rebellion is so difficult. What with the loyalty of the slaves from Keld and the chance that a slave born on this continent would trade in his countrymen for a little luxury."

"How could any slave conspire to escape or do injury?" Gravel questioned sarcastically.

"Well, he would have to try talking to virgin meat captured recently and be careful never to say anything too inflammatory," Army reflected.

"Keep his identity and face secret?" Gravel wondered.

"Yes, friend," Army paused for a moment. "Of course, one might wonder why anyone would be so foolish to contemplate resistance at all. Especially when anyone can betray you."

"To do nothing is to betray yourself," Gravel hissed.

Haddad realized the chance the two men were taking. He was marked for special consideration, and they stood in considerable danger. But since he had survived the first weeding out on the plains, he was probably more subtle in rebellion than the soldiers devoured by birds.

"Greetings, warrior," Army said loudly. "We are to take this slave to the Artificer Latulla's household. We are waiting for escort."

"A few minutes more, slave." The Keldon warrior loomed before Haddad. His helmet and armor were black in the sun, and Haddad could smell leather as sweat and water ran down the warrior's uniform. A canteen swung on the warrior's belt, wet from being refilled in the water-carrier's bucket.

"Malk!" the warrior bellowed. Another Keldon, yards away, turned from an unloading barge. At the shouter's gesture, Malk came striding over, the butt of his spear leading the way as he shoved slaves aside. His exit left a gap in the line that slowly closed as warriors shuffled into new positions. This reorganization opened another hole in the guard line, and a woman threw herself through the gap.

She was fair and blonde and might have been pretty without the fear distorting her features. The line of women that Haddad could now see was screened from sight as additional warriors moved into position. The Keldon who let the woman through turned to follow, rage at being outwitted plain on his features. The angry warrior would not have caught her except the woman bounced off slaves and then tripped, sprawling to the ground. The slaves, such a formidable barrier to the woman, parted instantaneously before the angry Keldon following her. The warrior stooped to haul the woman to her feet, but she flailed with such energy that he could not get a grip. The woman scooted away, kicking at the Keldon's face, cloth tearing as the warrior snatched at her limbs and clothing. Haddad wondered how someone so rash had escaped becoming meat for the parea.

"She will bring fierce warriors into the world, Malk," the sweating warrior said as Malk arrived and turned to see the struggle. The street was a stadium with the audience watching a farcical battle. The slaves on the street showed nothing, but Haddad could feel their cheers for the futile defiance the woman showed. The Keldons found the battle amusing as well because the slave was so overmatched but still battling a warrior to a stalemate.

"Perhaps there are still heroes born here," Malk said facetiously as he watched the exasperated warrior, bent over and pursuing the woman. Haddad was reminded of a housewife chasing down a chicken, though the final fate of the chicken was a grim counterpoint to the scene in front of him.

The warrior hovering over the woman still couldn't get a good grip. Long tattered strands of cloth whipped into his face, and the woman's garments tore in his metal gauntlets. Laughing warriors surrounded the pair. Haddad could see a tight cluster of spear points moving through the crowd and approaching the struggle. The Keldon warriors moved aside for greater authority as the slaves had parted for the warrior trying to capture the fleeing woman. Then the guard hit the woman with a closed fist.

Everything seemed to pause. The woman lay on the ground, her body limp as blood poured from a gash the gauntlet inflicted. Her face was washed away as blood covered her features and pooled on the ground. The laughter on the lips of the guards watching the fight disappeared in a disbelieving gasp, and then every Keldon—except the guard kneeling with horror over the injured woman—drew and raised weapons.

"Stop!" The voice was high, and Haddad wondered what slave dared speak. The cluster of spear carriers forced its way to the woman, and the guard line opened. A Keldon woman stood revealed. Smaller than any of the warriors around her, she nevertheless dominated the Keldons and slaves as surely as a giant. "Care for the girl, now."

A stretcher team, composed of slaves, was there in seconds, and the guards stayed still, tense with expectation. Haddad was shocked to see a slave place his hand over the kneeling warrior's face and shove him away like a bothersome sheep. The slaves applied compresses to the woman's head and rushed her away. The warrior who injured her hurried to his knees and knelt before the woman of his race.

"Who commands this trash?" the female Keldon demanded, gesturing at the kneeling warrior. "I want him before me." The attentive guards rushed off to do her bidding as the slave woman's blood soaked into the offender's clothes. The warrior had knelt directly on the site of the struggle, as if trying to erase the evidence. Haddad was mystified. With all the casual and deliberate brutality he had seen, why should this woman's injury matter?

"I thank the gods I am not in that squad," Malk said quietly as he watched the Keldon warriors searching for the commander of the man who incurred such wrath from the crowd. The warrior guarding Haddad shook his head in agreement.

"To strike a cradle woman in the presence of a midwife. To call down the curse of all women upon him and his fellows." Haddad's guard knew some of the warriors effected, and it showed in his tone. "All crafts and worked goods are turned from them. No luck on the battlefield, no chance to sire future warriors until the curse is repealed. No provocation is worth that." The Keldon spat on the ground in contempt.

A large Keldon warrior pushed his way through the crowd, his finer armor showing high rank. The leader bowed his head without word or salutation and stood ready to accept whatever the midwife might say.

"You have failed Keld. One under your command struck a future mother because she showed the spirit your subordinate so sorely lacks. You will excuse yourself from the ranks of warriors and report to the ship bound for Keld when you have finished your current business."

"Yes, Midwife," the commander replied. "I will attend you tomorrow."

The woman spat on the Keldon kneeling in the blood while his commanding officer looked on. Rage made the commander's face into a demon's mask. The midwife and her retainers withdrew, the circle of spears working its way back through the crowd.

The now disgraced leader pointed to the kneeling warrior rocking back and forth in silent distress.

"Hold him and still his tongue." Five warriors attached themselves in an instant—one for each limb and one gagging the prisoner with leather laces.

"I strike twice as is my right," the leader half-screamed, and blows from an armored boot crippled the prisoner, crushing the knees and tearing the flesh. Haddad could hear a muffled scream of pain as the commander gestured for the rest of his unit to approach.

"In striking a cradle wife this scum struck at Keld, at my honor, and at the honor of all his comrades. Return the blows that he has inflicted on us all." The surrounding warriors converged and began a slow, measured barrage of kicks to the body on the ground. Haddad could hear individual blows breaking bones as the slaves and the two Keldon guards led him away.

"I almost joined his attack group," the unnamed guard said as they walked away.

"You were lucky to escape that stain," Malk replied, jabbing the butt of his spear into the ground as a sign of agitation.

"Still," the other replied, "the commander could have tried to keep some honor for his warriors if not himself."

"You know the saying about midwives," Malk chided. "In all but battle they speak loudest. Better to plead and bargain tomorrow when her words do not echo. Perhaps some of the warriors will be able to serve worthy commanders. Anyway, some words are better spoken in privacy." Malk tried to surreptitiously wave at Haddad's face and the purple and red mark imprinted there. Malk's nervousness taught Haddad that he might have some power, even as a slave.

* * * * *

The dwelling of Latulla showed Haddad that he was to serve an important power. It was another walled compound with a large house and outbuildings. The main structure was multilevel, and in the entire town only a few buildings were equivalently high. The foundation and first story were rough-cut stone. There were two more levels of windows and balconies facing the gate and the sides of the compound. The roof was massive, a huge, steep tent about to settle over the entire house. A steep roof was necessary where large amounts of snow fell, but Haddad was astounded at the waste of materials and labor in building such a roof in these warm lowlands. In fact, the entire complex was too substantial for the few years that the Keldons had been here. Most of the materials did not look local except for the stone. How much shipping had been dedicated to this construction, Haddad wondered.

Keldons and slaves stopped at the gatehouse. A richly dressed human servant stood between two guards. Over the gate hung a round black shield with a single complex character of red and purple, an emblem Haddad realized must be replicated in the complex bruise on his face.

"We have brought a slave at the artificer's orders," said the Keldon escort, and Gravel and Army threw him down before the servant. Barge slaves and warriors left, and Haddad was at his new home.

"I am Briach, chief among Latulla's slaves," he intoned. "And while your genuflection is flattering, I require only simple courtesy." Haddad drew himself to his feet and stood before the gate.

Briach was tall and pale, dressed in a simple short robe of medium quality. His hair was red and freckles covered his face, a coloring common to many slaves from Keld as Haddad would find out. On his right arm was a bronze armband, richly worked with a scattering of stones. Threaded through his belt was a short, heavy club. While Haddad had seen knives and other possible weapons in the hands of slaves, they had all been tools. The club was a weapon, and it showed this slave had unusual trust and authority in the town.

"Come with me," Briach commanded, and Haddad moved at a half-run to catch up.

"You have been very fortunate . . ." Briach paused, and Haddad almost ran into him. "What is your name and profession?"

"I am Haddad, and I am a League soldier," Haddad replied, trying to sound proud. "I maintained the war machines and fought with honor."

"Your old life is dead, Haddad," Briach said as he continued walking. "Your life is now service to Keld and to Artificer Latulla." Briach stopped before the steps of the house and gestured widely. "This is your home, and here is your loyalty." Briach grasped Haddad's shoulder and lightly touched the massive bruise already starting to fade. "You are marked, and service is written on your soul. You have no family, no nation, no purpose apart from Latulla." Briach started walking around the building, out of sight of the gates and the guards standing watch at the small gatehouse.

Benches were placed outside the rear of the house, and the cackling of chickens sounded from a coop against the rear enclosure wall. Haddad and Briach sat down, and Haddad said nothing, instead looking at the grounds as a prospective battlefield for his freedom.

"Is it true that in the League, city has fought city?" Briach asked.

"Yes, the cities have battled, though they fought in the field rather than on city streets," Haddad replied. In the presence of an invasion it was an embarrassing historical note.

"And is it true your fighters may move from army to army?" Briach continued. Haddad decided to play along rather than educate Briach in the complexities and shifting loyalties that in the recent past governed military employment.

"Yes, allegiances change all the time." Of course, inter-city fighting disappeared with the current Keldon incursion.

"Then you are lucky you have this chance to serve Keld." Briach stood and stared north. "The strength of Keld will sweep down upon your cities and crush your armies. You have been given a precious opportunity to see the completion of a great destiny. You are honored to serve one of a special class. Artificers create new weapons, new engines of destruction. Fired by the 'Heroes' Blood' and the will of our warriors, Keld will sweep over the world!" Briach's eyes were shining, and Haddad felt his gorge rise at the sight of a slave in love with his masters. In the League, a military defeat only meant a small loss of status or position. Briach was talking about the total destruction of Haddad's city, nation, and culture. Haddad hoped he died before he wished for such a foulness to grow.

"What do you mean, 'Heroes' Blood'? " Haddad wanted Briach to keep talking but couldn't bring himself to agree with the chief slave's mad vision.

"Long ago when the land was newly born, gods and heroes stalked the land. Each stood taller and mightier than any who walk today." Briach swung and gestured westward. "But an evil came into the land and corrupted the gods, turning them weak and twisted in hate for all living things. They swept over the land, and death flew with them in slaughter and disease. The people writhed under the feet of their murderers. The gods' betrayal festered and poisoned mortal men until they joined the forces of darkness."

Haddad was impressed with Briach's storytelling skills but had no idea what the loon was talking about.

"The Heroes fought against false and treacherous gods. The swords of right spilled waves of blood, but each victory or stalemate only delayed evil's triumph. The Heroes saw all turned against them and sent their people fleeing north, telling them millennia must pass before they could return home. Those remaining battled without any thought of restraint. Every battlefield drank Heroes' Blood and the tears of fallen gods. Now evil was besieged at every point as men threw themselves against their betrayers, smothering and caging fallen gods under piles of bodies and then bloody bones. The final battle vanquished evil but at the cost of every warrior's life. Only the corpses were left in a poisoned land." Briach sat down and spoke more quietly.

"The land was empty for centuries. Time covered every victory and defeat, changing the remains of slaughter and sacrifice into power waiting to be picked up by the children of heroes." Briach's tone turned sour. "But escaped slaves came to the empty land and found the blood of heroes. They used it to fertilize fields, to power wagons and ships to carry cabbages. The scum fed off the land left behind by the fathers of Keld. And so the Keldons have returned to reclaim their heritage.

"Each victory, each barrel of tufa, each war manikin fed by Heroes' Blood brings all of Keld closer to a holy war. Each slave who completes his task brings that day closer," Briach exclaimed.

"The Keldons want to sweep over the world," Haddad repeated. "But if what you say is true, then they are centuries late in arriving here. Why are they here now?"

"Because you are stealing the Heroes' Blood!" Briach snarled. "The tufa your League pulls from the mines is composed of the blood and gore shed by the Heroes and their enemies. Each concentration marks the remains of battle and power run amok. What you call tufa is the matrix holding Heroes' Blood." Briach stood and turned to the west.

"The Kipamu League," he spat, "mines the greatness and legacy left to Keld by the ancestors! Heroes' Blood was laid down in battle, and your kind uses it to nurture crops! We have come to reclaim the inheritance and use it for war. Laid down in battle, the Blood will be expended in battle!" Briach walked to Haddad and gripped his shoulders tightly, as if to force his vision into Haddad's body.

"The Keldons are the chosen people!" Briach frothed. "They are a race of heroes drawn from every corner of the earth! Only in the last few years have they remembered the greatness of their forefathers here! Time and the blood of other lands have made the Keldons worthy to rule here and every other land! The final days are upon us and we are ready to take back the world!"

Haddad wondered when, exactly, Briach had lost his mind. The dead and brutalized League citizens in Haddad's memories were the victims of barbarians, not saviors. Haddad realized that Briach needed to serve heroes in his own mind. The steward was trying to convince himself as much as Haddad.

Briach came back to the present and prodded Haddad toward a workshop. "Remember you serve a great people. Now Latulla will see you and induct you into the house."

The workshop was the size of a large barn with a high peaked roof, massive logs and great stones forming the foundation and the walls. The workshop, even more than the house, squatted like an invader on the land. When he reached the open doors he found the interior well lit. Windows and skylights let the sun shine on the tables and benches inside. Haddad had assumed the building would be as dark as the magic and rituals he imagined within.

Instead, there were tables with carefully organized apparatus everywhere. Shelves of meticulously labeled bottles stood against the walls, and a large dispensary could be seen at the back of the shop. Pegs held stools and large pieces of gear up off the floor and out of the way.

The second story was an open loft without partitions. A rope-powered lift to raise and lower materials from the upper floor was to one side. A series of stalls with iron locks and cryptic symbols was on the other. Some of the stalls were barred with bedding inside. Why would Latulla keep prisoners here where they might disturb her work? Haddad realized that captives might be at the heart of Latulla's work and wondered how long they lasted. Haddad wondered if he would die here. His heart nearly stopped as he walked past a trough with a body in it. He stopped, looking down. It was not a body, he realized with relief, but a mechanical model that looked like a man. Haddad stared at the clumps of leather and flesh attached to the metal skeleton and wondered what purpose it served. Briach shoved him forward, stopping his inspection of the "body."

Latulla stood examining equipment Haddad recognized from his unit. She picked up a manual on maintaining war machines and turned the pages. The text she only glanced at, but the diagrams drew her interest as the two slaves stood before her. She closed the book and looked one final time at the army emblem on the front cover. The same emblem was worked into Haddad's shirt to show his military specialty.

"So you are an expert in the crude abominations of the enemy?" she asked.

Haddad nodded vaguely, unsure of her meaning and his expected response. Briach cuffed his head strongly when Latulla looked at him.

"Speak when spoken to. You are in service now." Briach sounded as if he wanted to curse in anger.

"I maintained war machines," Haddad ventured.

"I may make use of you then." Latulla lifted a plate at her side. On it were a crust of bread and a cup of wine. "Open your mouth and eat." Latulla stuffed part of the bread into his mouth and watch him gnaw off a piece of the stale loaf. After several painful chews she poured the sour wine into his mouth. He almost gagged.

"I take you into my house. I provide you nourishment. I give you purpose and meaning." Latulla threw the plate and cup down as if they were soiled. She turned her back to them and went back to examining her loot.

"Take the dishes away and teach him what I expect. He may be called to serve as my aide. Brief him on his responsibilities and the punishments for failure." She spoke without even contempt, as if Haddad were a dumb animal she would need trained.

You have enrolled a viper, not a beast of burden, Latulla, he whispered in the back of his mind as he picked up the two pieces of pewter. He and Briach left. Haddad talked and asked questions all the way back to the main building that night, gathering information to feed his treachery.

CHAPTER 4

Barrin looked at the sea. The surface was covered with a light chop. The small spots of white foam were the most interesting things he had seen for hours. He had arrived at Teferi's island expecting to rest after days spent traveling. He was instead told that Teferi was out on maritime patrol off the mainland. More hours of flight before he could finally commence his mission. The gray-haired wizard rolled his head, stretching his aged limbs to ease their stiffness.

The wings of the ornithopter beat relentlessly as Barrin's pilot, Yarbo, followed the homing signal. A rangy, athletic man in his twenties, the pilot had volunteered to fly for the duration of the wizard's stay in Jamuraa. The ground crew at Teferi's base camp was able to give Barrin and his pilot a device to find Teferi's craft, handing it up as the last of Barrin's cargo was unloaded. The lightened machine flew faster and was more responsive as it flew over a gray sea.

Yarbo pointed left and down, signaling he had spotted Teferi's vehicle. Barrin waved for the pilot to circle, and Yarbo immediately banked. Barrin could now see Teferi's craft.

Teferi and his crew were in a long gondola slung below the gasbag of a blimp. The blimp was smaller than the dirigibles that flew in Tolaria, but any lighter-than-air craft is huge when compared against an ornithopter. The blimp was well over five hundred feet long and was a mosaic of pastel red and orange hues. Barrin wondered why such an abstract color scheme was used as Yarbo began to lose more altitude until they were directly across from the gondola.

The gondola was more than a hundred feet long and was segmented in several places. Bare metal and more of the pastel cloth winked a cryptic code as the lowering sun reflected off it and the windows. Barrin could see the crew waving through the windows. He also noticed that while the crew smiled, the long snouts of launchers at the front and the back of the gondola followed the ornithopter in its flight. He could feel the magic of the craft, and at least one spellcaster was holding power for a possible battle. Teferi was involved in a war, and Barrin was here to observe it. It seemed a poor reason for a reunion to Barrin.

Yarbo banked the birdlike machine and signaled for rendezvous. An agreement came from the blimp. Barrin waited for Teferi. If the planeswalker had not been on the other craft, getting aboard would have been vastly more difficult.

Barrin patted the thick case slung on his shoulder. He had received it when meeting Teferi's intelligence officer to coordinate the flight. Though the planeswalker had ways of communicating at all times, security and limitations on how much information could be cast back to the mainland meant a thick stack of documents still needed to be physically carried back and forth. Barrin hoped that he was carrying good news.

Barrin felt the surge of energy and a moment of envy as Teferi, the planeswalker, appeared before him. The increase in weight momentarily interfered with Yarbo's control of the craft despite the fact that he was expecting it.

"Hello, Barrin!" Teferi called out as he crouched. The noise of the ornithopter's flight diminished as Yarbo cut speed to make speaking easier. "How was your trip? Shall I get your luggage?" Teferi was smiling, and Barrin smiled back. The planeswalker's black-skinned face was youthful and jovial compared to the wizard's care-worn visage.

"It's all back at base, so no tip for you." Barrin always enjoyed Teferi's sense of fun in comparison to Urza's permanent glower. Teferi proved being a planeswalker was not the source of Urza's melancholy and lack of people skills. It was only because Urza radiated such unrelenting purpose that so many people followed him.

Teferi crabbed over and laid his hands on Barrin as he prepared to leap back to the blimp. Teferi jumped. There was a moment of disorientation as Barrin's body changed to a different shape in a different dimension. It was a skill that was minor to Teferi but a mountain to Barrin. When they appeared in the wardroom of the gondola, Barrin's entire being exhaled, returning to its familiar form.

The first thing Barrin noticed was the quiet and stability of the craft. There was only a faint drone to signal the presence of working machinery. Except for the noise and the excellent view, Barrin could have been on land or a seagoing ship becalmed.

"Welcome aboard the *Hunter*, Barrin," Teferi said as he gestured around to the men. The men nodded in greeting but kept their stations. "The *Hunter* is the lead ship of the Mushan class. We are trying to build them as large as your cargo dirigibles, but we still have a ways to go." Teferi's every movement showed pride in the creation of the craft. "This is the biggest thing flying in the hemisphere until the new Negria class flies next year."

"It's a fine craft, but how does it do as a combat vessel? The *Weatherlight* would swat this out of the air like a gnat, and even an ornithopter would eat you alive. There may be a future in cargo and patrolling, but you should concentrate your flying efforts on ornithopters." Barrin could tell he had ruffled the feathers of an enthusiast.

"Of course the *Weatherlight* would destroy us. But it is the only one of its kind, and it took the power of a collapsing plane to charge its engines. Hundreds if not thousands of these can be built. Right now the Keldons have few if any flyers," Teferi replied. "These blimps are not as vulnerable or useless as you contend." Teferi turned and waved for Barrin to follow.

Teferi moved through a partition and gestured in a wide circle. "Cargo space and the ability to carry tons of it long distances." The shelves and bins were all locked tight, each labeled according to its contents. Large pieces of equipment were securely webbed down, and seeing the stringency of the lashing, Barrin wondered how rough the ride could get.

Teferi pointed to the ceiling. "Up there is the heavy machinery which provides the power and much of the passive defenses. Enough energy for months of flight."

Barrin stretched forth his senses. He could feel magical energy encased in tanks and drums, and thin lines carrying power in several directions. But he also felt the balloon and the envelope above him. It was subtle, but the same power trapped in the heavy tanks seemed to float in a huge, diffuse cloud over him.

"What exactly are you using the power for?" Barrin inquired as he sampled the texture of the energy being used.

"The liquid in the tanks is a concentrate refined from tufa and stabilized in a liquid form. Using this power we have quickened the fabric making up the envelope, balloons, and cabling," Teferi replied. "The material is in some sense alive and acts to maintain its own integrity. There is an additional benefit in that water is misted up into the balloons, and the material separates the water into hydrogen and oxygen. The oxygen is vented into the atmosphere and the hydrogen is contained to inflate the balloons. As you know, the shortage of ballast and lifting gas is usually the determining factor in how long we can fly. In effect, the water we take on board performs a double duty. We can even pump in a fresh supply by dangling a long hose. Endurance is enhanced." Teferi's eyes shone as he regaled Barrin with the details.

An airman interrupted Teferi before he could continue. "Sir, we have news of enemy craft to the east. Communications wants you immediately." Teferi strode to the front of the craft and called for a report. Barrin followed.

"The *Grey Dove* is reporting one Keldon ship so far. Their pilot has called for assistance, and we are moving to support them." Barrin could feel the blimp vibrating as their pilot went to maximum power and altered course.

"It appears you will have a chance to observe operations

sooner than I planned. The *Grey Dove* is a Kashan class blimp—smaller than the one we are on now—that was coming in from patrol. We are the only ship this far east that can support her."

Barrin looked at the broad expanse of coast on the map. He was astounded by the amount of coastline not covered by patrols. Teferi picked up on his question before it could leave his lips.

"You obviously haven't gotten the news. The airbase that housed the blimps for this area was burned six weeks ago. For at least the next year, the east will have inadequate coverage." Teferi looked grim as he remembered the recent raid.

"I thought these blimps had endurance." Barrin wanted to lighten the mood, but his primary mission was to collect information for Urza.

"The blimps need to rearm and perform maintenance. Also the semi-living nature of the fabric requires special maintenance facilities, and we don't have means to provide this without substantial new construction," Teferi explained.

Their pilot interrupted them. "Blimp sighted. All hands to battle stations. Cease hydrogen production. Engage all defenses. Communications, what's their status and where the hell is the ship they're attacking?" The pilot reduced speed, and two men came forward. The whisper of power they exuded alerted Barrin that these were combat mages, readying themselves for action.

"The *Grey Dove* is low on gas and ballast but is committing to an attack run. Look forward and starboard for the Keldons," the communicator responded, even as he continued broadcasting details of what has happening to other airships far to the west.

Barrin picked up a pair of magnifiers and looked for the enemy ship. One of the combat mages finished his defensive preparations and was looking as well.

"Try to spot distortion or a patch of mist. The Keldons have been hiding from surface forces and masking their movements," explained one of the battle mages.

Barrin leaned forward as a ship congealed on the ocean's surface. It was long and low slung. The figurehead was a dragon belching painted fire, and he wondered at the incongruity of flame cleaving a gray sea. The ship was crowded with Keldons, and on the bow there were several war engines Barrin did not recognize. A poor place to put heavy equipment, thought the old mage. In the front of the ship it could unbalance the boat.

"Doesn't look very impressive, does it? But it's the troops on board that are the real threat," the combat mage said while preparing for battle. His comments were addressed less to Barrin than to the world at large.

Suddenly one of the engines on the Keldon ship discharged high into the air, the projectile a flaming mass. It burned so brightly that even when Barrin looked away he could see the trajectory's afterimage superimposed over his vision.

"Oh, those swine!" someone in the cabin swore.

Barrin looked again. The fire had been cast at such a high angle, he thought the *Grey Dove* safe, but at the apex of the trajectory the compact ball of fire expanded and altered shape. A cloud of fiery green and yellow streamers glided down. For every foot they fell, the flaming projectiles moved yards closer to the smaller blimp. Then the streamers collapsed and rained fire down over the pastel envelope. Barrin imagined the crew burning as he waited for the explosion—but the explosion never came. The envelope was burning, smeared with fire, but the flames weren't spreading. In fact, they were starting to slowly diminish even as he looked on.

"Told you the defenses make a difference. The engines are spraying a mist that retards combustion. As long as the fuel holds out, or they don't lose power, the flames should be controllable." Teferi sounded relieved, but he immediately turned grim. "The pilot, however, has no business being that low over the water. He is going to get another volley from that ship if he doesn't break off soon."

While Teferi talked, Barrin shifted his glass from the blimp to the ship. The Keldons were moving erratically on the deck, and as the *Hunter* closed, he could detect the marshalling of magical power aboard all the craft in the area. The *Grey Dove* began to point down in a shallow dive, and Barrin saw ballast being dumped aft. The nose of the blimp dipped toward the surface.

A hail of projectiles poured from under the blimp. Dozens of rockets leaped at the ship, leaving ribbons of smoke and light as they accelerated to a high velocity. Dark vapors poured from braziers on the Keldon ship, forming a cloud in front of the attack. If it served a defensive purpose, Barrin had no idea what it was. The projectiles were not effected at all and beat the water into froth as the spikes nailed the sea and part of the ship's deck.

"We'll follow his bombing run and finish what's left," the pilot called as he adjusted course to over-fly the Keldon ship.

The *Grey Dove* dumped bombs, but only four dropped from its bays. The smoke from the Keldon ship went black as coal as the bombs entered it.

"The Keldon mages are still working on the ship. Either

the rocket darts missed or there were a lot of mages on board," the pilot reported.

Barrin's eyes dipped to catch the bombs as they exited the cloud of smoke, but the explosives failed to fall through. They reappeared after an obvious lag, falling farther to the rear than the bombardier had intended. The bombs exploded into giant green discs, covering the stern of the Keldon vessel. The ship listed to the port side, its steering apparently gone and the forces propelling it uncontrolled.

"*Grey Dove* says its remaining bombs are hung up. They will turn to support our attack if they can." The attacking blimp was on the right side of the *Hunter* and beginning a turn to follow the larger aerial craft in. The bomb doors were still open, and the combination of poor aerodynamics and unexpected weight meant the ship was much lower than intended.

Barrin saw the attack, but it was so quick that he was unable to respond. The envelope of the smaller blimp was smashed and the rigging tangled in an instant. The next strike he saw clearly. A drop of water leaped up from the sea. It was the size of a bathtub as it smashed the gondola into wreckage.

"Sea archer!" shouted the navigator.

Barrin could see the monster now. It body was reptilian and was at least sixty feet long. Its hide gleamed a dull, hideous shade of green with flashes of color as it reared out of the water. Its head was long and narrowed to an incongruously small mouth. The creature circled under the Kashan blimp it had just attacked.

Barrin could feel the bank as the *Hunter* turned. The monster submerged and then resurfaced, its head questing toward the sky. The skull seemed to compress, and the monster nearly disappeared at the recoil as another blast of water sheared into the *Grey Dove.* Debris poured from the stricken blimp. The rear of the gondola shattered, and huge sheets of its envelope spun down into the sea. Three crewmen were tumbling toward the water as the airship began to rise, the sudden weight loss sending the blimp higher. Interior balloons inside the blimp burst, and all the lift shifted to the front of the vessel. The nose of the blimp jumped toward the sky. More debris and personnel fell from the dying craft.

Teferi shouted, "I'll get—" and disappeared.

"You would swear the sea beasts are fighting for the Keldons," the navigator whispered as the sea archer struck at everything falling into the water.

"The enemy just throws bodies overboard, and monsters leave them alone," the pilot replied.

Teferi had jumped to the debris falling to the water and had grabbed a crewman, jumping back to the wardroom. Teferi disappeared again as the scream of a rescued man filled the cabin. It took a few seconds for the *Grey Dove* crewman to realize he was comparatively safe, and then Teferi jumped back with another crewman.

Barrin tried to find some magical hold on the beast but there was none to be found. The sea archer was hunting prey for its own reasons.

The nose gunner of the *Hunter* turned his launcher and sent a stream of rocket darts into the water. The single tube began to glow red from the heat, and Barrin could hear the man cursing as he corrected his aim. The monster lurched as two shots pierced its body. The well-placed darts smashed ribs and exploded tissue as they exited the other side of the beast.

Barrin had spread his mental net wide, trying to snare

the beast from the non-existent Keldon influence. Now he threw that net of calling out into the ocean. From miles around, sharks answered Barrin's summons, converging on the injured beast as a blood slick spread around the thrashing body. The water roiled, and the sea archer disappeared under the mass of hungry predators.

"Gunner, aim for the Keldons right now!" the pilot screamed into the launcher compartment underneath the cabin. The beast's attack and Teferi's ongoing rescue of the crew had given the raiders too much time. The Keldon ship was only seconds from being under the *Hunter*'s bomb bay. Suppression fire was vital. The enemy ship heeled hard as someone regained steering and overcorrected.

Barrin felt the rush of energy even as the men below were pitched off their feet by the sudden change in the ship's direction. The Keldons fired, and Barrin braced himself for a hit as a ball of brilliant fire arched into the sky. By design or luck, it struck the *Grey Dove*. The hydrogen in its remaining cells ignited and leaped to the heavens in a sheet of flame, then the fuel and remaining armaments exploded, and the craft disappeared in a rain of fire.

Teferi appeared, disoriented and dazed, in the command cabin, a charred body clutched in his arms—a final desperate attempt to save more crew from the doomed ship. The crew of the *Hunter* was shouting and trying to get to the planeswalker. Barrin, knowing how tough his friend truly was, moved up to the pilot's chair.

The front gunner was now firing into the Keldon ship, stabbing repeatedly around the bow area, searching for an enemy mage. The pilot looked at Barrin as he set the bomb bays for drop.

"I don't think we can allow those fellows to live," he said softly and tripped the release as they passed over the

Keldons. Barrin could feel each bomb dropping away. He was consumed with witnessing every moment of the battle and ran to the rear gunner's compartment, the floor jumping as the ship raced to the sky. He passed Teferi without a glance and levitated over the still crewmen rescued from the *Grey Dove*. He reached the blimp's stern and the gunner's station.

The bombs hit as Barrin peered through the window. Five of the projectiles missed, and huge columns of spray lifted high into the air. Three of the bombs smashed into the ship and plunged through the deck to explode in the holds. Then the Keldons' fuel and weapons added their power to the holocaust. Gouts of flame flew high into the sky, blooming into flowers of twisting fire and color. The ship lay hidden behind the smoke and spray. When the scene cleared, Barrin could see the Keldon ship had been shattered into a spread of floating timbers and bodies. Were there any survivors?

The rear gunner must have thought so, for he aimed and fired. This launcher was bulkier than the *Hunter*'s forward weapon, and an assistant had to elbow Barrin aside as he loaded another shell. The clumps of debris continued to spread out as more wreckage and gear sank to the bottom. The gunner fired again. The shell exploded into a large net that fell to the surface. Barrin watched as a man thrashing in the water tried to get on top of a barrel. The net covered everything and detonated in a flash. Barrin's eyes jerked away, and nothing but fragments floated where the Keldon had been.

"That isn't necessary, Gunner," Barrin said, numb after observing the battle. The gunner didn't say a word, but the loader inserted another shell into breech. The gunner fired the round before answering.

"We can't rescue them, and nobody is in sight. If I had a choice between getting eaten and getting shot, I'd take shot." Barrin remembered the small mouth of the sea archer and the sharks converging on the area from his call. The long-lived mage said nothing as the gunner took aim again.

CHAPTER 5

Haddad hated serving as Latulla's aide. Her one redeeming feature, in Haddad's eyes, was the small freedom she allowed him to leave her presence. As long as he performed the tasks she set and averted his eyes downward when she looked at him, he could avoid supervision. But serving as her aide meant long periods of time in the company of Keldons, and that was always dangerous.

Haddad had learned something about Keldon society. There were levels of challenge and dominance. A Keldon did not have to meet the eyes of a superior or attack an inferior to express the power. Sometimes warriors attacked the equipment or a slave of another Keldon. Haddad saw servants cuffed, beaten, and even killed to express power or belittle a superior without a full challenge. Latulla was a master of this technique. With a single well-placed blow of her staff, she could lay out a slave for days in excruciating pain without permanent harm. It wasn't kindness or pity that pulled her blow. An injured slave was a constant reminder of her authority and power. An inferior Keldon could not afford to kill one of a limited number of slaves. Latulla's every cruelty was calculated for maximum pain and effect on those involved.

"We will be taking one of the small land barges today. Find the duty crew and instruct them to ready themselves," Latulla had directed. A slave who ordered or commanded a Keldon warrior always risked death. The fact that Latulla could use slaves to carry orders reinforced her authority in the camp. It was a delicate balancing act that Haddad must perform. Too submissive and Latulla would punish him. Too forceful and the barge captain might kill him for presumption. As Haddad considered Latulla, he knew he would err on the side of arrogance rather than risk her displeasure. Besides, it was one of the few chances Haddad would get to tweak a Keldon's flat nose and not lose his head for it.

Haddad had seen other sections of the camp since his inclusion in Latulla's household but had never ridden one of the small barges. The first step was finding where the small barges were located. Haddad stopped a slave he recognized as a crewman from his apparel and the tools in his belt. Barge slaves were allowed instruments that were considered weapons in other hands. The sharpened quill or hollow awl was sturdy enough to punch through leather armor. It pierced seals and drained out the magical elixir powering the Keldon barges. It was also used to fill reservoirs and refresh fluids quickly with the attachment of a simple bulb. He asked directions to the barges and their commanders in the extended camp.

"This morning they've shoved us over toward the corrals. The fighting broke out again and disturbed the colony." The slave gestured to the empty pack he carried over his shoulders. His body was scarred and bruised by the casual brutality many of the lowest status Keldons expressed, both to reinforce authority and prove their own positions. "I'm to bring cheese back, if I can get any. There are ships coming in, we heard, and the storehouse may be relaxing the rations." The slave stepped off for the warehouses.

Haddad felt a little jealousy as he watched the man striding away. What was the man's name? He realized with shame he hadn't thought to ask. He was seeing more and more signs that life in Latulla's household was changing him. The little courtesies were draining away and leaving watered down Keldon arrogance. The man had obviously suffered more physical abuse than Haddad had, but despite his bruises, he was in better spirits. He was happier as a worker for the lowest commanders than Haddad was as Latulla's voice. Haddad wondered how his own soul would fare a year from now as he set off for the small barges.

Shouting and the odor from livestock pens were pervasive when Haddad finally arrived. The warriors here appeared only a little different from the slaves working on the barges. Haddad spotted the small purple standard flying over the overlord's tent. Lord Druik was reclining and napping in the surrounding noise. Haddad considered the titular commander of the small barge fleet with interest and a little wonder. Druik was huge, even for a Keldon. Muscles rippled as he stretched a little, his hand moving slightly as he dreamed. Druik's entire left side was damaged. His arm was missing from the elbow down. A hook was strapped on tightly, the straps circling the Keldon's chest with studs liberally applied to the harness and cup over the stump. The lower leg was likewise encased, and there were sheathes for two knives on either side above the knee. Haddad wondered why anyone with one hand would have weapons in so awkward a location. Druik's ribs on his left side were twisted and covered with scars.

Druik was an anomaly to Haddad. Every Keldon he had ever seen held his place by force. Physical contests of strength were common even up the line of command. The jockeying went on at the highest levels of Keldon society. How a crippled warrior held even the ceremonial post of small craft commander was a mystery.

A wave off to the side of the small tent caught Haddad's attention. A dainty table with a clerk sitting behind it looked over the stockyards and the men hauling away dung. As Haddad approached, an especially pungent waft of stench set him coughing as the fitful breeze turned, putting the tent downwind of the smell. Haddad's eyes watered as he stood before what must be the first real bureaucrat he had seen since he left the League territory. He couldn't believe how happy he was to see a petty official.

"What do you want?" the little man droned as he shuffled some papers, suggesting his time was valuable. "I don't have all day, you know." The official was looking right at him, and Haddad was now more accurately remembering the aggravation petty officials could give.

"The Artificer Latulla commands a small land barge and crew be assigned to her convenience immediately for a trip to the interior camps. Additionally, I would like to know what you are doing here." Haddad could not keep hidden his admiration for the small scene of authority any longer.

The small man smiled widely, his teeth coal black and his tongue a grotesque purple. He nudged a desk stool out and waved for Haddad to sit. His smile was amazingly ugly, but the good humor in it was a tonic to Haddad. He even offered Haddad some nuts as refreshment.

"If you don't mind a smile like mine, these are really tasty."

Haddad only nodded but declined to sample the dish. The official was quite tiny and fine featured. His eyes appeared to squint in the light, and his skin was pale.

"My name is Fumash, originally of the Kipamu League Customs Service. Captured by long shore raiders as I inspected a cargo in harbor." Fumash was pensive, his hands slowly touching everything on the table as he spoke. "Not to dwell on the past, I arrived as one of the first slaves to this lovely port and started at the bottom of the bottom. The Keldons had just landed and were setting up. The imported slaves thought me above myself, and so I ended up here." Haddad looked around at the small comforts Fumash arranged for himself, even an awning to be set up if the sun grew too strong. Fumash saw his disbelief.

"Don't be fooled. This is the bottom of the line. The Keldons on the other side of this tent have no status and fit into no clan or structure. They man small land barges, able to carry a few tons of cargo or a small squad of men. They are warriors, but they operate in very small groups. They are constantly being reassigned to any higher status Keldon who needs temporary transportation. They are nearly civilians." The hands searching the table found a thin sack of wine, and Fumash dumped out the dregs from a cup and offered a drink to Haddad.

"Yes, please." He was grateful for the human gesture. Fumash paused in his story, and Haddad realized he should savor the wine. "Please continue," Haddad requested after a final swallow.

"Well, you have a large number of Keldons constantly changing assignments in very small groups. Of course there are a huge number of fights." Fumash shook his head at the foibles of his masters. "Every night they tried to fight out a new structure, each morning about a quarter of them were smashed up with new crews forming and new conflicts arising for the next night. I don't know how it was in Keld, but here it was a mess. The slaves were even getting involved, trying to increase the glory of whoever their master was for that day. I wasn't doing very well."

Haddad had to appreciate the man's sense of humor. Any Keldon would dwarf his small frame. In addition, human slaves working the vehicles could be rough indeed. But many officers curbed excessive discipline and valued the loyalty and service that a slave could bring to small crews. There was still an ample supply of sadists and thugs working at the low end of Keldon society, but a master who valued you and considered you more than an animal could be found.

"Eventually they put Druik in command. He was a hero in their homeland, you know. He has close ties to several commanders and warlords from his younger days, so everyone respects him. He might have had high office if he had remained on Keld, but he had to leave for some reason. But to the common warrior, he has achieved an automatic reception of support and loyalty. Even if someone were to challenge him, the other Keldons would pull the challenger down. Besides, he can still fight fairly well, enough to kill most warriors." There was an undertone of fondness Fumash soon shook off.

"Now Druik keeps all the barge crews in stable units. The warriors still fight over duties, but there is less violence even if the arguments are just as loud. I was drafted to keep the records and clerk for Druik. I am also the official recorder of bets," Fumash said.

Haddad had to laugh. "A gamemonger! How could you, a slave, ever get the money to cover bets?" Haddad couldn't imagine any slave having real power.

"I record the bets and oversee the gambling the warriors do to establish status and decide duty schedules. By having them compete against one another, the urge to dominate is assuaged, and the loser is willing to accept a loss. He knows there is a chance he can win back his place tomorrow. The actual loss of warriors and slaves to dominance fights are lower than any other section of the camp. I also receive some advantage since I record and adjust the odds for many of the bets. As a representative of Druik, of course." Fumash apparently realized how long he had been talking and got back to business. "The land barge under Cradow is on service today. He is at the back of the field, the figure of a toad on the body and shield of his craft. Best you seek him now and ask him to report before the artificer grows impatient. Good luck to you." With that, Fumash began reorganizing his slates after checking off what must be Cradow's craft.

Somewhat nonplussed by his abrupt dismissal, Haddad rose and set the emptied wine cup on the edge of the table. He walked to the back of the tent and saw the small barges, only three times the length of freight wagons. The Keldon warriors were working on their combat gear and ordering slaves to do maintenance. He turned one last time to look at Fumash and his small table embodying the height of human authority that Haddad had seen in the colony. For all of the small man's good nature, position, and acceptance for his work, Fumash still set up his table so he stared at the dung and stench of the stock pens rather than the Keldons he served.

Eventually Haddad found the barge with the toad on its upper shield. The Keldons and the slaves looked at him with hostility as he called to see the warrior in charge.

"I'll get Cradow then," a slave said. He walked back to the barge and shouted into its hold.

Cradow was slightly smaller than the average Keldon, and he only grunted and muttered something about terrible luck as Haddad presented his authority token from Latulla.

The barges were scattered all over the field in no particular order that Haddad could discern. Each crew camped in and around their machine. Haddad could see arguments and shoving breaking out as crewmen moved equipment to stake out their space. The barges were tiny castles, and each had its independent army trying to conquer as much space as possible. Haddad wondered what it looked like before Druik and Fumash "organized" the barge crews.

"Come on up, whelp," Cradow called. "The rest of you lot get ready to depart at once."

Slaves and warriors began breaking down gear and throwing it into the barge.

"Artificers hate to wait," Cradow explained to a warrior who was snarling as he did a slave's work in moving gear into the barge. The Keldon's comment was a common saying, judging from the nods of everyone within hearing distance, and Haddad had to agree as he gave directions to Latulla's dwelling.

* * * * *

The barge traveled for hours in almost utter silence with only occasional orders from Latulla to Cradow. The normal chatter and noise of a working crew were swallowed up by the silence centered on Latulla. When they began to draw near their destination, Haddad felt relief, even if the omens heralding their arrival were poor.

It was the ungodly smell that signaled the camp. Haddad had seen massacres and smelled rendering yards, but the sheer scale of this stench rose far above any odor he had ever encountered. They were traveling down into the bowl of a long, stretched-out valley. There should have been a lake or a stream exiting toward the sea. Instead there was a temporary barn surrounded by a wall of thorns and vines. There were animals caught in the spikes and tangles of the surrounding barrier, and there were also the bodies of slaves and even one Keldon guard trapped in the deadly brambles. The dead warrior's head slumped as if in sleep, the flesh rotting and tattered from the efforts of scavengers. A gate broke the mounds of brush, and Cradow directed the vehicle with particular care as they entered. A bandaged and filthy Keldon left the darkness of the rough structure. He supported himself with a staff as he came to meet them.

"Who comes to the Clinging Bogs?" he intoned as he shielded his eyes from the dim sunlight. He leaned on the staff and showed none of the vitality Haddad had seen even in the most crippled warriors back at the landing.

"I am the Artificer Latulla, and I come for an accounting from the leader of this . . . fortress." She looked around. There was only a great barn and nothing else—no barracks, cookhouses, or latrines. It was just a shell surrounded by disgusting mounds of decaying flesh and razor vines. "I wonder at the lack of guards. In fact, the smell is the only thing the enemies of Keld must fear. Where are your warriors?"

"I am Lord Urit, and my warriors are where they are needed." Urit drew himself up a little straighter. He was shorter than many of the Keldons whom Haddad had seen.

His face was gaunt and distorted by heavy brows and a massive jaw. His hands were huge, and swollen knuckles gripped his ebony staff. Haddad could see fine clothing under the mud, and he wondered how a commander could get in such a poor state. Urit gestured at the green wood and piles of rotting vegetation, his staff dripping as it swung to emphasize his words.

"This is just a way station and doesn't need fortification or guards. If enemies ever try to burn it, I wish them luck. Only a mage could start a fire that can burn in these swamps. If I had more men, perhaps I could post a proper guard instead of trusting slaves!" Urit reined himself in with difficulty, and the passion that had animated his speech drained out of his face and posture. Latulla was nonplussed at the near tirade, and Haddad wondered how she would react after her anger had festered for a while.

"Certain changes must be made to your vehicle before you can continue," Urit announced as slaves opened large doors in the central building. "Without new traction devices fitted to your barges, you would mire before you reached the workings. I can provide some refreshment while the changes are made to your machine."

"I am unfamiliar with the operations out here. I thought the pits themselves were some miles farther on." Latulla, grim as she was, faded into the background in the all-pervasive gloom. "Who oversees the actual diggings?"

"I am considered master of these bogs, Artificer. If any can be called master." He walked farther out to the gate. "Don't touch anything on the mounds, and try to walk on bare soil or mud."

Some of the barge slaves drifted closer to the wall of greenery and were waved back.

Lord Urit turned and called to the sheds, "Bring out the

prisoner. I want to show our guests the strength of our 'fortress.' "

The prisoner was tightly bound hand and foot and gagged for good measure. His Keldon guard was forced to carry him, and at every step the captive bucked and fought with a strength that would have seemed lunatic anywhere else. In the poor light and the surrounding desolation, the slave's energy seemed almost demonic.

The guard threw the prisoner down. "Please get rid of him now, Lord Urit. I'm sick of him."

Lord Urit leaned on his staff and shook his head in agreement. "Call out everyone. A lesson isn't worth much if no one sees it."

The guard turned to fetch the compound's slaves, and Urit reversed his staff and pinned the prisoner down. The slave was filthy and foul looking, his features shadowed by mud and stained with juices from cut vegetation. The mud marked everyone in the camp, and the slaves slowly gathering were as dull as the dirt that flecked their faces and collected on their clothes. Even the Keldon guards seemed lethargic. Lord Urit's stooped demeanor was replicated in his guards, and even the promise of a punishment excited little Keldon interest. The slave to be punished was different in the energy and frenzy of his movements. There were ulcers and sores on his limbs, but they were distributed all over, and Haddad knew it was more than the chains of slavery that had punished his body.

Everyone was out of the shed and formed a rough semicircle with Lord Urit at its focus. He leaned on his stick hard, and Haddad heard the slave gasp as the haft dug into his belly.

"We are here to punish a slave who would run. He tried to cheat the Keldon nation and everyone here of his labor.

This sin merits death because his despicable act effects us all. Without loyalty, without the will to endure, we die. His death is more merciful than what he wished to inflict upon us." With that Lord Urit bent and picked up the slave. He raised him over his head and slowly walked toward the gate. He was unsteady, and the squirming of the victim threatened to overwhelm him. He cast the slave onto the interior slope of the mound with great force, and the body sank deep into the piled vegetation. It stuck there, and Haddad could hear a faint crackle and could see liquid soaking the clothes and limbs of the slave. There was a high keening and the body vibrated. How any sound could escape the cruel gag was a mystery, but Haddad could hear the snapping of bones as the tension in the slave's muscles went past the endurance of mere mortal flesh. Lord Urit and Latulla watched the body until all life left it. Urit watched with weary eyes, but Latulla seemed to savor every tremor of pain and muted scream. Urit gestured to the body.

"The vegetation that we piled up is thorny and poisonous. The animals of the land avoid it, and I thought a mound around the shed would make a fine fence. Unfortunately, it has taken root and new plants have begun to grow. Some are covered in a sap that grips tighter than a vise anything it touches. The other puts forth pods or buds filled with poison and seeds. When these touch flesh they break, soaking into almost anything and driving tendrils throughout the victim's body. I've thrown a chunk of firewood and found it rived by fronds in seconds. If we could, we would burn it and forget walls altogether, but it is too wet to burn and now too dangerous to cut and remove. We merely keep the interior of the circle clear, and I wonder how much longer that will be possible," Urit said, the hate thick on his tongue.

"Burn it? Something so efficient and elegant in its operation? I think you overwrought by your isolation, Lord Urit," Latulla said, enraptured by the sheer deadliness of the barrier. "I believe these mounds serve your camp better than stone or wooden palisades."

"As I said before, this is not the main camp. The barrack and my quarters are located three miles up that rise." Urit pointed up the slope of a gentle hill to where a muddy trail went up and over the side. "We had to go that far to get away from the stench and find ground firm enough to build on. I also wanted a well with water I could trust."

"Interesting, but I didn't come here to get a history. I came to find out why production is so low. The largest concentration of tufa within easy distance of the camp was detected here, yet nothing has come out of these bogs despite the numbers of guards, slaves, and materials you have requested and received." Latulla was calm in her delivery, but the threat and anger behind her words was clear.

"I am not sure we will ever get any Heroes' Blood from this land of muck." Urit was intense and livelier as he defended himself. "As foul and difficult as the land is here, it is much worse at the workings. Until you have seen them you can understand nothing." Urit gripped his staff tighter and met Latulla's eyes directly. "I will escort you myself. You will see that whatever your desires, the land will not meet them."

* * * * *

Lord Urit said not a word as the modifications to the barge were finished. Each leg of the machine now ended in a large shoe that reminded Haddad of a pontoon. The slaves finished tightening the last few bolts very slowly even after seeing the slave's death.

"We work in a land more treacherous than any enemy's heart," Urit explained. "Without additional support the barge will bog down even though it was designed for any terrain. I often wonder how the Heroes' Blood was laid down in this domain of mud. The bravery and power of our ancestors was greatest in reaching the battlefield."

Latulla took exception to this blasphemy. "You forget yourself, Urit," she exclaimed. "The Heroes' valor in battle is our legacy, not the conquest of a marsh."

"You will soon see how hard it is to conquer a mere marsh," Urit replied. "Like any war, each battle with the mud has taught us new tactics—the additional traction devices for the barges, new methods of excavation, and trying to preserve the warrior spirit in a land that mires every step. We are fighting, and no one outside the bogs seems to realize how desperate that fight is."

Urit boarded the barge without permission from Latulla but seated himself in an inferior position. However the lord of the bogs viewed his challenge to Latulla and her ideas, he was playing a balancing act. Haddad couldn't read his intentions, but looking at the miserable countenances around him, Haddad realized that losing his life and position was not a realistic threat to make against the grim lord. The odor of rotting animals and bodies caught in the razor vine wall faded as they left the great shed behind, but the insects grew steadily worse, settling on everything like dirt in a dust storm.

It was only twenty minutes before the barge moved into another cloud, this one of stench, of rotting flesh worse than the odor from the mounds around the transport shed. Cradow stopped the barge at Lord Urit's signal. Haddad got his first real look at the work site they had traveled so far to see.

The centerpiece of the site was the system of cranes. They loomed over a pit, each resting on pilings and pontoons set into what looked like solid ground. Every structure reminded Haddad of piers and bridges set over water, as if the builders thought the ground might liquefy and try to swallow the mining camp at any moment.

Even as he watched, one of the cranes began to move. The network of cables and counterweights jerked into motion. The bottom of each crane was connected to a long base that extended quite a distance behind the structure. A huge upright wheel on struts provided motive power. The wheels were very much like the prison wheels Haddad had seen illustrated in a manual on power transmission. Prisoners were forced to walk and climb for hours inside them until legal reforms and better engines ended the practice. Haddad was relieved to see each of the crane power wheels was connected to a small barge. Latulla was also observing the site and tilted her head at the innovation.

"There is always a shortage of slaves," Lord Urit explained, "and the wheels went through them too fast. Besides, the insects drove the workers crazy when heavy lifting was called for. We had heat exhaustion and dehydration cases the first day workers were in the wheel. I ordered our technician to rig up a power transfer so we could use the barges."

One of the active towers sent a large hook into the pit, and Haddad could hear shouting, then the application of power. There was a sound of suction being overcome and then the load eased. Slowly a large corpse rose out of the ground. It was several times the size of an ox. Mud dripped and water fell from the carcass as it finished rising out of the ground. The cable stopped rising, and there was a soun gears and levers being thrown. Haddad lowered his eyes a saw men working inside the base of the crane. The clus of machinery was obviously some sort of transmission t transferred the power of the wheel to the different cab and gears. Haddad could hear the gears engage, and crane began to turn, swinging the animal slowly over t giant stoneboat with very wide skids.

"That's part of the reason work has been slowed. The b has sucked down creatures of every size for uncounted m lennia. Some of them weigh tons. They have never cayed. We've run into hundreds during our digging."

"Dig somewhere else, on firmer ground," Latulla order

"Doesn't anyone receive the reports I send?" Lord U was exasperated and reigned in his temper with difficu "The ground is too unstable for another place to be bet This bog alters ground consistency almost daily. What firm today may run like water tomorrow. In fact, I reques additional lumber to lay out walkways at this site because unpredictable ground consistency. This was the best pla to dig, the artificers themselves said this was the clos point to the Heroes' Blood." Lord Urit started picking way to the pit. Latulla and Haddad followed.

The pit was actually walled with heavy planks. T instability of the soil forced the Keldons to shore up t sides as they dug down. The interior of the pit had seve spars crisscrossing the interior as it sank. Hoses and ha ing belts worked to keep water and mud flowing o Haddad could see the corpses of many dead anima entombed centuries ago and now exposed to the air, lo ing almost alive though covered in filth. A huge hog w almost completely exposed, and slaves called down a cra hook to lift it out. Haddad winced as the crane cable beg to scream under a load. Latulla suddenly pointed off to the side of the pit.

"What are they doing there?" she demanded in an angry voice. She was pointing to a small group of slaves and a Keldon overseer that were an island of calm in the thrashing, chaotic floor of the giant pit. The group seemed centered on a young girl, still splotched with mud but almost pristine in comparison to everyone else working. She was blonde and pale. She raised up her arms, her voice cutting through the pandemonium of the working slaves. Latulla tensed as she did when working magic, and Haddad wondered what spell she was readying.

"The pit witch is conducting a ceremony to stabilize the soil in the pit and the surrounding ground, Artificer. Even with her spells, we still have to pump out water and reinforce the walls," Lord Urit replied. "If you are worried about her abusing her power, we have her family held at a remote location as a surety of her cooperation."

"I don't care if you have a knife at her back twenty-four hours a day. She's flaring like a bonfire, and it's bound to attract something. She's uncontrolled." Latulla spoke as a professional criticizing the technique of an amateur.

"It's true whenever she conducts a ceremony we get more insects and animals coming into the area, but it is a small price to pay to keep the digging going," Lord Urit spoke flatly. "Unless you can replace her, we need her magic."

"You know we can't send you artificers or magicians. They are too rare to spend on a project even this important." Latulla was pensive as she considered how overextended Keldon capabilities were on the continent. "Perhaps when you reach the tufa detected in the bowels of this swamp we will be able to shift real spell users here instead of slave trash." She paused, and Haddad saw the end of the ceremony. The ground everywhere in the work site seemed to quiver slightly, and on the pit floor, workers no longer fought suction as they moved soil and animal bodies to pallets to be lifted out. The soil being turned and moved could have been from rich farmland instead of a near swamp.

"It's temporary, of course," Lord Urit said as even more frantic activity began on the pit floor. More workers were moving down ladders bolted to the wooden support walls. All the cranes were lifting out soil, and gangs of men at the rim moved wooden support sections to be lowered into the pit. "In less than an hour the ground will start turning into mud, and the pumps will be losing ground. It keeps getting worse the deeper we go, and we still don't know where the bottom is."

"It is that fact which will keep this a low priority operation, Urit," Latulla replied. "I will report home you are doing your best, but success is unlikely. For now, conquest of the western mines is a surer supply of tufa than your diggings here."

Urit bridled at the statement that what he was doing was not very important, but remembering Latulla's power and position, he merely looked to the side. The inspection was over, and the artificer turned and walked quickly to her vehicle.

Haddad ran ahead to ready the crew. Knowing the importance of this place, he continued to look around, memorizing the layout for the debriefing he would receive if he ever managed to escape. It was his eye that spotted movement outside the camp first. He stopped just as he reached the craft. Cradow was overseeing maintenance and followed Haddad's eyes as the slave skidded to a halt.

"Darba!" Cradow cried in a voice that resounded over the entire camp. The Keldon shouted with such force that when he tried to order the crew, he could only gape like a fish for a few moments.

Haddad saw a creature related to the parea—a giant carnivorous bird, but as it came closer, he gasped at its size. The monsters of the plains were flocks of chickens in comparison to this beast. It was at least twenty-five feet tall. Its feathers were green and brown, decent camouflage, perhaps, when it was a chick, but silly on a bird that could snatch up an ox. It moved toward the mound of dead animals hauled out of the pit. The huge muddy pile was obviously awaiting transport to a distant dumping site, but the bird had homed in on this pile of carrion rather than the huge mound of corpses that must exist somewhere else.

"Ready for battle!" Cradow croaked and scooped up Haddad, throwing him into the barge as the crew scrambled among the gear. A large ballista was yanked from a crate and set on a stand bolted to the floor of the vehicle. Keldons from around the camp were converging on the vehicles and yanking out weapons and armor, but all the other barges were secured to cranes supplying power or attached to trailers piled high with debris. Only Cradow's craft was ready for quick action. Haddad had no idea what to do, so he helped another slave move a heavy spear and put it into brackets set into the floor. The craft sprouted lethal quills as Cradow called for action. Haddad gripped the deck as the barge began to turn, and he could see Lord Urit at the base of a crane trying to get a barge unhooked. Latulla retreated to the edge of the pit.

"Hurry securing that bow!" Cradow directed the slaves. "Find the bolts and ready for a run." The two men he was pointing at stumbled to the gear and began digging for the bolts buried under Latulla's baggage. They tore loose the restraints, and the containers spilled throughout the interior as Cradow increased speed.

"Throw that crap over the side," he commanded Haddad and another man. Haddad was throwing out Latulla's cases before he realized it. Perhaps he would die and the artificer would be unable to punish him.

They completed their turn and were aimed at the carrion collection. The bird was pecking at the mound of flesh. Haddad was surprised to see the bird's wings holding the carcass of a great hippo. The wings were canted forward unnaturally, and Haddad noticed what appeared to be arms at this angle. The bird cut another chunk off and then fully extended its neck, regurgitating what it had eaten in a spray across the pile of meat. The corpses had not aged to the bird's taste while entombed in the mud.

The movement of slaves caught its attention, and it turned and stepped quickly to the pit. Those still standing dived into the excavation. The fortunate were climbing down the walls or sliding down cables—the screams of the unfortunate cut off as they reached the bottom ahead of the rest. The Keldons were roaring defiance, and a group under Lord Urit charged, the rush accelerating until it reached the creature. The beast's head dipped down, and it snared a pair of warriors. One was crushed to death, and the other looked like a doll caught by its arm as the darba's head rose out of the crowd. The victim's screams and the warrior's desperate attacks against its beak irritated the bird, and its forelimbs stabbed talons into the body, stilling it as the bird gulped down fresh meat.

"Get out of the way!" Cradow boomed as he directed the barge after the bird. The predator stalked through the heart of the camp, its head diving to snare a victim and cut the man to pieces. It killed without eating, leaving a trail of body parts. The camp slaves who fled from its attack were blocking Cradow's path. "Fire the bow, you cowards!"

The ballista was finally mounted and discharged. The darba's call of pain drowned out the rest of the camp as the bolt punched through the muscles of its leg. "Aim for the body, you idiots," Cradow ordered.

"We're too close, ash face!" a slave screamed back, the moment overwhelming healthy survival instincts. The ballista was powerful enough to kill, but the angle was too steep to hit the vital organs of the bird while the barge was so near. Cradow's response was to ram the great bird.

The barge came to a near halt as it hit the monster's leg. The multiple legs of the barge pushed up hummocks of dirt as the vehicle tried to trample the darba. The bird slammed down on the barge's overhead shell. The wooden canopy above Haddad's head proved stronger than the League technician had feared, withstanding the weight of the giant monster. Unfortunately, the weight was too much for many of the barge's legs. Haddad heard seals exploding under the sudden spike in pressure. The bird rolled off the top of the vehicle to the ground. Haddad could smell leaking Heroes' Blood as the bird struggled upright.

"Get some distance before we lose all power!" Haddad shouted. If the barge stopped dead, the bird would dig out the crew like the meat from a nut. They needed more time and distance for a ballista shot. The slaves manning the weapon were dazed and scrambled to load another bolt.

"Maybe the artificer can kill it," someone said, and Cradow sent the machine in a curving run along the edge of the pit. The collapsed legs gave the barge a rolling gait, the crew stumbling as the deck pitched beneath them. Haddad could see Latulla with her staff raised for a blow and wondered if her usual method of chastisement could work on a creature weighing tons. As the Keldon's stick fell, a wave of fire built and raced toward the creature. Unfortunately, the barge's malfunctioning controls took it into the spell's path. The men working on the ballista flamed into charred husks, and their bodies broke into pieces as they fell. Haddad looked out the other side of the barge, following the fire line as it converged with the darba, but the fire slowed and subsided as it reached the creature, the flames seeming to sink into the ground. When it hit the bird, it was far smaller and slower than Latulla had planned.

The spell covered the bird in fire, and Haddad believed the battle over. Then the flames died and left the monster standing. The feathers that covered the bulk of the bird's body were carbonized, and as it took a few breaths, most of its feathers fell like melting snow off a roof line. Its flesh was red and burned, and its cry squealed through the air. The line of fire had crossed through the barge, and when the beast's head dropped down, Haddad knew who it blamed.

"Try to get a bolt loaded," Cradow said almost calmly as he took the barge out of the camp at the highest speed he could manage. Haddad looked helplessly at the charred and twisted weapon as the sound of the bird's charge echoed across the site behind them. All the slaves readied personal weapons. They would be useless, but that was all they had.

Haddad's stomach seemed to fall, and he was stunned as the barge did likewise. They had run into a sudden mud hole that had appeared in their path, and the barge's limbs beat futilely as they dug the craft deeper into the mud.

"Come on!" Haddad screamed to the man beside him and flung a small trunk as hard as he could off the side of the barge. He jumped out after it and landed on his belly, forcing out his breath. The mud seemed very hard as he eeled forward without air. He reached the crate he had flung with such hysterical strength and hauled himself on top of it, out of the mud. He sat with his head down between his legs, trying desperately to breathe, ignoring the world around him.

When his head came up, the barge showed only the peak of the upper shell. Men and a few Keldons were throwing themselves through the mud in a mad attempt to escape from the darba. The monster had chased the barge and become mired as well, but it still struck at the men unfortunate enough to be too close. Slaves and Keldon warriors rushed from the work site and threw ropes to those stuck in the mud. Barge crew were pulled out of the mud and dragged yards over the surface. The pain on the faces of those rescued as their bodies were torn out of the mud stilled Haddad's urge to call for help. Hopefully, after things calmed down, more care would be used in rescuing people.

The pit witch was standing and chanting, directing her attention to the ground around the still struggling darba. Haddad now realized why the ground had suddenly given way beneath the barge and the giant bird. He was feeling grateful to be alive when he saw Latulla force her way through the crowd to the edge of the new mud hole. She was almost white with rage at her failure to kill the bird. Haddad saw her swing her staff high and bring it down. Knowing his mistress, he curled his limbs on top of the crate and closed his ears. The explosion of steam and mud blotted out all other sounds, and he swore as the effects of Latulla's angry strike washed over him.

* * * * *

Haddad came to on the floor of a land barge.. Outside he could hear Latulla and Urit talking, and he slowly sat up to observe the conversation. He winced in pain and wondered at the numbness of his hands and face. His arms were smothered in some medicinal salve, and he knew it must be numbing extreme pain.

The entire encampment was getting into wagons and sleds hooked up to land barges. The site was closing down for the night and the workers were getting ready to move to the firmer ground of the housing camp.

"We must have more barges and war manikins," Urit was saying. "The losses would have been much smaller with decent heavy weapons. This is the first time a darba has gotten into the site, but we have seen them before. Send more material." He was emphatic, but his lowered eyes spelled out his inferior status before the artificer.

"Keld cannot afford to reinforce failure. You will have to succeed with what you have before we can move more equipment to you." Latulla looked over the site one last time. "Dismount all the barges supplying power, and go back to using slaves in the wheels. The barges' weapons can kill the birds if you use them properly and at a distance."

"But that means more slaves will die, and we'll have to implement harsher discipline to keep them at work," Lord Urit replied. "It is more cost effective to use machines if possible."

"We can always find more slaves," Latulla said derisively. "We expect to have more prisoners coming in soon. Until then, make the mud witch work harder. You must succeed in producing tufa from the depths of the swamp. I or another artificer will be out here in a month to see that you do."

CHAPTER 6

The Keldon fleet was coming in. The ships in port were not the fast sailors that Haddad expected to see, considering the distance that they had supposedly come. Perhaps the more seaworthy craft were keeping out to sea, patrolling for League vessels. The ones that had pulled into the port were tubs. Wallowing in the water, they were nothing like the rakish raiders that Haddad heard stories about. As the crowd grew on the docks, Haddad drifted to a higher vantage point. He climbed to the veranda of a house and was surprised to hear his name called from the crowd. He looked down into a wide black smile.

"Fumash!" Haddad exclaimed. "Why aren't you outside Druik's tent? You didn't have a problem with the general, did you?" Haddad was expansive with this stolen moment of freedom and even a poor joke seemed humorous.

"He'll be here later," the clerk replied. "A hand up wouldn't be refused."

Haddad bent down, and Fumash seemed to fly up as Haddad pulled.

"Look's like a lot of activity out there. More gear coming in," Haddad said as stevedores unloaded one ship. The Keldon warriors and sailors began to disembark, kicking aside the slaves trying to unload the ship. "I despise them, I think." Such sentiments were dangerous to say aloud where someone might hear, but Haddad felt he could trust Fumash, though he realized he was taking a chance with someone he barely knew.

"We all despise them," Fumash replied. "Only a fool loves slavery. I serve a master who is comparatively kind because I provide clerical skills not commonly found in the camp. Yet his kindness is due to his lack of interest in overseeing me, not any innate goodness. As long as sleep and drinking with old cronies engages him, I am safe. But he has severely injured slaves when drunk or angry. Perhaps in Keld their servants love them, but not here." Even as Fumash spoke his bitter words, he smiled and nodded to the crowd, not wanting to appear furtive. "Look attentive, Haddad. We are looking for our masters from this high point. Remember?" He even pretended to point, then shake his head as if he was mistaken. The habits of deception were deeply engrained by now.

"Fumash, we both hate being here. If we don't like it, perhaps we should leave." Haddad kept looking over the crowd and speaking in an even tone, but surely Fumash knew he wasn't talking about the balcony.

"Why haven't you left before now? If you are looking for something, you should have spotted it by now and been on your way," Fumash said. Now he was swinging his wallet around and drew papers out of it. He held them up to the sunlight as if reading them, but his eyes were focused inside rather than on the paper.

"I am ready to go but need aid in finding the way." Haddad thought of all he could relate to League forces and moved his head closer to Fumash's to confer more privately.

"Keep your distance, sir," Fumash said almost primly and handed another document to Haddad. "Two birds close together can mean a nest and something hatching, as any bird watcher could tell you." The man's chin jerked to the crowd and the Keldons organizing the square.

"Bird watching is an excellent hobby, though it is quite dangerous around here. A man would get only a few miles before something snapped him up." Haddad kept his tone light and stared through the paper as he jerked his chin briefly at the growing organization in front of them. "Perhaps bird watching might be easier at sea. *If* the watcher knew how to use a boat." Haddad was a landsman through and through, but the dangers of fleeing overland seemed too great. Better to risk the unknown.

"A man familiar with boats might spot quite a few birds if he was far enough out to sea. The waters around here are too dangerous, but out where there is sea, one might spot all manner of interesting birds. And of course, many shores are safer for the bird watcher than this one." Fumash took the paper out of Haddad's hands and stood up, folding the paper and placing it in his wallet. "I myself will be putting to sea in the near future, accompanying Lord Druik back to Keld. I might do some bird watching, looking for nocturnal flyers. Perhaps you will accompany your mistress on the trip as well. It would be very useful to have someone besides myself helping me, carrying supplies, jotting down notes and so forth." Fumash finished arranging his kit and then waved as if to someone in the crowd. Haddad accepted the information that he might be dragged thousands of miles without blinking an eye.

"Perhaps we will be able to find something interesting at sea." Haddad also stood and waved to the crowd in general before following the little man down. Of course, considering the number of people Haddad had seen devoured by parea, no one would have accepted his interest in bird watching as likely. The habits of deception were becoming engrained in Haddad as well.

Haddad went only yards before another slave hailed him.

"Latulla has tasked all members of her household to finish unloading the barge. Absence will be noted and punished, so you best get there quick." The slave pointed to the emblem on Haddad's clothes and continued on his way, looking for other members of the house who had not received the news.

Haddad stepped smartly, knowing the thoroughness with which Latulla could express herself. He had not been on the docks themselves, only viewed them from a distance. The pier was rough and already showing signs of weathering and peeling that signaled the hurried construction. The Keldons suffered that failing on many construction projects that used locally "acquired" labor.

There were two ships at dock. The overseer of the nearest asked Haddad his name and marked it off a list. He was relieved to see that he was not the last to arrive and should escape Latulla's displeasure. He was waved to the ship farther down the dock. It was wide with stubby masts fore and aft, and it was tied to a thick bollard on the pier. Haddad expected to see the stub of a broken middle mast, but instead there were a series of hatches. He joined a work party and passed a line of slaves carrying sacks that strained their backs, turning their faces bright red. Haddad couldn't help thinking that a crane would be of more use here than stuck in the bogs farther inland.

The crew chief called them around and shouted over the groans of the other work parties.

"We will be assisting a mage moving warriors out of stasis. Work as directed, and you may ask questions freely. We will have no accidents. Any accident or damage to the warriors will be severely punished. Now come on." He turned and walked down a steep stairway that led to the hold. The chief cuffed and bludgeoned his way through the slaves, then led Haddad and the rest below decks.

The hold was dark, and they went to a corner farthest from the light. A comparatively slender Keldon sat on his heels as slaves removed the last of several sacks from pallets and moved everything away from the hull. All Haddad could think of was coffins as he looked at several dozen long narrow crates stacked and tied down with cargo netting. They were even corralled by brackets secured to the body of the ship itself.

"Move the first one down carefully," the overseer instructed.

Haddad noticed that all the slaves were in good shape and took it as another sign of the value of the cargo. Four men moved in concert, talking to each other as they carefully unhooked the nets and unscrewed the brackets that locked the crates into a single static unit. They moved the top crate slowly onto a set of supports. The crew boss broke the seals and swung the lid open. A Keldon warrior in full armor, weapons, and other gear filled the interior of the crate.

"What the nine hells is going on?" he whispered to the man beside him. Given permission to ask questions, he was definitely going to take advantage.

"Just watch. It will all become obvious in a minute," the slave replied, though he too looked on in obvious interest.

The Keldon mage rose off his heels and approached the body. The slaves cleared away though they stayed close in case they were needed. The mage reached under his cloak and pulled out a censer and tinderbox. It took him a moment to light the censer, then he swung it just over the head of the still warrior in very small arcs. The smoke poured into the crate slowly, like thick honey, and seemed to be absorbed by the body. The mage chanted quietly but lacked the tension that Latulla exhibited when she practiced magic. When the apparent corpse opened his eyes and began to breathe deeply, Haddad was startled but not totally surprised.

"Welcome to the Land of Heroes," the mage said and continued to swing the smoking censer. "It will be at least a few minutes before you may rise. You and your brothers will find glory and honor in these lands."

The crew chief motioned for another crate to be set down.

"I am always surprised they wake up from that sleep," the slave standing beside Haddad commented as they waited their turn to work. Already another crate was being opened.

"The first time I thought it necromancy, as did you, I am sure." The sailor looked not much older than Haddad, but he sounded richly paternal as he shared knowledge with one who was ignorant.

"Keld is thousands of miles away, and they don't have the greatest ships despite their reputation as pirates. They could never ship enough people and supplies to this base without some tricks up their sleeves. The warriors without sufficient rank or power are boxed up like cargo and shipped here. They ingest a philter of a drug that freezes them in a death-like state. The warriors lie down in crates, are dusted with certain powders, and then sealed up. They travel here without having to eat, drink, or engage in other activities."

The mage was chanting again and swinging the censer.

"A magic user isn't even necessary. It's the smoke that does the job. I've seen crewmen wake up warriors in transit without any magic at all. Just a match and a handful of leaves."

The crew boss waved Haddad and three others to replace the previous team. Haddad instantly realized why the slaves were all in good condition and were being rotated on the detail. The crate was solidly constructed, and the Keldon inside was not light. The slaves all exercised great care, realizing that their punishment would be swift and sure should they mishandle anything. Even with the weight and danger of punishment, the job soon became simple repetition. However, as Haddad and his crew reached the bottom layer of crates, the job became anything but routine.

Haddad was opening a crate, and as he began to lever up the lid, he noticed the smell. The stink of the bilge prevented his nose from noticing before. It was semisweet, but it tickled the back of his throat, and he had to repress the urge to gag. Remembering the permission granted him to ask questions, he spoke to the overseer.

"I think there's a problem here."

The crew boss was talking quietly to other workers on the detail but came over instantly at Haddad's interruption. The mage also rose from his crouch and approached.

"What is it?" the Keldon demanded.

"It's an odor, Lord. It is only noticeable up close but seems very strong," Haddad explained.

They had been working for quite some time, and the hold was deserted. The mage called for another light to be lit so he could see the crate. He held the lantern and inspected the crate closely. His cry of anger drove most of the other slaves away. Haddad knew it was dangerous, but he had to know what provoked such a reaction. The mage turned and loomed over Haddad, his face flushed and dark as a storm cloud.

"Get it open, right now!" he hissed, trying to reign in the usual Keldon impulse to take out anger on his inferiors.

Haddad silently set the point of his crowbar into the latches and threw his weight onto it. Unlike the earlier crates, there was no rush or puff of air as a seal was broken. The smell grew stronger as he worked the other latches, each release seemed more odorous than the last. When the last catch was thrown, the mage could restrain himself no longer. He reached past Haddad's shoulder and threw the lid wide open.

It took Haddad's eyes a moment to evaluate the contents of the crate. The slaves with the lamps retreated as Haddad tried to puzzle out what the warrior was wearing. Then a lamp holder moved closer, and the technician could see clearly. The coffin was alive with insects and maggots. The insignificant creatures retreated under and into the body as the light drove them to cover. The features of the warrior were twisted, and he seemed to grimace as parasites under the shrunken skin moved. Haddad looked on in horror for only a moment and then turned his head aside. He fell to his hands and knees. Everything he had eaten that morning spewed out as spasms racked his body. When Haddad could finally stand, he could see the other slaves had retreated away from the mage. The Keldon's body radiated tension that usually signaled magic. The less knowledgeable slaves saw it as blinding rage. Haddad wondered which it was as he spat and tried to clear his mouth, wishing vainly for some water.

"Filth," was all the mage said as his hand pointed at the corpse, but Haddad felt the flash of heat rising from the crate. The sound of the body cooking and the destruction of the parasites in the crate were the only sounds. Haddad could see the wide eyes of the other slaves as they realized the danger of such magic in the confines of the ship's hold. Then the smell of meat cooking hit his nostrils and sent him to his knees again. He could think of nothing as his body tried to empty a vacant stomach.

Shouts of panic, Keldon panic, made him look up after vain attempts to be sick. One of the awakened Keldons had heard the commotion and then had seen the body and its heat treatment. At the sight of a magic user destroying the contents of a transport crate, the warrior drew a long knife.

"What are you doing?" he screamed, tottering forward to threaten violence. "Warriors to me!" The strange sounds and odors from the hold were ignored by the deck crew, but a direct Keldon appeal for aid brought several sailors with knives sliding down ladders and stairs into the hold, throwing slaves out of the way to reach the mage and the warrior.

"Stop!" the magic user said loudly. "This crate was infested, and the occupant was dead. The slaves can confirm it." Haddad and the rest nodded their heads and prayed to be outside as several Keldons swore and looked at them closely.

"There may be other crates whose protections were violated," the mage continued. He pointed to a Keldon sailor. "Go to the Artificer Latulla, and tell her to come with a group of controlled slaves here." The sailor departed at a run.

"Take these other slaves on deck and hold them there," the magic user directed. "Latulla may wish to interrogate them."

The Keldon sailors immediately began to cuff and shove Haddad and his fellow slaves toward the main stair. The slaves ran up the steps quickly as the sailors relayed the order to hold them on the ship. The slaves were hustled forward until they were in the bow. They crowded against a set of holed benches over the water, and Haddad realized they were in the latrine.

The slaves sat down en masse, and no one spoke. Haddad could clearly see the gangplank. Latulla strode aboard and into the hold, closely followed by a group of slaves. Each slave wore a bracer or armband of metal. Haddad had seen slaves throughout the camp with such but never assigned much meaning to it. Now he realized that it conferred some special status, and he wondered what that status was. The mage requested controlled slaves even though Haddad and the others showed no sign of rebellion whatsoever. How were these new slaves different? What power did the Keldons have over these slaves beyond what they held over Haddad? He pondered these questions in silence as the day passed.

Throughout the day slaves used the facilities so conveniently close by as they waited in the sun. Water and food appeared, and Haddad nodded his thanks as a cook's assistant for the ship distributed rations. One brave or foolish slave started to ask what was happening, and the butt of a Keldon spear hit his temple before more than a few words issued from his mouth. Haddad and another man lifted him up and carried him to the very bow of the ship. They signaled another slave to keep him quiet and hoped that any sound the man made when he regained consciousness would be too quiet to invite more punishment.

Night arrived, and as the guards changed, the cook's assistant passed out blankets and more food and water. Haddad knew from the anxiety on the man's face that he was doing it without any orders and wondered at the man's quiet courage in caring for others.

At midnight there was a guard change, and Haddad thought he recognized the soldiers. They were among those awakened from stasis during the day. They seemed to stare at the opening to the hold more than they watched the prisoners. Haddad could guess what they thought. Each guard must be thinking about how easily he might have died. Two of the warriors talked, only stopping when other Keldons came close.

"How could it have happened?" asked one. "I was told it was safe."

"It is safe!" the other excitedly replied. "I have been in stasis several times, and there were no problems. I know warriors who were down as long as a year and there were no deaths." The more experienced warrior looked coldly at the slaves sitting on deck and spoke quietly, though Haddad could still hear him.

"I think it was sabotage," the guard said. "Someone put those insects in or violated the seals to kill the warrior inside. It may have even been done during the voyage by one of these slaves." Both warriors were fingering their weapons now. Haddad wanted to explain there was no way he could be guilty, but three things held him back. First, he would be passing blame onto other slaves. Second, he was glad to think that a slave had killed a warrior and probably got away with it. Third, drawing attention was suicide in the presence of two angry Keldons. Haddad felt relief when the guards were replaced. The new warriors were not so vocal in their suspicions, though their hands caressed the hilts of their swords. Finally, too bored and cold to worry, Haddad drifted off to sleep.

CHAPTER 7

"Get up! Get up!" The shouting woke Haddad, and he scrambled to his feet. A sailor stood before the slaves. Crewmembers helped stiff longshoremen up and collected the blankets and the buckets of fresh water provided them the night before.

"You are to return to your quarters and say nothing of what you have seen or heard. Tell your master that you have been ordered by the Artificer Latulla to reveal nothing." The sailor pointed to a man setting up a table and book by the gangplank. "Give your name and master before leaving the ship, so your story may be confirmed. Now get off the ship."

Haddad was in back, and it took quite some time before he was walking down the gangplank and toward Latulla's quarters. Though the sun was still being born in the east, the docks were crowded. Wagon after wagon lined up along the streets and every driver cursed the delay. The ships were reloading as crews and longshoremen toted their loads aboard. Once a wagon was empty, it was put to work hauling away cargo from ships that came in the day before. Haddad wondered at the level of activity, because usually it was days unloading a ship, and the screaming Keldon overseers wanted it done in hours.

He struggled his way through the current of wagons and slaves. When he arrived at Latulla's quarters, he found the gatehouse open. He could see wagons being loaded by exhausted members of the household. Lamps and torches were still set out and burning. From the faces of Haddad's fellow servants, the work had been going on all night.

"Haddad! Where the devil have you been?" screamed Briach. The chief servant was drawn and his eyes red with lack of sleep. He stepped toward Haddad, his hand going up for a cuff, but Haddad snarled back. The technician was too tired and aching from a night on deck to take abuse from another slave.

"I was kept by Latulla's orders, and that is all you need to know!" Haddad clenched his fist and tried to rein in his temper, but he found it difficult. "Where is Latulla? I will need to report to her now that I've finally been released."

Briach's face went still as he took in Haddad's defiance. "You will find the mistress in her workshop." Briach gestured to the outbuilding up against the compound wall. Haddad turned without a word and strode off, kicking the ground in anger.

"Keep a civil tongue, or she'll have it out," Briach called after him when he was a safe distance away. Haddad heard only the rumble of hunger from his stomach and wondered if he would be able to find a meal in the chaos of the morning.

Latulla was directing the packing of various projects as

Haddad entered the workshop. The shutters were thrown wide, and lamps were burning, but it was still dim inside. Haddad did not know the slaves in the room by name, but he recognized them as the banded slaves from the night before. They must have arrived with the ships just come in, and they had already displaced Latulla's regular helpers. Once again Haddad wondered what special talents they possessed.

"Finally you're here, Haddad." Latulla turned around, her hands full with apparatus that she was packing herself. "We are leaving with the fleet in only a few hours. Pack up your tools and manuals and anything else you will need for working on war machines. Bring the instruments you would need for fine work."

Haddad turned and slowly walked toward the locked cabinets holding his personal gear and tools. All the cabinets were open, and manuals and workboxes from other members of his old unit lay out. His eyes misted as he looked on the remnants of his former life.

"Most of the parts are already crated for shipment to Keld with us," Latulla called after him. "Hurry packing, and you can catch a meal before we have to pull out." Haddad turned and stared. Surely someone else was speaking. Latulla was almost smiling as she directed slaves doing the packing. Consideration was something he never expected from the artificer, and it left a strange taste in his mouth. He started packing a crate and writing an inventory of the tools and books he sealed away.

It took hours to finish loading. Haddad barely managed to get food and his personal kit before reporting outside. Latulla ordered him into the wagon for the ride down to the dock. Walking would have been quicker and more comfortable, but he was tasked with preventing theft. The material was all to go to Keld. Though warriors had picked over the booty when first captured, many wanted a last chance to snatch a piece before it headed north. Haddad bore Latulla's emblem, and her sigil on the wagons kept the warriors away. Except for Haddad, it seemed no other member of the household would be traveling north with Latulla. Haddad prayed that he would not have to serve as her personal slave. Haddad would miss Briach's unseemly passion for slavery if he had to constantly attend to Latulla's needs in the steward's place. Reaching the dock, Haddad could see the frantic pace of loading the ships had slowed. Latulla's wagons were among the last to be unloaded by exhausted longshoremen.

"Hurry up you fools, we need to depart immediately." The style and dress of the Keldon speaking suggested that this was the ship's captain. If so, Haddad hoped he could read the sea better than he read Latulla's uncertain temper.

"What did you say, Captain?" Latulla called as she stalked up the gangplank, her hands grasping her metal-shod staff.

"I apologize, but we must set sail immediately." The captain sounded rushed rather than apologetic as Haddad slung his personal gear and bedding onto his shoulder. "We were late getting in, and if we take too long we'll have League trouble for sure."

"I thought their ships stayed out of these waters?" Latulla leaned against the rail and watched Keldon crewmen running crates and sacks of her gear up the gangplank. The sight of the gray-skinned sailors doing slaves' work showed Haddad how short time was.

"You can't find a ship, but their cursed aerial patrols are starting to sortie from their rebuilt base out west. Someone will need to burn that out or shipping is going to cease." The captain gestured to the men forward to prepare to cast off.

"Still, why the rush?" Latulla eyed the final stragglers coming aboard and some of the longshoremen held each other up as they almost fell down the gangplank. A crude temporary crane dropped a wagonload into the hull with a crash.

"Haddad," Latulla called. He stepped closer and wondered if he would be preparing her cabin. "As soon as the last crane load is in the hold, go down and see to the storage of the cargo. I want a check of the inventory and description of any broken containers. Draft sailors to aid you as necessary." The captain finished signaling his orders to the crew, and she turned back to him with an expectant air.

"There are supposed to be long-shore raids today through the dawn in the far west," continued the captain. "It should drag their air patrols away and mask our departure. But until we rendezvous with the war ships in a week, we have no protection against attack. We need to get away from this port. All ships are to sail alone in case some are discovered, and I want to be ahead of the rest. Now I suggest that you make sure you have your gear onboard because I want to make way the second we can." Haddad saw that there were only a few loads left to go and went to start his task.

His first discovery in the hold was a pleasant one. Fumash, the small customs inspector, was looking over the cargo, checking its condition and security in case of storm. A broad black smile showed as Haddad hurried forward to talk to the little man.

"What luck!" exclaimed Fumash. "I was just wondering who might help me in the difficult execution of my duties. Who should appear but my good friend Haddad?" He turned to a crewman assigned to help him. "Go back to your regular duties, please. Your aid is appreciated, but your own tasks must surely call to you."

The crewman looked exhausted from working all night and most of the day preparing for departure. He only shook his head and stumbled deeper into the hold, looking for an out-of-the-way spot to catch a nap.

"Shout when you are through," the crewman called back.

"Trusting soul," Haddad said, thinking on the probable punishment for napping on duty.

"The tired do not think clearly. Besides, the rest of the crew is working farther forward, securing gear in the second hold." Sunlight shadowed the pair as they crouched, checking cargo ties among the crates.

"So Druik is onboard and bound for home," Haddad inferred. "I was surprised not to see him on deck." The cargo they were now processing bore Latulla's mark, and Haddad began to write on the slate he had grabbed from his gear. The words were almost illegible in the poor light. "Still interested in the birds of the outer islands?"

"Master Druik is in the cabin he and I share. I am checking his personal baggage." Fumash began chalking on a slate that squealed piercingly as he wrote. "And I am always interested in birds, though I doubt this is the time to discuss any expeditions."

"When would be a better time?" Haddad looked around and motioned Fumash to crouch behind the crate so they might talk freely. "The crew is completely exhausted, and we are unobserved for the moment," he whispered. "The captain said the ship sails alone for the next week. The farther we sail the more difficult it will be to find our way to the League. Do you want to wait until we reach Keld to escape?"

"Sea air has made you far too trusting," Fumash whispered back. He rose, and Haddad followed though Fumash only went a few steps before crouching out of sight again. "We are inspecting the cargo, remember?" Once again Fumash began scraping on his slate, though only random lines.

"Perhaps the sea air has affected me as well," Fumash continued. "I have long since had my fill of Keldon hospitality. We will go three nights from now."

"Why so long?" questioned Haddad. "The crew is tired now and will be busy getting the ship ready for the voyage." Haddad swore loudly then, as if discovering some problem. Fumash glanced up to check the hold for anyone else.

"Because no matter how tired the crew is, the captain will maintain a careful watch as long as we are in coastal waters—both to prevent escape and spot League air patrols. In three days we will be far enough from land that he will relax his watch. We'll grab a boat and sail for the eastern islands. We'll hide there for a few days and gather as much food and water as we can. If the Keldons are practicing raids, we'll wait a few days and then run west. In the deeps maybe we will miss some of the monsters that exist inshore. If we are lucky, we'll be spotted by our air patrols." Fumash signaled that their conference was at an end. "Don't stock up any supplies. It's too likely to be spotted and warn the guards. Besides, we'll grab food just before we leave." Fumash began to walk away, and Haddad could still barely hear his last whispered comment.

"If we are really lucky, the League won't sink us when we are spotted."

* * * * *

The dawn of the second day found Haddad slowly going mad with impatience. He spent hours slowly reviewing what he knew of the Keldon plans. While he knew the physical layout of the military colony quite well, he was unfamiliar with the Keldon tactics. Just how useful he would be as a source of military intelligence was open to question. Still, any idea of what lay at the heart of the Keldon incursion would have to be useful.

Haddad walked by a ship's boat one more time. He was unable to stop himself from inspecting the boat, so he rationed his glances. For cover, he toured the entire ship. He even got down to the power source for the ship's propulsion. He expected to see a shaft or moving machinery, but even with his background in large machinery, he was mystified at how the engine worked. It appeared that there were no working parts, no hydraulic transfer of power, and no powerstones. The engine just sat in the middle of several tanks like a pile of scrap. There was no sound of load or power. Something in that assemblage of parts was slowly and steadily assisting the sails in pushing the ship north, but he still wondered if it wasn't a trick played on him.

The crew, both human and Keldon, seemed merrier than the people he knew on shore. Perhaps it was because the line between the races blurred under the demands of shipboard life. The equality that Haddad saw working subtly in land barges was much stronger at sea. Part of it was the elevation of knowledge or skill that allowed slaves a new level of freedom in working the sails and managing the deck gang. Haddad thought it might also be because this was a transport vessel, and the Keldon identity as warriors just wasn't as valuable when the primary responsibility was transporting cargo. When he heard women usually oversaw such supply responsibility, he was surprised. The only Keldon women he had seen were midwives or artificers. Some of the slaves educated him when he eavesdropped on a conversation.

"Of course it's better to serve on a male-commanded vessel," one crewman commented to another as they checked coils of rope and prepared to wash down the decks. "You there, Haddad." He was waved over and wondered if he had revealed his interest in the conversation.

"What do you want, crewman?" he asked, already thinking of the lies he would use.

"We want you to settle an argument. I say it's better to serve under a male, even if he is more brutal, than under a female, because they strive to show authority at all times." Haddad took several moments because none of his ready answers addressed this unlikely question from a slave.

"I believe that Latulla is a special case, and it would be unfair to consider her as representative of her gender." Haddad tried to sound respectful of his mistress, but his eyes watched the unfortunate steward that the captain had appointed to wait on Latulla. Bruises and a general furtiveness gave the man a hunted look as he waited on deck to put off talking to Latulla as long as possible. He had tried to switch positions with the other sailors, but so far he had no takers.

"You're right. It wouldn't be fair to use her as an example. She has special demands upon her as part of her position." Each excuse was more forced than the last; each trying to overlook the fact that Latulla was unusually cruel even in a race that rewarded such cruelty.

"Usually women give lots of verbal abuse and scut work. When clear of military duty, a woman may have warriors underneath her, but very few males are capable of much outside of military action." The sailor spoke with the knowledge of experience evident in his voice, and Haddad took a chance to learn more before he left the Keldon world.

"Why don't we see more women then? Almost all of the bosses are male, regardless of the activity they oversee." Haddad had not considered it unusual, but he did not see the Keldons as anything but monsters most of the time. Trying to see them as a race or people was painful and jarring. "Where are all the women if they are so skilled?"

"Haddad, the town you left is a military base. Military action is the provenance of males. Our captain and officers are male because this is a combat area." The sailor smiled smugly as he revealed his superior knowledge. "Furthermore, this incursion is not totally supported by the Keldon nation. Most of the warriors are of inferior status and from secondary clans. The males you see commanding work details are from clans too poor to maintain a proper distribution of work between males and females. But if the loads we bring in are as rich as the one we're hauling now, there will be serious interest in colonizing."

Every time Haddad ran into slaves who supported or approved of the Keldon cause, he wondered what flaw warped their minds. Ignorant as he was of Keldon culture, he was sure that human males sat at the bottom, and that made him even more determined to escape and fight for the League.

It was late afternoon before Haddad found free time. Latulla ordered him to repack several crates they had hurriedly loaded to make the sailing date. The inventory was blatantly incorrect, and Haddad considered the man who packed it lucky indeed to avoid Latulla's grasp by staying on land. Of course, any mistake that Latulla could not instantly address tended to fester. Only a shipwreck would stop a sure reckoning upon her return. The artificer even designed a new loading scheme, so Haddad had to draft several crewmen throughout the day to dig crates out of tight quarters.

Haddad was taking a break on deck. Not a large risk because a meal would be served soon, and Latulla preferred to be in her quarters when the deck was crowded with men.

The helmsman and officers were in the raised stern, and Haddad wondered how much longer he could escape notice. The crew was taking a break, and each man had his cup ready as the galley workers brought up buckets of beer. Fumash was near the rail and looking over the sea. As Haddad approached, several sailors started a round of singing as their ration of spirits was distributed. Haddad had lived on coffee and weak beer for most of his life, but the strength of the spirits the crewmen routinely consumed was a source of amazement.

Fumash threw a bucket on a line into the water and drew it back up. He carefully poured a little from the bucket into his fresh water ration.

"I thought drinking seawater would kill you," Haddad said.

"You can add seawater to fresh water to stretch out your supplies as long as you dilute enough. Besides, it's a convenient source of salt." Fumash added to the concoction a small portion of spirits and then drank the mixture down. "Tastes as bad as always," he said with a smile.

Haddad could see hints of white teeth and wondered if the drinking was scouring away the deposits left by Fumash's nut habit. It would certainly be more difficult to procure a supply of them if they arrived at Keld.

"The captain doesn't look too concerned about League airships," ventured Haddad.

The ship commander was talking to Druik. The huge Keldon was on deck without the customary armor of a war leader, though the spike and long blades on his artificial limbs certainly gave him a martial air.

"He has to look brave under a war leader's eyes," Fumash replied. "We are heading northeast and should be outside the regular patrol areas. By tomorrow it will be just navigation watches, and we'll turn to the northwest the day after. It should still be calm if we are lucky." There was no wind, and the sails hung slackly. Those crewmen with needle skills worked their way through the ship's sails and signal flags. Maintenance had lagged, and Haddad wondered why. The ship glided forward slowly and without sound over the still sea.

"So we change course tomorrow," Haddad said, nodding slightly at the boat only a few feet away.

"As long as we are not spotted we should make a clean break." Fumash was growing nervous and stood with the bucket in hand. "How about a little sea water to cut your liquor ration?" He threw the bucket over, and it hit with a splat rather than a splash.

"What the hell is that?" The customs man was leaning over the side and sounded so puzzled that Haddad and another sailor looked over the side as well.

The water shimmered with faint glints of color, as if a sheen of oil lay on the water. It was a thick patch that the ship had hit in only the last few minutes. It was a large slick, and Haddad thought it strange that none of the lookouts spotted it. Perhaps it was common enough that only a landlubber or coastal sailor would be surprised by its appearance. The sailor's reaction put that theory to rest.

"Captain!" he yelled in a near falsetto, "we're on a gastro-jelly!" His cry sparked a round of confirmations as the various lookouts turned their eyes from the sky to the water about the ship.

The captain took only seconds to look over the side and then started shouting orders. "Change course hard to port! All hands fetch boarding pikes and prepare for jelly drill! Cook!" he shouted as the first serving of hot food was brought on deck, "start boiling soap! We've jelly to deal with!"

The cook dumped the rations on the deck and hurried into the galley, screaming orders to his assistant as he went. Haddad turned to the sailor who was sweating and holding a boarding pike.

"What is going on?" He looked at the water. The colors were now rushing toward the hull, and deeper, more-vibrant colors were starting to well up from the depths. The sailor seemed calm but expectant.

"It's a gastro-jelly, a type of jellyfish larger than the ship." He shook his pike at the disturbance under the water. "Right now it's turning over so it can use its tentacles. If the course change doesn't break us free, we'll be scraping it off the sides in a few moments." Haddad had seen monster attacks, but this one was so leisurely that he had a hard time feeling any fear. Fumash was confused as well, and Haddad was pleased not to be alone in his ignorance.

"Why haven't I heard of it if it is so dangerous?" Haddad asked as he took a pike.

Lord Druik was shouting and making the rounds of the railings as well. The words were forceful exhalations and grunts that Haddad couldn't make out, but the exhortations served to energize the Keldon crew. Each touch of Druik's hand as he walked left a more confident warrior behind.

Even Haddad could feel something, a call to battle, a shout of defiance against an enemy.

"A gastro-jelly usually isn't dangerous, but this hulk is too bloody slow, and we've caught the central mass. If those blind morons on watch had spotted it, we wouldn't be in any danger at all," the sailor said.

Latulla was now on deck and talking to the Keldon mate, trying to find out what she could do.

"Fire is not something we use next to the hull, Doyenne." The officer fidgeted as he talked to Latulla instead of rushing to his duty station.

"Well, it's almost impossible to target the jelly. There's nothing solid to hit," Latulla said, looking over the side.

"It's turned," went the call, and thin tentacles began to rise up out of the water. They were small and fragile looking, and Haddad wanted to laugh at the excitement they inspired. Then they began growing, and Haddad joined the rest of the crew in fear.

The tentacles grew in different ways. Some swelled until they were as thick as anchor cables. Others flattened into a rough sheet that coated the hull as if mechanical grease. And still others extended in sudden spurts of a few feet. Each sailor along the side broke off tentacles into the sea, some shaking and tugging their pikes as they became entangled like a bough attacked by a climbing vine.

More warriors rushed to the sides, and Druik began a war cry as each new fighter joined the attack. The hollering was in a dialect unfamiliar to Haddad, but the rhythm reminded him of a marching song, the melody uniting different parts into a single, focused whole. Keldon warriors roared in a brutal harmony, and some used bare hands to clear the sides of the ship. But being inspired by Druik did not make them invulnerable, and a single touch of jelly to bare flesh was something no amount of singing would overcome. Druik used his artificial arm to clear the sides and called out to the other warriors.

"Don't touch it, just peel it off the ship!" he yelled. "Use a spear, or lash it off with a rope." One warrior quickly picked up a coil and flailed it against the hull. The rope broke tentacles and tubes free of the hull with every strike. Other warriors drew swords and scraped the sides, others smashed barrels to use the staves. Despite the enthusiasm, the jelly sent up more and more extension, trying to pull itself aboard. The ropes were coated with jelly, and they dissolved. Warriors dropped weapons and rope overboard as the juices ate away at whatever they covered. Now crewmen stripped their clothes and armor to use against the monster. Druik's arm was covered, and Haddad could see jelly flesh eating away at the Keldon. Chunks of the beast were flung up on Druik's skin at the fury of his attack.

"I hope the cook hurries with the lye," the sailor said as he peeled away a long, gooey tentacle that spurted almost to the rail. Haddad and Fumash ran back and forth along their section of hull.

"What does it do?" Haddad asked as he darted several feet to slice a limb off the hull.

"Poisons it." An explosion made Haddad look over his shoulder before going back to his own battle. Latulla's spell had cleared the ship's side like a barber's razor, the line of fire hugging the hull and searing the monstrous flesh. Now several warriors ran to help other men clear their sections of the ship's side, while a few stayed to repulse any new assault.

Haddad turned as a warrior shoved him aside. The warrior used his shield as a giant spoon to scoop runners of jelly free and back into the sea. Latulla stood with her staff raised, and a growing nimbus of fire enveloped the wood and her arms. Then she struck, and the fire dived into the sea, burrowing into the monster beneath the ship. But the jelly had no complex organ center to destroy. Her explosion, while impressive, didn't win the battle, but its aftereffects did change how the battle was fought. The screams started seconds after the blast. Haddad turned to see men writhing all over the deck in agony. Latulla's explosion had hurled the jelly's flesh and digestive juices over the crew. The assault on Haddad's section of the hull abated as suction from the explosion pulled the tentacles back into the water. Haddad turned all the way around and started to run to the other side. Tentacles were over the rail, and Haddad could see the contractions as they pumped a living pool of acid over the deck.

Crew ran toward the cook who came on deck with a mixture of soap and water. The sight of men splashing almost boiling lye into their faces and on their wounds made Haddad determined that he would not touch the flesh of the gastro-jelly. It was Lord Druik who turned the battle.

There were bodies now on deck—slumping piles of flesh that poured red into the tentacles and pools. The bodies emptied out like wineskins, and a rich wave of color raced back over the side into the sea. Tentacles draped down into the hold, contracting and raining more juices and jelly below with each second. Druik knocked men away from the cook and splashed his leg with the remains of the bucket.

"Bring the rest up, damn you!" he screamed. Then the Keldon walked through the pooling jelly with a sword scraping along the railing. His body received several jets of fluid, but he only laughed and called for the men to fight. "Fight or cut your throats, cowards!" More buckets of diluted lye came and were sluiced over the deck. The tentacles withdrew or shriveled under the attack, but Haddad doubted it would be enough. Then he remembered the supplies that Latulla had packed below, and he called to her. She was crouched on the deck, and he could see the wood slowly charring as it heated around her. The jelly gave her a wide birth, but her defense would rapidly become a threat to the ship if she didn't stop.

"Latulla, did you pack anything poisonous or reactive?" She glanced up at his shout and narrowed her eyes at his failure to use her title.

"Yes, in the second crate," she called back. "The sacks are marked 'catalysts.' " Haddad threw himself into the hold before common sense could stop him. The area was dark with only a few shafts of light coming in. Most of the deck hatches were closed, and Haddad prayed he wouldn't be knee deep in jelly before he could find what he was looking for. The second crate was one that he had moved, and he hoped Latulla had given him the original loading number rather than one under her new scheme. He could see tentacles beginning to edge out of the bilge, and he skinned his hand badly as he hammered the seals loose with the butt of his knife. He threw out the containers, hoping he wouldn't poison himself as pottery and glass shattered. The interior of the crate was full of smaller crates that nestled Latulla's work in shock resistant packing.

Finally he recognized the symbol for catalyst and broke the container open. Two large satchels lay inside, and he looked for a glove or scoop to spread it around. When tentacles forced him to hop onto another crate, he decided to chance death by poison.

He cut the fasteners loose and took out a handful. It had the consistency of fine sand, and he threw it wide in a circle. Whatever it was, the jelly had no love for it. Where the sand touched, jelly flesh liquefied and then crusted over. Haddad began shouting as he rushed toward the open hatch where he had jumped down.

"Fumash, I've found the answer." He hurled the fine sand to either side. Fumash looked down then skidded around to the other side of the hatch in response to the jelly flowing over the deck.

"Then you better tell me now because I'm not going to be around much longer," Fumash shouted down. He had lost his pike and was holding a mop that scraped along the lip of the hatch. Haddad swore as the jelly fell toward him, and he nailed it with a pinch of the catalyst.

"Spread this all around," he called and threw the sealed bag to the customs man. Fumash caught it and then drew out of sight.

"Who's got a god-cursed knife?" he shouted on the deck, and Haddad heard shouts of relief as crewmen converged on Fumash. Remembering the mop laden with jelly, Haddad decided to head back up the hold for a stairway rather than trust a ladder. He had no desire for a jelly shower, and he dusted his way back up the hold even as shouts of triumph and victory began to sound on deck.

When he reached the stair he had almost completely emptied the bag. He could only hope that it wouldn't be needed on deck. The shouting had died down, and he was careful to have a fistful of catalyst when he stepped into the afternoon light. The deck seemed safe, with many sailors tending the wounds of others. The captain was examining the deck and exterior of the hull carefully as he talked to Latulla.

"I thought we were finished until that slave started using your powder. It's amazing stuff. We should carry it whenever we sail." His relief was obvious, and he still had the occasional tremor as his body shook off his adrenaline.

"That catalyst was very valuable and difficult to obtain," Latulla stated, prodding the crusty remains of the jelly as she followed the officer. "It would be more effective to whip the lookouts so they carry out their duties."

She looked at Haddad and the catalyst slowly dribbling from his hand. He immediately threw it into the sack and sealed it. He knew there would be no thanks or praise for his actions. He had gained her notice, however, and wished that he could reclaim her indifference. He left to find Fumash, wondering how his friend had fared. He couldn't find him as he went over the deck. His circuit took time as parts of the ship were covered with crusted jelly, and, dead or not, he was reluctant to walk on the remains. Approaching a crewman who was washing and bandaging another man's wound, he asked where Fumash was, fearing him lost.

"The little fellow is fine, but his master, Lord Druik, took terrible wounds." The man's patient hissed in pain as a bandage was tied over his salved wounds. "They took him to his cabin, and you should find your friend there." Haddad thanked him and crossed to the other side of the ship, trying to stay out of Latulla's eye. The cook was just leaving Druik's cabin, a bundle of bloody clothes in his hand.

In the dim light, Fumash was bent over the war leader, his hands gently smearing a thin paste over the Keldon's ribs. Long gaps showed muscle and even a glimpse of bone before Fumash's small hands covered it with paste. He looked up at Haddad briefly.

"Give me another pad of gauze." His elbow knocked an empty bottle of brandy as he gestured to a pile of medical supplies on a chair opposite the bed. "This stuff is supposed to be good for burns. Maybe it will help." His shoulders tensed, and each move was deliberated.

"Of course," Haddad said, handing another roll to Fumash, who started laying pads of the coarse weave over Druik's torso. The seeping wounds and salve glued the fabric down like patches on a coat. Haddad's eyes finished adjusting, and he considered Druik. Half-crippled he may have been before, but Haddad wondered how the Keldon could still be alive.

His stumps from past amputations were wrapped and already treated, but the artificial limbs thrown to the side had seen hard service. The metal studs and buckles on the prosthetics were only lightly discolored, but the leather was eaten through in several places. Half of the straps lay open, and Haddad at first thought Druik's caregivers cut the limbs free. A closer look revealed that the jelly had dissolved right through the straps. If more had given way, Druik would have fallen face first into the digestive mass of the beast.

"He was lucky," whispered Haddad.

Fumash slapped him, hitting hard enough that Haddad tasted blood as he looked at his friend.

"Lucky?" He pulled aside the sheet that half-covered Druik's good side. The arm was already wrapped, but even through the bandages Haddad could see how misshapen it was. Dimples and pits showed on the surface of the cloth and hinted at the gaps beneath. Druik's leg was still mercifully covered, but the heavy spotting on the clean sheet and the strange lay and contortion of the limb hinted that Druik had lost it as surely as he had lost his other leg in a battle long past.

"Someone has got to take it off." Fumash nodded to the

limb. "Chances are almost sure that I will get stuck with the job." Haddad swallowed his gorge at the thought. By viewing it as just an image, he could control his stomach, but the thought of doing more damage made him sick. At the sight of his distress, Fumash managed a small grim smile.

"Lift his torso up. I need to wrap his ribs." Fumash was holding a long linen wrap that he had picked up as Druik's injuries hypnotized Haddad.

"Shouldn't a surgeon be doing this?" Haddad asked, though he slowly moved into position to lift at the shoulders.

"As a slave, I am in his household and responsible for caring for him," Fumash replied as he twirled the wrap into a roll that could easily pass under Druik. "And if there was a way to get someone else to help with these little jobs, I wouldn't be talking to you. Now lift," he ordered.

Haddad slowly raised the Keldon's upper body. Druik made no intelligible sound, but Haddad could feel each breath and the warmth of the gray living flesh.

"Why isn't he screaming with pain?" Haddad asked as the breathing continued without interruption.

"He's had enough drugs and alcohol that I think he's going to die," Fumash replied as he continued to wrap the form of his master. "If he lives, it will be in spite of my ignorance, not because of my doctoring. Besides," he continued, "I certainly wouldn't want to live in this condition."

Haddad looked to the door, hoping no one was within hearing distance.

"Don't say that," he whispered to Fumash. His friend misunderstood him as he continued his task.

"He's been a good master in comparison to some, but I am not here by choice," Fumash said as he began to secure the sheath of cloth with a series of strategic tucks and a long pin. "I might even like him, but he is the enemy, and I would leave him dying if offered the chance."

"What do you mean?" Haddad said, forgetting circumspection. "We're leaving tomorrow night. The crew has fought a battle, and we need to leave before they recover."

"The captain will be especially vigilant after this, and there is no way I am going to sneak out of this cabin. I am on a deathwatch and will be expected to stay here until he dies or recovers. Even if he dies, death rites will demand my presence." Fumash was bitter, but his hands motioned Haddad to gently lower Druik to the rough mattress. "If he survives at least two more days, I might be able to leave. You will have to escape for both of us." Fumash tried to give Haddad a smile but couldn't manage it.

"I can barely stand in a small boat," Haddad said, "much less sail on the open sea. If you don't go then I can't go." He realized that bolder action would be required. "We go in two nights or die trying. If you are with someone, slave or Keldon, kill him and meet me at the ship's boat. I am not expected to serve Latulla and am not closely watched. I, too, will kill if I must."

Fumash was doubtful about their chances, and it showed. He had been a slave for a longer time and was used to pushing hope farther and farther into the future.

"We have to leave, Fumash." Haddad gripped his own shirt and it tore as he tried to rein in the anger threatening to explode at this sign of doubt. "Every day that we stay we shrink and lose a little bit more of ourselves. If you don't run you'll be as crippled and helpless as Druik is now." He laid his hand on his friend's arm and finally received a nod of agreement. The decision and near-resignation was plain in Fumash's eyes as he turned to the medical kit and began withdrawing implements for amputating the destroyed leg.

A Keldon guard came in as Haddad tried to nerve himself up for the possible operation. The warrior advanced into the room with his head lowered as a sign of respect for the fallen lord.

"You are commanded to appear before your mistress, slave," he said to Haddad. Despite the harshness of the words, the Keldon sounded almost polite. The warrior turned to Fumash. "I will assist you in what needs to be done."

Fumash gave Haddad a quick nod and showed two fingers where the guard could not see them.

"Two days," the small man mouthed.

Haddad nodded quickly. Two days until escape from the ship. As Haddad left to serve his mistress's pleasure, Fumash turned back to the instruments.

* * * * *

"You've been down in the hold since the attack," were Latulla's opening words. "Was there any damage to the cargo besides the crate you broke open?" The lack of gratitude firmed up Haddad's plan to escape even over her dead body.

"I don't know," Haddad said as the injustice of her implied criticism sank in. "I was busy trying to kill the beast and help save the ship." Latulla's flat stare reminded him that he lived at her sufferance.

The captain and Latulla stood at the entrance to the hold after finishing the survey of the deck. Haddad could see two sailors down among the cargo searching for more remains of the gastro-jelly, the nearly empty bags of catalyst ready in their hands.

"Considering how much damage it did to the crew and ropes up here, who knows how much cargo was devoured when it pooled in the hold?" The captain had survived the attack but worry about his cargo threatened to overwhelm his relief.

"Fetch the inventory that you prepared, check my crates, and then the rest of the cargo," Latulla ordered Haddad. "Report to me as soon as you and the captain are finished. I will be in my quarters or with Lord Druik." She turned and walked away.

Haddad waited until the warriors in the hold finished their search for any living jelly. He didn't care how quickly Latulla wanted him to get to work. After the all clear, he went carefully down into darkness with other crew who the captain detailed to the task. Haddad set lanterns alight in the dark corners, and no one gainsaid him even though light poured in through the open deck hatches.

Except for the one Haddad broke into, Latulla's crates survived the battle without a scratch. In the farther hold it was a different story. The monster had poured through the upper hatches and landed on the supplies of biscuits and other provisions. The mound had spread over other crates, and a few had given way, their contents strewn among the remains of the beast.

"We need to clear this hold and check everything," said a Keldon mate. The first few attempts to shovel the monster's remains into a barrel for disposal were very tentative. The odor and settling of the remains when the first shovel broke the crust sent men stumbling back. But under the repeated orders from the Keldon mate, the crew began to collect the mess and put it into barrels. A winch was quickly rigged on deck, and the barrels began rising out of the hold to dump their contents into the sea.

"What shall we do with the stores that are contaminated?" asked a crewman who uncovered a container of cheese. The mate looked at the rounds covered in muck. He cut a wedge and saw how trails of digestive juices had eaten their way through like worms.

"When in doubt, toss it out." Supplies went into the barrel and then whole containers of food were hauled up. Perhaps the captain disagreed with the mate when he saw containers of meat going up, but his own investigation of its purity overwhelmed even his iron stomach. It took hours to check every barrel and cask. Eventually the provisions not violated during the attack were separated out. More than half of the food, water, and spirits were emptied over the side, and the sober faces of sailors told Haddad that things were serious indeed.

The corners of the hold were filled with crates that seemed to have escaped the touch of the devourer. But even after the long day that the crew had put in, there was no break. The captain rotated men from the deck to the hold. Haddad continued working except for a few trips to the deck for relief. He devoured an issue of rations that he ordered from the cook, letting him think that he was carrying it for a Keldon down in the hold. Latulla had tasked him to remain until the survey of damage was done, and his bravado wasn't yet strong enough for him to disobey.

Haddad became more nervous when a wall of crates came down. Behind the booty stolen from the League were stasis boxes. The image of the eaten corpses he had found in another hold mingled in his mind with thoughts of the monster's ghastly appetite. He really did not want to open the boxes. Of course, the mate overseeing the crew did not solicit his opinion.

"Crack them open," the officer ordered. He motioned

two Keldon sailors forward, their strength necessary in the tight quarters.

"All of them?" one of the Keldons asked incredulously.

"Just the ones marked as occupied, fool." The mate pointed to a circle on the foot each of the forty or so crates. Most of the circles were broken, an arc left out, and Haddad quickly realized that only those with closed circles needed inspection. "We'll do those on top and several from the bottom." The crates were stacked three high and a cargo net was attached to cleats and bolts to prevent shifting in heavy seas.

"You will open them, slave," the mate said and handed a lever to Haddad. The two crewmen swung a crate down, and Haddad set the iron bit in the latch. He levered it open in a rush, then took a deep breath as he forced the lid up, expecting a corpse. Instead there was only an armored warrior in stasis. A great sword lay clamped at his side, and at the warrior's feet lay a bag of coins spilling out stolen League silver. A Keldon warrior going home with riches squeezed from Haddad's homeland. No breath or movement from the body, but even as tired as Haddad was, he could tell that the man wasn't dead. There seemed to be an air of satisfaction and expectation to the still warrior. The Keldon lay ready to arise and conquer, and Haddad hated him. It was the same as they went down the line, until Haddad felt nothing except exhaustion as he opened the boxes to reveal the sleeping warriors within.

"We'll need to check the bottom one just to be sure." The mate pointed to a single crate with a complete circle with two crates on top of it. He ordered two more crew to replace the sailors working with Haddad. Even for a race with gray skin, the two sailors looked listless. The mate did not relieve Haddad however, and the captured League soldier leaned against an open crate, trying not to collapse.

Haddad couldn't muster the energy to think as he threw the last series of catches. When the lid opened, he looked on in confusion at the contents. The "body" had arms and legs and a head, but it wasn't alive. There were weapons and pieces of armor in the crate, but it was no Keldon warrior. Despite the brick colored skin that covered muscles and bones, Haddad was unsure if the figure had ever been alive. The body's skin looked like leather and was tightly drawn. The joints were swollen and the hands were a collection of walnuts strung together. The head was enclosed in a helmet, and Haddad felt his gorge momentarily rise. The body had no lower jaw, and Haddad felt sick at the thought of such an injury. But the skin and lines of the neck showed no trace of injury. Finally, the eyes were spheres of glass or crystal, and they stared out of lidless sockets. Haddad looked to the mate in confusion, and the officer advanced to get a better look at the contents.

"A war manikin?" he exclaimed. "Why would anyone put a war manikin in a stasis box?" He stooped and looked over the humanoid device in puzzlement. Haddad gnawed at the inside of his cheeks, trying to wake up, to get a close look. The mate stopped Haddad's inspection as he closed the box, taking the lever from Haddad's hand to throw the latches shut.

"One of the warriors in stasis must have decided to bring it home with him," the mate said out loud. "Actually a clever way to smuggle it back to Keld if he can get around the wake up ceremony when we reach port." He motioned for the crew to secure the crates again with the cargo net and bolt. "We'll leave it alone. None of our business, anyway."

The crew was finished, and finally they all trooped up onto the deck. Haddad realized that night must have fallen hours ago, but he had lost track of time as lanterns were lit, and the work moved farther and farther into the depths of the hold. His exhaustion clouded his mind.

"The captain and the artificer have retired," the sailor standing watch informed them as they stumbled around in the darkness. "They'll take reports in the morning." Haddad was thankful and followed the rest of the crew to bed.

Haddad lay in his hammock minutes later, dreaming of the gastro-jelly eating and dissolving men until only a crippled Lord Druik was left, surrounded by ranks of what the mate named war manikins.

* * * * *

The morning found Haddad barely aware but already ordered to report to Latulla. He was surprised to find the morning half gone and most of the company on deck standing beside empty stasis boxes. Many of the Keldon warriors who came aboard with Lord Druik were in armor and standing ready as if for battle. Haddad checked the horizon for signs of an enemy, but nothing was visible. It seemed a perfect day. The captain cleared his throat and addressed the company.

"We took several casualties in the battle yesterday, but the ship has survived due to your efforts. I am proud to have you aboard as my crew." Hollow cheers sounded, but most were exhausted from the battle and its aftermath, and enthusiasm was lacking in their voices.

"In spite of your bravery we still lost a substantial part of our cargo, and so we will all have to work harder and make some sacrifices." He looked to the horizon and spoke in a more serious tone. "We were carrying supplies for the ships we are to meet in three days. Keld needs those ships sailing and raiding in these waters. They can't withdraw to resupply without jeopardizing important plans. So to provide them with what they need we will have to transfer part of our own rations." A low murmur sprang up, but none of the crew seemed particularly surprised or upset.

"We've neither the funds nor time to buy or raid for more, so we will have to consume less." He gestured to the stasis boxes. "We will put as many in stasis as we can. When we meet the fleet, we will take on their empty boxes and sail with as small a crew as possible. Lord Druik has volunteered to be first."

Haddad doubted that Druik had spoken since the battle. High-ranking Keldons almost never entered the boxes because of the danger and loss of control that they experienced. It was means of cramming low-level warriors into ships and restraining supply costs, but pride overrode the economics. The crew murmured again in real surprise at the thought of a lord willing to endure a process that they were happy to avoid.

When Fumash backed out of the cabin holding one end of a hatch cover, Haddad realized that the captain was serious and that Druik had survived through the night. Fumash and the crewmen helping him used the cut hatch as a crude stretcher. Once they were out of the hatchway, Haddad could see that the Keldon war leader had grown easier to carry. Fumash had amputated the leg, and Druik's remaining arm looked foreshortened as well, though the layers of bandages made an accurate assessment impossible. The fallen hero was still insensate, and Haddad hoped he stayed that way. He couldn't imagine waking up with his limbs gone. He was frankly surprised that someone had not eased Druik's passage into the next life already.

"Bring him here." Latulla was standing beside the first open box. A burning censer and several bottles rested on a table moved up on deck. She was clad in her finest robes, and she laid a gold-embossed cane on the table. She began to arrange the ingredients.

Fumash and the others shuffled up to the box, and at Latulla's wave, two of Druik's armed retainers advanced and slid his shrunken form into the box.

"To sleep in the dreamless void," Latulla intoned as she opened a bottle and placed it between Druik's slack lips. The lord coughed as the liquid poured into his mouth and into his lungs. Latulla was muttering before he finally swallowed a proper dose.

"He shall need no nourishment for a year and day." Latulla forced a second bottle and gave the lord a draught. Haddad could see the form stilling as each second passed. Finally, Latulla was satisfied that Druik was under. Haddad wondered how difficult it was to figure the proper doses for a man without limbs.

"Finally, protection from decay, from the mouths of worms and the companions of the dead." Latulla picked up the censer and then looked at the flags and emblems on the masts to evaluate the direction of the wind. She shifted to keep the wind at her back and raised the censer. The crew shifted away from the path of the smoke, Haddad following and trying to move to the front of the group for a better view.

Latulla hesitated and then waved Fumash closer. Haddad managed to reach the front rank and could hear her as she whispered to Lord Druik's personal slave.

"The bandages need to be cut and more of the flesh

exposed." She handed him a small knife and motioned him to begin. Fumash bent over the still form of his master and began cutting through the wrappings that he had so carefully tied over his master's wounds. Druik was totally removed from time but there was still fresh blood soaking in the pads placed over his wounds. Haddad turned his eyes and counted the boxes awaiting bodies. Almost thirty were open, and Haddad wondered how many more would be filled after they reached the supply point. At last, Fumash finished his task and stepped back from Druik.

Latulla must have added something to the censer while Haddad was lost in thought. The censer boiled over like a kettle on the fire, and the smoke poured over the sides like water, filling the stasis box and hiding Druik from view. Some smoke lapped over the sides of the box and seemed to crawl like a snake over the deck before collapsing and disappearing. Latulla grew irritated as crew tried to avoid the excess vapor. If there was more to this internment ceremony, she cut it short and swung the heavy box lid closed. Fumash threw the final latches.

"His guards will follow him into sleep now." Latulla waved the guards forward as a group and there were no more words as she processed them all at once. Each guard drank from a bottle and then quickly lay down in his new home. Latulla went down the line, forcing the second potion between their lips. Haddad could hear the bottle jamming and levering against teeth as Latulla acted with her customary regard for others. Then she stoked the censer till smoke geysered out. She walked it up and down the line of boxes as if watering a flowerbed, and finally the guards were closed up in their boxes.

"It is fitting that Druik's servants travel with him."

Fumash froze as other slaves advanced to stand before

empty boxes. Latulla gripped him by the throat and sharply struck his hand with the base of a potion bottle. The knife he used to cut Druik's bandages fell to the deck. Haddad could only watch the surprise spreading slowly over Fumash's exhausted features as the potion poured down his throat. Latulla pushed him into an open box, and he fell into oblivion. Latulla administered the doses, and Druik and his entire household were sealed up.

There were still a few open boxes, and from the restlessness of the crew, it was obvious that a new crop of bodies was going to be laid to rest. The captain walked toward the group and drew out the unwilling volunteers by touching their arms and pushing them toward the open boxes. A mate selected crew to transfer the full boxes to the hold. Latulla called Haddad forward. He advanced, but his eyes were locked on the boxes as he walked closer. Latulla smacked his head with her cane from the table. After his vision cleared, she thrust a small container of paint and a brush into his hands.

"Check the latches, and use the paint to close the circles." She turned to process the crew waiting for her and her potions. Haddad knelt down by Druik's box and checked it thoroughly. He dipped the brush into the inky black paint and closed the circle at the box's end. He went down the line of boxes quickly but paused when he came to the one containing Fumash. All of their plans had been ruined by this mischance. When they first plotted to escape, Haddad had expected to taste freedom tonight. Now his chances were much slimmer. He didn't know sailing or the surrounding waters, but he must make the break alone. Fumash was going to Keld, as surely as a doomed soul sank into the underworld. Haddad continued past his friend and soon caught up to Latulla. The last few crewmen waited to be processed, and Haddad was surprised to see Latulla's personal steward from the ship's crew among them. He was smiling—the first happy man Haddad had seen lowered into a box. Haddad thought sourly that he would be waiting on his mistress now and understood the man's happiness. The fading bruises Latulla had provided the steward stood out against his pallor as Latulla finished administering the second draught. The censer streamed smoke, and Haddad swung the lid closed on the steward. The captain approached Latulla as Haddad closed the latches and prepared to close the circle with an arc of paint.

"It's going to be difficult working with a crew this small after all the casualties and filling up these boxes." The captain patted the back of the crewman waiting to enter the last box.

"Of course I realize the difficulties, Captain," Latulla replied, resting the now quiescent censer on the deck. "That is why I have decided to make my own sacrifice to the common good." She rested the shaft of her cane on Haddad's shoulder with a gentle tap.

"My last personal slave will rest in one of these boxes till we reach Keld to give you another able seaman." Her words were expansive and generous sounding, but the metal figurehead on the cane's end rested against Haddad's Adam's apple. She drew him upright and close to the box. The denial and fear in his eyes didn't surprise Latulla, and she twisted the metal head of the cane under his jaw, forcing his head back to administer the sleeping draft. She pushed him into the last box, and his skull rang off of the bottom. He opened his mouth to yell, and the second drink was poured down his throat. Latulla was standing over him and watching his sputters and tremors of fear with a smile. Had she discovered his plans for escape or was this payback for his perceived lack of respect? He saw the enjoyment in her eyes as his limbs grew heavy. She enjoyed the fear he radiated as his entombment continued. His eyes were only starting to close as the smoke from the censer obscured his vision. He could feel the heavy vapor settling over his clothing and coating his face as he heard the lid swing shut and the latches close.

CHAPTER 8

When Teferi sent Barrin to the blimp hangar construction site on the eastern frontier, the wizard considered himself fortunate. Barrin's task was to learn all he could about the systems supporting Teferi's military and to perhaps adapt what he had learned to Urza's forces. The building of a new hangar complex gave him that chance.

Teferi was kind enough to 'walk Barrin to his ornithopter—in mid-flight. Yarbo started as Barrin appeared with the planeswalker, and then Teferi vanished back to his blimp.

"Fly us to the new airbase," the wizard ordered, and the pilot turned the craft. Soon the coastline appeared, and Barrin compared it to the maps he had received. Yarbo winged inland, arriving over the growing base in minutes. He put the machine down on a landing pad. People converged on Barrin as he exited his craft.

"Tell me you are here to take over this madhouse," a man said as he rushed to the landing craft.

"I am just an observer, here with Teferi's approval," Barrin replied.

"Another little job for me to handle!" the man shouted, and he began stomping around the ornithopter, cursing. Several other members of the construction team hurried up and began unloading the baggage and gear. Barrin noticed several tubes of plans being unloaded and turned to his pilot Yarbo for an explanation.

"Since I was flying to pick you up, I was asked to bring a set of plans to Willum, the master builder." Yarbo looked at the apparent madman still stomping around in a circle. "That must be the man you are supposed to observe and copy." At Barrin's look of ire, the pilot quickly grabbed his personal bag and ran after the withdrawing construction workers. Willum orbited back to Barrin, and the wizard quickly schooled his face into its usual serious mien.

The man was short and his skin red from recent exposure to the sun. He was heavy and in the rough work clothes of a skilled construction worker. His limbs were thick with muscle but lacked the definition of an athlete. His expression was angry but seemed directed at the world at large, not at Barrin standing before him.

"Willum is the name. I manage the circus you've come to see." He extended his hand as he spoke, and Barrin gripped it. The wizard could feel the calluses and the strength behind them.

"I am Barrin, and there is no need to dance attendance on me. I am here to see how things are done. I'll just follow along or perhaps you can gift a junior with me if you are busy." Barrin wanted a smooth working relationship with the people he observed, and the impromptu war dance suggested he might spend more time fighting with Willum than learning from him.

"If you want to learn about the whole operation then you better stay with me," Willum answered, turning and beginning to walk to the construction site in the distance. "I am tasked with putting this together and am the best authority you could hope to find here. Besides, maybe you can help me." Barrin walked quickly to catch up. "I've yelled long enough," Willum continued, "it's time I took a break." He chuckled, and Barrin realized that Willum's temper was a tool as carefully wielded as any other in finishing the job.

"Okay," Barrin said. "Then perhaps you can answer a question for me. Why is a base for naval patrols so far from the sea?" They were almost twelve miles inland, and a range of low hills blocked easy access to the ocean.

"We're an airbase, and while we work in conjunction with surface units, none are based here." Willum walked the site perimeter. "We have sea access and shipping from a river about a mile north of here." He pointed to a graded and graveled road that entered a screen of trees. "Remember that the former eastern airbase was burned by raiders. It's rugged country if they come from the coast, and the river adds miles to the trip inland. That's if they get past the fort we placed at the mouth." Willum spoke with pride as he considered the defensive arrangements. He stood on a low berm and gestured in all directions. "This is the best point to see everything," he said.

Barrin stood beside him and looked to the road that carried cargo from the river. A collection of tanks and piping sat in a depression. Barrin noticed the fresh sod and the regularity of the slope and realized that massive amounts of dirt must have been moved to create the dip.

"Why did you lower the ground there?" Barrin asked. The works served no obvious defensive purpose, and while the strange construction was hidden from a distance, aesthetics was an unlikely reason for so much labor.

"That is where we will be breaking down and refining the tufa," Willum replied as he looked on the workers connecting pipes and digging additional pits for storage. "The stuff it throws off is pretty volatile, and I decided that lowering the works would help protect the rest of the site in case of accident. Also, some of the vapors can be dangerous even if they don't burn, and the geometry of the digging sends the fumes out toward the trees instead of the hangars. The biggest trouble was making sure we had year-round drainage." Willum kicked at the turf that his men cut and laid down after they finished building the rise. "The ground can turn to quicksand in rain, and during part of the year there's a lot of standing water in this country. I didn't want a part-time lake interfering with refinery operations.

"But the hangars are the real heart of the operation and the bottleneck to the whole naval strategy," Willum said as they walked into the site. As they got closer, Barrin began to grasp the sheer scale of the endeavor, and it was impressive even when compared to the huge air sheds maintained for the dirigibles that flew under Urza's flag.

"We have already set the foundations for two hangars," Willum said. "Each will be almost a thousand feet long and nearly two hundred feet high at the roof." Barrin could barely grasp the scale of how huge the buildings would be. An army of thousands could be massed in each of the buildings with ornithopters flying inside. An entire fleet could be constructed from the wood used on site. Within the year, ten acres would be domed over.

"Why so large?" Barrin asked. "Surely building on such a remote site makes this type of construction almost impossible."

"Teferi states that we are building for the ages, and we shouldn't let the flock of small craft we fly now limit the size of our facilities," Willum answered. Barrin thought of Teferi's heavily armed whale of a command ship and wondered just how large the planeswalker's dreams were for his aerial fleet. "As you can see, we are setting up the door supports for both hangars before we begin construction of the walls."

Four sets of wooden structures laid out the corners of the hangars to come. They were all set on massive concrete pedestals. Men were completing work even as Barrin watched. Huge cranes overtopped even the soaring gate towers.

"Unfortunately, we don't have adequate men or materials to work on both structures at once with all the auxiliary buildings we are constructing." He gestured toward a barrack, the new wood looking raw even from Barrin's distant viewpoint. "If we can increase the flow of supplies, maybe we can start construction on the second hangar."

The field along one side of the proposed hangar was covered with stacks of lumber. Groups of workmen were bolting and fitting together huge sections of arches. As they drew closer, Barrin saw three great cranes being positioned with the largest secured close to the field.

"The timbers are all precut, and once they are assembled, the large crane will pass them along to the other cranes, and then they will all be raised at once."

A network of narrow trenches crisscrossed the ground

before them, and Willum turned to walk the length of the proposed structure. At Barrin's glance, he briefly explained, "Drainage, remember. Eventually I'll receive a load of sewer pipe and be able to fill them in. Right now, it's trust a plank or jump over them." Willum demonstrated that he was able to navigate the hazard by leaping over a water-filled obstacle as Barrin followed.

"This is all very impressive, but I am more interested in the problems you're having now than the plans you have for the future," Barrin told him.

"My problem is we are out in the middle of nowhere, and everything has to be brought onsite." Willum waved at the stacks of cut lumber. "We've trees all over this country and upriver, but because I can't get the men or materials, there's no way to cut and mill them." He pointed in the direction of the river. "Every stick and brick I need has to be barged from along the coast to the western ports and then hauled upriver and trundled along one road." He began to stomp heavily, showing his temper. "The stinking sea monsters and the bloody Keldons seem to sink about one in three before they can get here, and you can imagine how that screws up my schedule." Barrin wondered how many men were dying for that schedule.

Willum clenched his fists in frustration. "Not that I have enough men for the materials I do get. I've scraped through every city to find decent construction workers, and I have them cooking, gathering firewood, and trying to get around a lack of basic necessities." He was beginning to wave his arms now, and Barrin prudently stepped away to avoid an unlucky blow. "We need a town and farms here, or this base will never get done in time or keep enough blimps flying."

"Surely you have communicated your problems to Teferi."

Barrin placated the distraught man. It only provoked heavier stomping and wider gestures.

"I'm not a fool. Of course I've communicated my concerns to higher command, and I received one blimp for escort duty." Willum considered the blimp in the distance with narrowed eyes. "One blimp that is available perhaps two weeks a month because it has to fly west for maintenance and rearming. I can barely get it to deliver my mail much less protect my shipping. The rest of the air fleet is always far out at sea or flying from western ports. Hell, this airbase is supposed to stop Keldon raids, and until I get it constructed, I'm naked." Willum seethed at the paradox that only *after* he constructed the airbase would shipments of building supplies become sure.

The builder turned to Barrin with intensity and decision plain in his eyes. "If you want to see and do something important, figure out how to guard my shipping or there won't be much to see."

Barrin wondered how he could control a stretch of nearly deserted coast for hundreds of miles with only a single blimp and a heavy ornithopter. The blimp left on patrol before he could interview its crew. As he thought, he realized that he didn't need to patrol the open sea. What needed air cover were the supply ships. Barrin resolved to fly to the shipping port to get a handle on the supply problem.

* * * * *

The morning was crisp as Barrin walked to the ornithopter. The ground was covered with a light frost melting in the early sunlight. The shipping port of Kitani lay only an hour's flight away. It was time to take command of the supply line and expedite construction of the airbase.

Teferi was counting on patrols flying out of the hangars, and their construction depended on timely shipments. Barrin was going to convince the shippers to be bolder. As he clambered into his ornithopter, he wondered how angry he should be when he met the leaders of Kitani.

He settled into his machine, and it rose into the air swiftly. He looked at the airbase shrinking below him and saw once more how isolated it truly was. Barrin flew over the sea of forest green and soon the gray of the ocean was beneath his craft. The coast was rocky, and Barrin glanced at the waves beating on cliffs and narrow beaches. The violence of the waves evoked images of the Keldons waiting to attack these shores. The raiders must be stopped out at sea, or, like a tidal wave, they would wash over the coastal towns. This land was under his protection now. He thought on how to defend it as the flight continued.

The first sign that something was wrong was a magical call that washed over him like a bucket of ice water.

"This is Kitani. We are under attack from Keldon raiders. At least two ships have landed, and warriors are inside the city. Any League forces within range. This is Kitani . . ." The message repeated, an ethereal cry for help. Barrin thought on how thinly stretched the League was and realized that he might be the only aid the city could expect. He accelerated to his maximum speed and wondered if he would reach Kitani in time.

The port city appeared in the distance. Smoke was beginning to rise, and Barrin could tell that fires burned in several places. Soon piers and docks showed, with many of the warehouses and boatyards engulfed in flame. Two Keldon warships were tied up, their decks nearly deserted.

The raiders must already be in town, Barrin thought. But where are the League forces?

Then he saw flames devouring wreckage on a beach outside of the city. A blimp had crashed and was burning. The pile of debris suddenly shattered in a series of explosions as munitions cooked off. The flames were green and purple and rose toward the heavens. The concussion rocked Barrin's ornithopter as he swooped to land. Then flaming fragments struck his craft as he hit the ground in a controlled crash. Flaming brands fell everywhere, and he knew that his first priority was stopping the fires or he would lose the town.

Barrin threw himself outside and coughed as the smoke and haze swept over him. He steadied himself and cast his magic into the sky. His power ballooned over the town and his mind peered down into the city streets. Fighting spread from house to house, but it was the fires that grabbed his attention. The figures of League marines faded from his thoughts as he grounded his power into the sea. Now clouds filled the sky and the sea steamed as water catapulted itself into Barrin's dome of power. The sky was black and rumbling with thunder as more and more water collected in the air. The sky reached maximum saturation, and then it released as the storm began. Water poured in, driving rain that extinguished many of the fires in an instant. Fighting in the town slowed as men flattened under the force of the water. The most intense conflagrations were hit harder as Barrin concentrated on them. Wind threw a river of water into buildings, and the hiss of steam could be heard over the storm. Barrin turned his attention to the Keldon ships, but even as he concentrated and rallied his power, another magic user latched onto the storm.

Fountains of power reared up on the docks and congealed into crystalline towers of magic. Barrin could feel the sharp recoil as new magic speared the storm. He readied for a counter stroke, but the taste of the magic was so familiar. He realized that it reminded him of the League distress call. Lightning flowed from the storm into the crystals, and then arcs of energy sheared into the Keldon vessels. Decks seared and exploded as the power flowed over the ships. Sailors were charred as the Keldons rushed to respond. Barrin felt admiration for the unknown ally, but he could feel the Keldon mages preparing a response as the League magic cleared the decks.

"We have no time," Barrin said as he detected more fighting within the city. People were dying, and Barrin resolved to finish the Keldon ships now. His mind clenched, and sheet lightning blinded him as he directed his will. The energy surge hit the crystal towers, and they detonated in a white flash, tearing through the Keldon ships. One craft exploded as Keldon magic interacted with Barrin's strike, and debris flew everywhere. The other ship was gutted as a wound opened from stem to stern. Keldons died in agony as arcs of power played over them. The sea filled the hull almost instantly, and the ship settled, its decks soon underwater.

Barrin gasped, bent over with strain as his mind disengaged from the sky. The storm continued, but the rain lightened as his will no longer directed the deluge. Barrin straightened and headed into the city, preparing himself to meet the Keldons at close quarters.

The streets were narrow and cobblestone. The buildings were stone and timber, and rain poured from tiled roofs. Here and there structures smoldered and stank as the continuing rain drenched materials that had burned only minutes before. Barrin turned a corner, and suddenly a sword flashed. But the attack stopped before Barrin responded. A League marine stood before him with a small target shield, his sword ready. Water poured from his helmet and armor as he saluted.

"Sir, if you would come with me to the captain, sir!" He turned and ran deeper into town. Barrin followed, bemused by his instant acceptance. The marine went past a series of barricades, and Barrin could see corpses as they continued up the street.

"How did you know I was coming?" Barrin asked. The marine paused to check around a corner before continuing.

"We have scouts running the roofs, and they reported you landing," the marine replied. "We assumed that you had something to do with the storm."

Barrin nodded, but the marine darted around the corner before he could continue. A long street lay before them, and a barricade was at each end. A company of men and war machines stood ready, and Barrin got a glimpse of more soldiers in other buildings.

"The magic user from the beach," the scout reported to the officer in charge. Smoke and ash had darkened the officer's skin and uniform, and he grinned as Barrin came up.

"Excellent attack, Lord Barrin," the officer said, noting the mage's surprise. "All naval and marine commands were notified of your arrival on the coast. Can we expect more reinforcements soon?" He peered behind Barrin as if watching for more arrivals.

"I'm afraid that no one else is with me," Barrin stated. "I wouldn't count on any more help for quite some time."

The officer swore and turned to consider the street. The marines were armed with swords, shields, and light armor. Several stood ready with short bows, and Barrin could see other bowmen creeping along the roofs on one side of the street. Barrin regarded the war machines that he could see. Most were steel ants, the machines dripping water and some lubricants. Most were battered, and a few were missing limbs. Barrin wondered how heavy the fighting had been. Two machines towered over the rest. These were marine mantises—six-legged bodies at waist height with rearing towers for torsos that overtopped the marines standing beside them. Their heads were insectile and large with great mandibles covered with blood from today's fighting. Each had the two arms folded against its body, and Barrin could see flesh and cloth caught in the barbed surfaces. Then Barrin detected the rising of familiar magic and walked closer to the barricade, stepping up onto a cart for a better view.

Standing on the other side of the barricade was an athletic-looking Jamuraan woman with straight black hair. Barrin could feel the power rushing through her frame. She was wearing a soaked blue cloak with an intricate black and white checker pattern across the front, and she looked tiny—nearly lost—under the wet cloth. Two marines crouched next to her with large shields, tensed as if waiting to interpose themselves between her and danger. She flung her arms wide and three crystalline tops appeared and raced down the street. Each top spun and glowed with inner fire as they dodged around bodies, heading for the open doors of a building midway down the road. Suddenly shutters flew up, and Keldon warriors stood revealed, hurling weapons and debris at the tops. Two shattered, and the pieces tumbled to the ground before dissolving into the aether. Marine archers on the roofs of the buildings across the street shot volleys of arrows, sending warriors for cover. The surviving top curved into the entrance and exploded. Barrin could see blue knives of crystalline magic flying back out of the entrance and thudding into buildings across the sheet.

"Damn," the woman swore as she crouched behind the

shields her two marines had raised. "I thought I'd get two inside." The marine captain stepped forward and waved her down.

"This is Alexi, Lord Barrin," he said. "She was a mage on a blimp and had the misfortune to be shot down outside of town."

"Lucky for you I survived," she said hotly. "I wonder how you would have done without me." She glowered briefly. "I've been making those swine pay for my crew all afternoon, and if I could get some support we could finish them now!"

The captain shrugged and turned apologetically to Barrin. "We have pinned the raiders in the warehouses on one side of the street. We can't surround the building, and eventually the raiders are going to chop another entrance and escape."

"Why not blow open the buildings and send your machines in under cover fire from the archers?" Barrin asked. Alexi seemed powerful enough, and with his aid they could peel the complex like a grape.

"We thought of that, but the building contains essential supplies that explosions and heavy weapons would damage. The place must be taken by hand to hand, and storming the entrances is going to be bloody. I'd wait, but Alexi says there's at least one Keldon mage in there. He'll burn the place down, or his soldiers will, if we wait much longer. And without their ships they are going to try to destroy the rest of the town. We will attack in five minutes." The captain visibly tensed up as he prepared to give the order.

"Wait, Captain," Barrin said with authority. "If Alexi and I were to screen your attack until you entered the building, you could achieve maximum surprise and avoid casualties during you charge. Let me confer with Alexi for a moment, and then you can send your orders." The captain looked as if a division had appeared to support him and went to talk to his soldiers in better humor.

"Screen them how?" Alexi whispered as the captain withdrew.

"First, how many mages are in that building?" Barrin asked.

"There's just one opposing mage left, but those buildings are crammed with munitions, refined tufa oil, and essential naval stores. The first thing the mage will do is destroy it all, and perhaps the town, when we break in. We'll destroy the place ourselves if we throw anything too powerful. My tops and light-knives are as strong as I dare use." Alexi looked disgusted at the curbs to her power and thirst for battle.

"I can prevent the Keldons from seeing the charge, and I can smother the efforts of just one mage," Barrin said with confidence. "But I can't keep it up forever, so the marines need to take that building quickly."

"I will push the attack myself." She said. "When will you be ready?"

"As soon as I get into a better viewing position," Barrin replied and went to speak to the captain. Within minutes new orders were flying, and Barrin made his way to the roofs with the archers. He half-crawled over the roof across from the main warehouse entrance. He seated himself and began to call up his power. He imagined the world as a painting, scenery coming into existence as he maneuvered his imaginary canvas into position in front of the warehouse. Archers poured from the roof down stairwells as Barrin signaled that his illusion was in place. The League marines began to walk down the street quietly and carefully, a few soldiers left at the barricade making as much noise as possible to cover the shuffling of feet. Steel ants and the mantises were hand guided for maximum silence. Barrin felt the illusion firming, and he began raising more power. The most difficult part was masking his magic so as to remain undetected. Barrin infiltrated the warehouse with subtle spells, feeling for the knot of energy that was the enemy mage. More power licked into the structure as Barrin filled it with his awareness and will.

Alexi was with the column below, and she began the attack. Her power instantly created five spinning tops that darted into the entrance. They exploded into showers of blue knives that cut living flesh to ribbons. Steel ants followed the tops and mounted internal barricades manned by dying Keldons, falling upon warriors rushing to reinforce. Barrin's mind could follow the attack, and he watched as Keldons fell to pieces under metal mandibles. Shouting raiders rallied their men and charged the machines with swords and axes that smashed metal armor and removed mechanical limbs. Marines poured in and firmed the League lines. The mantises moved to attack the Keldon leaders, and the core of the defense broke as long steel arms darted out, lopping off limbs and heads of those opposing the war machines.

Barrin felt the rush of power as the Keldon mage acted to turn the attack. Barrin submerged the mage in a sea of stillness. The enemy mage drew more power but could initiate no spell against Barrin's might. Alexi was inside now, and her spells lanced into the Keldon line. Knives of light cut a bloody swath into the building. Barrin could feel the Keldon mage trying to cast a spell—any spell—but the power he had called to him had no outlet. The enemy wizard fell to his knees and clutched at his face, his eyes rolling back into his head. Smoke began to rise from the man's shoulders and limbs, and the Keldon magic user burst into brilliant red flames. Alexi and the other League forces gave the burning pile a wide berth as they closed on the remaining raiders. Then, just as suddenly as they had ignited, the brilliant fire went out, leaving only a huge black scorch mark on the floor.

Barrin rose and looked with his mortal eyes into the street and through the open doorway and shutters of the warehouse. Bodies lay everywhere with streams of blood connecting the corpses. The League had won but at a ruinous cost to the marines and the town. Now, more than ever, Barrin was determined to stop the Keldons at sea. He already knew the first thing he would requisition from this town. He went to inform Alexi that she would now be serving under his command.

CHAPTER 9

"Keldon coming in—about twenty miles south of your position," came the call.

"Finally!" Alexi exclaimed and ran from her bunk to the detector station. It had been nearly a month since the pitched battle at Kitani, and today's was the first enemy detected off the coast since then. Barrin had acted quickly in the aftermath of the battle and began patrols to intercept the Keldon raiders at sea. Shipments of materials to the airbase construction site were increased. No League supply ships had been sunk for the past month, but now the Keldons were renewing their attack as Barrin worked to reestablish command over coastal waters.

Alexi and Barrin were out on patrol in a Kashan blimp

screening a supply fleet hauling the last loads of vital construction supplies. The Keldons had chosen the perfect time to attack.

Barrin stood at the blimp detection equipment, casting a spell into a shallow bowl of seawater. His eyes looked out on a vast expanse of sea, and he could feel Alexi pushing her senses into the magic.

"Tell Yarbo we have the target and he is to search for supporting units," Barrin said to the communications officer.

Alexi ran from her bunk to the detection gear. Now that a battle was close at hand, she showed the streak of fastidiousness that Barrin had found endearing. It reminded him of his daughter, Hannah, when she was very young.

"How long till they're in range, Barrin?" she asked.

"If they don't try to shear off, ten minutes. Though they might not see us at all until it's too late." Barrin had worked with the crew in altering the natural color scheme of the envelope until it was harder to see against the sky. The *Avenging Cloud* was easy to lose against its namesakes.

"There it is," Barrin said and pointed down. Alexi regarded the images conjured up by Barrin. A tiny fleet of Keldon ships appeared to float in the bowl. Several ships were accelerating toward the League convoy. The ships began to spread out and hazy smoke began to rise from fires burning in great kettles on the decks. The bowl of water that Barrin held between his hands clouded and only glimpses of ships could be seen.

"They are spreading out to fall on the supplies," Barrin said to Alexi. "Tell the pilot to head northwest. We will take them on one at a time." Alexi ran forward to relay the order.

Barrin began calling for League reinforcements via magic, but the Keldons' spells of deceit were spreading everywhere. There was serious power aboard those ships, and Barrin decided that his power was better saved for combat than used to call for help that might not arrive. He directed the communications officer to send out a distress call, and the old wizard went forward and sat down in temporary seats close to the pilot.

"I'm taking her in a circle to come around the target," the pilot announced, and he cut the gas makers. There was a definite tilt, and the pilot let the machine rise a few hundred feet before the blimp stabilized. The copilot began the slow and steady dance to keep the blimp at the current level through small releases of gas and adjustments to the throttles. That dance would become frenzy once battle began.

Barrin closed his eyes, tapping the power of his home on Tolaria, and directed a hurricane of magic toward the rising smokescreen around the Keldon vessel. The deceitful smoke thinned as the enemy mages redirected their magical efforts.

"I don't see any signs of panic at all down there." Alexi was staring down onto the ship's deck.

Long and narrow, the vessel was crowded with warriors. Three masts rose, but no sails were raised even though the ship cut through the water, sending spray high into the air. Two concentrations of machines were at the bow and amidships. The men surrounding them fed fires with unnatural fuels and the blood of a slave. A body went over the side as a Keldon mage twisted the last drop of magic from a slave's corpse.

"They are heading straight for us. I don't like this. Widen the circle," Alexi ordered. The pilot obeyed. The gondola swayed as it went into a turn.

Barrin was aware of what was happening, but his mind searched for the rest of the enemy fleet. He was confident that Alexi and the crew of the Kashan blimp could handle one attacker.

"I don't suppose there are any pets you can throw at them," the pilot asked, hinting that Alexi could introduce a sea monster into the fight.

"No—and too strong a call might endanger the convoy." The blimp was swinging wider, and sailors began to move more rapidly on the Keldon ship as it began its own turn to bear on the blimp.

"They could care less about the convoy. We're the one they want," said the pilot. Suddenly a catapult on the ship below discharged, throwing an arc of fire into the sky. "Someone got a little too eager," the pilot guessed as the arc peaked well below their altitude and turned into racing ribbons of fire, spiraling down to the ocean's surface. The pilot smiled and altered his course to bear on the ship. Gas began emptying out of the bag as the area below entered the range of the rockets the pilot controlled.

"Firing," he called. From under their feet came a rapid series of thumps, and the nose began to pitch up. A deluge of rocket-driven darts rained down and emptied into the water and against the ship.

"You got something!" Alexi crowed, and the tattered ship began losing way. One of the smoking machines on the ship's deck was on its side, and crewmembers sluiced a spreading fire with seawater from pumps.

The copilot was checking trim and preparing to deal with the loss of four bombs. Barrin was easing his efforts to bolster the ship's defensive system, while Alexi was concentrating on sweeping the area for additional attackers. All the people in the control cabin prepared to savor a masterful attack run. The doomed ship below sent up another arc of racing streamers, but the pilot ignored the futile attempt to distract him. He was about to release the bombs when the copilot dumped ballast in a rush. The shock tripped the already primed bombing system, and four heavy bombs fell toward the ocean. The crewmembers watched in disbelief as the bombs went off in close proximity to the ship but did not strike a crippling blow.

"Why the hell did you do that?" Alexi cursed as she watched their only remaining offensive weapons expending themselves uselessly against the sea. The copilot only pointed to a fire streamer in the distance.

"It skipped." The meaning of the confusing statement became clear as the Keldon fire streamer gathered into a closed ball of flame that pulsed and expanded and then rose steeply into the air. Even after dumping the bombs and the ballast, the flaming ball was still dangerously close to the blimp. If the copilot had not acted, the flames from the Keldon weapon would be spraying over them now. The pilot, Alexi, and Barrin had all succumbed to target fixation, and only the copilot remembered to check around for other dangers. Barrin reminded himself to recommend the man for a commendation.

The Keldon ship was cutting through the water again and closing with the League supply fleet. Its bow once more sent up a wave of spray, and sailors swept bodies and debris into the sea. Flares began to rise into the air, and Barrin wondered if the ship was relaying orders or just trying to confuse its attackers.

"Whoever is commanding the ship is completely crazy," Alexi said as they raced to interpose themselves between the ship and the convoy. "He invited a rocket attack, and if we hadn't acted at the last second to save ourselves the ship would have broken up under the bombs."

"He may be crazy, but he came uncomfortably close to hitting us," Barrin replied, computing the distance to the convoy and how much time before the Keldons could attack. There were only minutes to act, and Barrin didn't like the situation. He had many direct magical strikes that would destroy the opposing ship, but he might need those spells later to deal with the other Keldon ships. Barrin needed to sink this vessel quickly and cheaply.

"Alexi, begin calling whatever you can. If you call up a kraken or a leviathan, I won't mind. Just send something against that ship," the old wizard directed.

Alexi began concentrating, and crystal spheres formed. The crystals began vibrating, singing to attract the creatures of the deep, but the violence of the battle made success unlikely. The Keldon ship worsened the situation by launching several skipping streamers of fire into the sky. The transforming balls of flame drove the blimp off and made it harder for Barrin and Alexi to act. Now the League convoy appeared on the horizon, and the Keldon ship launched three more streamers of flame high into the sky. The fire raced in the direction of Barrin's supply ships, and he acted to protect them. The clouds that laced the sky seemed to darken as if soaking up ink. A wind blew from the land out to sea. Barrin threw out pulses of power in short bursts, accelerating the process. If he couldn't find the Keldon fleet, he would clear the seas surrounding the League supply ships. The wind and clouds circled over the fleet, and waves mounted and shifted directions as the sea went mad. The League ships continued on in the eye of a growing storm. No more fire streams flew toward the heavens as the Keldons tried to preserve their ship and enter the calm of the eye.

"Keep us between the Keldons and the convoy, even if you dump us in the sea to do it," Barrin ordered the pilot. The wizard continued to pound and shape the forces of the air with his will.

The battle was a strange one. The *Avenging Cloud* kept station and moved only in response to the Keldon ship, which became increasingly hard to track. The Keldons' attempts to conceal themselves were amplified by the rain and wind that Barrin kept roaring over the sea. Alexi sent out magic sentinels to track the ship, but the violence of the wind shattered their crystalline structure. She was blind until the violence of the storm abated.

Barrin paused in his assault when he felt Alexi's efforts. "I think I detected another ship beyond the wind." Barrin battled with the storm, not the Keldons. The winds and waves seemed hungry for the ships that sailed in the eye. Barrin could not reply to another Keldon attack for some minutes. The blimp and the entire convoy were in a dangerous position.

"We have to sink at least one of the Keldons right now." Alexi stated the obvious.

"Can you call up anything?" Barrin asked hopefully.

"Right now, I couldn't command a goldfish," Alexi said with disgust.

"Then we will have to get as close as possible and attack the ship directly," Barrin declared. "Have the pilot take us down to just a few hundred feet above the water."

The storm Barrin had conjured was making the pilot's job much harder than the man was prepared to deal with. He was constantly adjusting the throttles and was green with nausea. The blimp flexed and rose with the vagaries of the wind, and the pilot retched over the controls as he fought airsickness. The pilot listened to Alexi convey the old wizard's orders as he fought a downdraft.

"He wants us just over the sea?" the pilot exclaimed. "With this wind, he wants us just over the water?"

"It's the only way to attack the Keldons. We need to stay low," Alexi ordered, visibly gagging from the odor of vomit. She returned to Barrin.

"I will support the defenses, and you must take the offense." Barrin was winded from his constant struggle with the storm. He needed a few moments to collect himself. "Hit them with a massive power strike the second you can see the ship," Barrin directed.

"You have more power than I ever will," Alexi confessed. "You'd have a greater range."

"If I thought you could juggle several spells at once I would switch places. Now get up with the pilot before some other disaster happens." Barrin's words came out all at once, as if he couldn't spare the time or energy to sustain a longer conversation. The old mage locked his arms to the side of the cabin, bracing himself for a long fight and against the gyrations of the blimp in the storm.

Alexi went forward. The pilot was empty, and his stomach contractions brought up nothing as the violence seemed to increase. Now each surge of wind induced storms of cursing as the pilot wrestled with the controls. The water jumped closer, and then the engines fought their way up.

"There!" the pilot shouted as a ship appeared less than a hundred yards away.

Alexi closed her eyes and let fly her attack. She formed her spell just outside the blimp. Her surge of power shattered the gondola's windows as energy speared the enemy ship. The concussion reverberated throughout the cabin. Alexi's strike split the masts on the Keldon raider and crushed many of the sailors fighting to keep it afloat.

The pilot tried to climb, but deafened and confused, he turned the craft and caught the wind. The *Avenging Cloud* began to retreat at a high speed, but not high enough to escape a counterattack. Alexi dumbly wondered how they kept the ammunition for the catapult ready in such heavy seas as a fire streamer covered the blimp. Fire ran like water over the envelope. The crew waited for the explosion, but Barrin powered the blimp's defenses against fire, and the Keldon flames washed over the gondola into the sea. Alexi sealed the shattered window with planes of magic glass, but she hissed in agony as a stray lick of flame played over her skin.

All of Barrin's energy focused on keeping the blimp whole, and the magical storm began to break up. Three battered enemy ships lay revealed less than a thousand yards away. Mysteriously, the Keldons didn't fire, and then Barrin heard the communications man shouting behind him.

"It's the *Hunter*!" he yelled. "They finally made it here!"

Teferi's blimp was thousands of feet up and behind the Keldon fleet. Even as Barrin watched warriors running to load catapults, the *Hunter* dropped four large objects that accelerated sharply and seemed to fly down to an enemy ship. Explosions smashed the Keldons to pieces, and the ship instantly sank beneath the waves.

Barrin could feel Teferi aboard the other craft creating walls of protective energy over the League supply fleet. A desperate attack from a Keldon caster hit Teferi's spell as a ribbon of flame, but it transformed into an explosion of cinders drifting down into the ocean. Barrin latched onto the dissipating storm and spun it into another of the Keldon ships. A twist of wind dipped into the sea and formed a great waterspout that moved over the ship and tore it apart. Flames from enemy spells filled the watery column and were sucked up into the clouds, exploding into sheet lightning. The concussion weakened the storm, and Barrin's blimp rose as the pilot aimed for a clearing sky. The final Keldon ship tried to withdraw, its casters throwing a huge display of fiery streams and cloaking smoke into the air. Barrin felt the planeswalker turn the smoke into an acidic rain that fell onto the fleeing Keldon ship. The liquid ate through the sailors and into the holds.

Barrin expanded the blimp defenses against fire, and the last few streamers sputtered and lost momentum long before they closed with the blimp. Alexi's bloodthirst demanded satisfaction, and she hurled exploding crystalline lances of energy at the retreating ship.

"Die, die, die!" she screamed as her attack penetrated below decks and started fires. The raider had fought heavy seas all day and was stressed beyond endurance. The sharp detonations of Alexi's lances began to break up the ship. It was already doomed when a great whirlpool called by Teferi dragged it beneath the waves.

* * * * *

The airbase would be completed within days. After the supply fleet docked, the final pieces of the tufa refinery were quickly set into place. The warehouses behind protective berms were now filled with munitions. While Willum oversaw the final touches before transferring back to the west, Barrin and Teferi retreated to discuss where to direct the League's growing strength.

It was hours later that an aide interrupted them at the map table. Teferi frowned with annoyance as the aide handed him a note and withdrew. The planeswalker suddenly grinned and rose from his chair.

"Come on, Barrin. Your reinforcements from home are arriving at the landing field. You should be on hand to meet them. In fact, you better carry the welcome." Teferi snatched up wine and a fruit bowl and shoved them to Barrin. The wizard rose slowly but did not protest. Anything that lightened Teferi's mood was welcome.

The passengers began to disembark, and Shalanda, aide to Barrin's wife Rayne, was the first to touch ground. She was tall and garbed in rough clothing. Her skin was a deep brown and her features were weathered by exposure to the elements. Her hazel eyes widened in recognition, and she walked toward Barrin with her hands outstretched. The old wizard saw the woman behind her and handed Shalanda the food and drink as he walked by.

Rayne embraced Barrin, and they held each other as the rest of the passengers flowed around them. Barrin hugged his wife fiercely, nuzzling her dark hair. He felt younger as he looked at her. Appearing only in her thirties, Barrin wondered at the decades of love they had shared and the centuries that would be theirs. When they finally turned their eyes from each other, only Teferi still stood on the field. The planeswalker looked envious for just an instant before he stepped forward to clasp Rayne's offered hand.

"I am happy to see you, Rayne," Teferi said as he let go of her hand and gestured that they should enter the offices.

"You should have come to Tolaria more often, Teferi," Rayne replied as she grasped Barrin's hand.

"You know that I prefer to take Urza in small doses if possible," Teferi replied as they arrived at the strategy room.

"Urza is rarely there, Teferi," Barrin explained. "My wife and I manage Tolaria. In fact, this is the longest I have been off the island since we battled the Phyrexians for it." Barrin pulled out a chair for his wife. He stood behind her with his hands on her shoulders. He could feel the tenseness in her muscles from hours in flight, and he massaged them. Rayne trembled slightly at the touch of his hands but reluctantly considered the maps and unit markers on the table.

"Barrin and I have been discussing a land campaign to the east," Teferi explained. "A counter invasion, so to speak. Barrin tells me that you will be ferrying equipment to support a Tolarian army in the field. When can we expect the first wave of forces?"

"We should see them arriving within the week." Rayne was oddly evasive, her eyes looking at the forces displayed and the long lines of advance that the two men had penciled in.

"We will have some difficulty integrating with League forces. As you can see, it will take weeks to concentrate the army on the frontier." Barrin reached for the list of towns and garrisons that would house the forward units even as he wondered what Rayne was hiding.

"Just what forces are you bringing?" Teferi asked.

"Two great dirigibles will be landing here. One with a cargo of light runners, the other with a load of power crystal and parts to help feed your own artificers. That's all." She seemed embarrassed to say it, and Barrin was stunned.

"Surely you mean that this is only the first flight, my dear?" Barrin asked. He thought of the tens of thousands of war machines stored on Tolaria and the terrible weapons that he had helped construct.

"There may be a few ornithopter flights of students, but the two loads of materials are all for now. The dirigibles will withdraw for a season, so you won't have them for transport," Rayne answered quietly and began to move a few unit markers on the board to represent the Tolarian forces.

"Why did Urza send so little?" Teferi wondered aloud.

"Urza considers all of Dominaria, not just a single continent. He has sent the equipment and students that he could spare." Rayne turned from Teferi and finished moving a last few markers.

Barrin tried to explain Urza's actions as he had so often over the years. "Teferi, I'm sure Urza has excellent reasons for what he has done—even as you have focused your attentions west and in the naval campaign." Barrin pointed at the coastal and river cities on which Teferi had lavished most of his attention.

"We are just beginning to realize how many troops and machines we will need to cover the frontier without committing any to combat. I am sure that his priorities will change once a clearer picture of our need is available." Barrin had counted on elite squads of war machines to head the offensive and provide him with an independent command.

"Teferi," Rayne said, "it is growing late, and it was an exhausting trip. This is also the first time my husband and I have met in months. Give us this night for reunion and leave the war for tomorrow."

"Of course." Teferi bowed to the couple as Barrin rose to escort his wife to his quarters. But even Barrin's joy at seeing Rayne after all this time couldn't drown his disappointment at the support he had received from home.

"Why did Urza send so little?" Barrin asked later. A lamp was burning on the nightstand beside his bed as Rayne unpacked her things. He could think of no reason for Urza to provide so little. He hoped that his wife could explain what was happening.

"I was never even able to speak to Urza. He reappeared on Tolaria in the middle of the night, read your dispatches, and ordered the limited reinforcement. He left before news of his arrival even reached me." Rayne shoved his clothing to the side of a wardrobe and began hanging her robes. Barrin watched as she integrated her things among his.

"If Urza isn't on the island, then what are you doing

here? Who did he appoint in your place to oversee the academy and the factories?" Barrin could think of no one that he would trust to replace Rayne and her expertise.

"Urza gave no orders—I came on my own," Rayne answered simply as she pushed a large trunk of her things to the side of the room. Barrin's chest of drawers was too small to allow her to unpack more. She turned and set herself for the coming response.

"What! You left everything on a whim? Just picked up your luggage and came?" Barrin knew from bitter experience how vast and consuming the responsibility of command could be in managing Urza's extensive operations.

Rayne's reply was calm but as implacable as any juggernaut. "Do you really think that I would leave you alone out here knowing how little support Urza sent? That I would stay behind safe while you and the students I encouraged to volunteer went off to fight a war?" Rayne gazed with love but more than a little exasperation at her mate. "Besides, how can you possibly coordinate missions from this airbase, work with Teferi as an advisor, lead a detail of artifact troops, and maintain the intricate systems the Tolarian war machines require?" Rayne stopped to smile. "The academy will survive on its own. Most of the real work has been completed, and the remaining students and scholars are doing mainly maintenance. Everything is going as Urza planned—except for this war." Barrin was visibly softening his resolve and coming to see the situation the same way Rayne did. "Whether you like it or not," she continued, "you need me to take charge of the artifice I just delivered. You can't do it all by yourself."

Barrin knew when to concede a battle. "You're right," he said finally. "It's just that the next phase of the war is so uncertain. I spent months focused on building and supporting this airbase. All that work, yet I am certain that this has just been a sideshow to the real war."

"As I said to Teferi," Rayne reminded as she sat down on the bed beside him, "leave the war for tomorrow." Barrin kissed his wife and forgot the world outside their room.

CHAPTER 10

Barrin and Rayne spent nearly a week together, but it went by very quickly. Soon the two of them were sucked into the madness of the war in Jamuraa.

Teferi came into the map room where the two Tolarian scholars were working. "I'd like to introduce you both to a good friend of mine. Barrin, Rayne, this is Jolreal, affectionately known here on Jamuraa as the Empress of the Beasts."

Beside Teferi stood a tall Jamuraan woman in ornate purple and green robes and a finely crafted headdress of feathers. She was very tall and slender and carried herself in a regal fashion, befitting her title of empress.

"It's a pleasure to meet you both. Teferi has told me much of you over the years." Jolreal bowed to her new acquaintances.

"Yes, well, let's leave the stories of my schoolboy antics until later," said Teferi, looking at Barrin and coughing into his fist. "Jolreal has agreed to do some scouting for us," he said, changing the subject.

"My friends make excellent spies." Jolreal lifted both of her arms, and from behind her robes stepped two gray wolves. The great beasts moved casually around their empress, and then they lay down at her feet, looking like tamed hunting dogs but with tremendous fangs.

The sudden appearance of the wild animals startled Barrin, but their passive nature soon calmed his fears.

"It seems that you have things well in hand," said the old wizard. "With such creatures on our side, we will easily fill in the gaps in our intelligence."

"Yes, Jolreal will be able to report on all the Keldon movements on the eastern perimeter, but Northern Jamuraa is a very big place, and even with her help, we still won't be able to cover all the land that we need," conceded Teferi.

"One of the Tolarian dirigibles is bringing in forty fast runners," Rayne interjected. "They aren't numerous enough to stiffen the army, but I believe they are the fastest light machines on the ground. Perhaps we could use them to fill in the gaps."

"I am a mistress of beasts, Rayne," Jolreal explained. "What do I know of maintaining artifacts? No matter how cleverly made your machines are, they will break down. Who knows how many would be stranded behind the Keldon lines?"

"Well then," Rayne said, crouching down to stroke the head of one of the wolves, "*I* will use them to fill in the gaps." She stood and placed her hand on Barrin's arm, silencing any objections her overprotective husband could raise. "I brought students from the academy as well as machines, and I can maintain the runners under any conditions," Rayne said with confidence. "You'll have no one stranded under my care."

"But why go yourself?" Jolreal asked quizzically. "Surely there is much you can do here?"

"I will not ask my students to do something I will not," Rayne said with intensity. "I have sat in an office too long, and it is time to see war's face."

* * * * *

Jolreal was impressed when she saw the machines that Rayne had ferried over to the League. The runners were bipedal, with the long legs of a running bird, and like a bird, each machine had a set of wings, but these wings snapped out of long depressions on each side of the runner like giant sabers. A battery of twenty bolts peered forward from the machine's torso aimed by the runner's sensors and the rider's direction. But to Jolreal, the most impressive aspect of the runners was their grace and economy of motion. Even fully loaded with a pilot and supplies of every sort, they accelerated smoothly, bounding and turning sharply. As rapidly as the deadly birds of the north, they covered ground in long lopes that outdistanced horses. The runners' sensors placed their feet faultlessly, and their speed over broken ground was unmatched. Jolreal shared Rayne's confidence that outrunning Keldon cavalry was not a problem. As long as the scouts weren't encircled by terrain or enemy forces, they would be able to escape.

Rayne felt only a little trepidation as she and her aide, Shalanda, readied themselves to ride out with Jolreal's scouting party. Barrin exited the building where he and Teferi conferenced when in camp, and he approached his wife.

"You are determined to do this?" he asked.

"Yes, my love," Rayne replied. "You fight where you can, and I can do no less." Barrin only grasped her hand and pressed a kiss to the inside of her wrist.

"Come back to me," he whispered. Rayne saw the other scouts leaving and followed.

"I'll see you in three weeks," Rayne called as she followed Jolreal into the eastern wilderness. Who knew what the Keldons were doing and who was stationed in the east?

One thing that was not out east was people. Within hours of leaving camp, the scouts began running across destroyed and abandoned property. It was a depressing look at the failure of the League to protect itself, and Rayne grew more depressed as they pressed farther east. A week of riding and still they saw only the leavings of the enemy.

"Where are the Keldons?" Rayne asked Jolreal.

The empress could only shake her head. "The signs all point to them drawing back and to the east," Jolreal stated. "Perhaps they are massing deep in their own rear area."

"Then perhaps we should turn north?" Rayne opinioned.

Jolreal shook her head again. "There's a chance that the Keldons might be advancing farther east. My other scouting parties can cover that area. We can afford to check the possibility."

The land grew rougher, and there were more and more trees. The scouts still sped over the landscape, detouring around isolated stands of trees that impeded their rapid passage. The runners sped around the obstacles and began to head north, looking for the enemy. What finally stopped them was the fresh sign of Keldon passage.

* * * * *

Jolreal followed the tracks slowly, watchful for members of the enemy party. On foot, the empress sent her power into the forest, trying to taste the passage of warriors and their beasts. The forest seemed distant and the flow of its power chaotic and confusing, but the signs of the enemy were plain enough. Rayne and the other scouts waited at the edge of the forest wall.

"Wait here while I scout ahead," Jolreal had ordered as she dismounted. The enemy had entered a path leading through trees. The path was narrow and almost lost among the giant forest trees. The Empress of the Beasts raised her hands above her head as she had the day she met Rayne. In the distance, along the path Jolreal had found, several sets of eyes appeared. She nodded and turned back to the rest of the party. "Now hide yourselves out of sight in the tree line and be prepared to run if necessary. We'll rendezvous at last night's camp if we are separated."

Jolreal stalked the trail, moving in and out of the forest, keeping out of sight as much as possible. Forests and jungles had always been her natural home, and she had friends here as well as in other places. Only minutes later she came across the Keldons.

It was the smell of the guard's leathers that alerted her. The odor of sweat-stained hide wafted from the warrior and revealed his presence even though he was hidden from sight. Jolreal slowly moved through the trees in an arc until she was behind the sentry. The Keldon sat behind several bushes in a small depression. Anyone coming up the path would have been spotted and the alarm given. Jolreal signaled for her animal escort to stay out of sight, noted the alertness of the guard, and continued carefully toward the main party. Soon she saw them.

A huge tree had toppled, knocking down several others on its way and creating a tangle of logs and smashed brush. There were thirty men in the temporary camp. Half seemed slaves from their ragged clothes and fawning manner as they served the warriors taking their ease. The Keldons sat in a series of small groups, conversing as their servants packed the camp.

A hundred feet away, the party's riding beasts milled as saddles were slung onto their backs. Horses and mules accounted for most of the beasts, but three huge goatlike creatures stood to the side. They were six feet at the shoulder and massively muscled. Armed with heavy curled horns, the rest of the animals nervously kept their distance. She had heard that Keldons in the far north rode such beasts. Colos, they were called. A warrior saddled them, pushing slaves out of the way as he separated the saddles from the rest of the gear. One group of fighters broke up and went into the forest. A Keldon passed within a few feet of her as she lay with stilled breath. The party was preparing to leave, and the sentries were being fetched in. She needed to get closer, to hear something. Like a snake she slid over the ground, moving slowly nearer to the men of the camp. Hidden behind a huge root, she could make out the low voices of the seated warriors. Her knowledge of Keldon was limited and laboriously acquired, but she could follow the talk.

"This great beast is not here," a voice said forcefully. "We are being dragged away from the advance in a futile quest for glory."

"And the statement of the elf prisoners?" another voice countered. "These beasts stand guard over ancient ruins. Perhaps the ancient heroes lived here millennia ago. Can you imagine standing on the streets where our distant ancestors lived and fought? Can you imagine the respect that would flow to us from the army and Keld? This would make us known in every cradle house and in the Witch King Council. It is worth missing the first few battles of the new offensive."

The only reply was a snort of disgust.

Jolreal carefully moved so she could see the speakers, but the warriors were standing up and moving toward the mounts. They knew something about the timing of the new Keldon offensive. She must learn more. Jolreal watched the warriors pulling themselves into their saddles. Slaves finished packing the last of the gear and threw it onto mules. A few minutes to let them ride on, and Jolreal would go back for Rayne and the others. It was vital that they capture one of the Keldons. A breeze blew over her, and she shivered slightly. The gap in the trees overhead allowed the wind to dip toward the ground.

Jolreal tensed, her blood beginning to race. There was something in the air, some odor. The Keldons and their slaves rose in their stirrups, their heads held high like dogs smelling the wind. The horses, mules, and colos breathed in the air as well. Like stallions to mares in heat, they began moving, their riders pulling briefly at the reins but soon losing themselves in taking deep breaths.

Jolreal's mouth watered as she inhaled the intoxicating odor. It took all her will to lie there and not look for the source of that delicious smell. She concentrated on her mission—find the Keldons and bring back information. But the Keldons were riding off, their noses questing for something. The colos shouldered their way to the head of the party and off the trail into the forest. Warriors and slaves jostled after them. Keldons swore as their fawning servants ignored their orders to clear a path. Jolreal followed the fragrant lure, dragging after the party she spied upon.

Everyone rode into the trees, spreading out as riders and beasts ignored everything in their rush. Jolreal was in the open now. She ran after them, still trying to use cover as her mind fought to overwhelm her instincts. She stumbled over roots and depressions, her usually invisible trail looking like the passage of a drunkard. The Keldons should have outdistanced her but each warrior and servant fought to pass by another, and the whole party began to string out. Jolreal raced to the side to get a better view. The colos and their warriors stopped in front of a soaring tree. The smell that had been so overpowering intensified as the warriors dismounted and tore into the trunk. The bark was ripped, and mushroomlike growth grew in giant clusters up the vertical slashes. The wounds continued high past the heads of the mounted men and the warriors drew swords to cut more of the spongy flesh free.

Jolreal's mind went blank, and she moved blindly forward. She was some yards away from the milling crowd and ignored the land around her. The pit was shallow and overgrown, left by a toppled tree, but it was deep enough to collect water, and her mouth and nose submerged in scummy muck as she fell. Swollen flowers and pitcher plants burst as her limbs churned the mud and rotting needles.

Just then she felt a tugging at the back of her robes, and her head cleared the water. The plants were acrid, and her eyes wept with tears even after she cleared the muck from her face. The crushed foliage wept potent chemicals, and Jolreal's nose filled, a headache pounding at her temples. A dire wolf, one of her escorts, had a firm hold on her clothing and was pulling her free of the trap. She was aware again and furious at her soiled condition, but a look at the Keldons made her glad for her accident.

The party members were fighting amongst themselves. As plentiful as the fungus encrusting the tree was, the greed of the men tolerated no sharing. Slaves tried to fight their way through to the tree. Knives used for cooking were yanked out of saddlebags and pierced living flesh as the former servants attacked their masters.

Jolreal watched the slaughter. Warriors went berserk as they turned on the men scrabbling to the tree. One Keldon grabbed hold of a slave and began hitting the smaller man with bone-breaking blows. Ribs shattered like cheap pottery, and then the warrior laughed as the dying man stabbed at the arm holding him up with a table knife. Kettles rattled against the shield of the apparent party leader as desperation overwhelmed the slaves' survival instincts. The huge whip sergeant swung himself off an unmanageably large colos as his bloodthirst overwhelmed the unnatural appetite inspired by the tree fungus. He did not even draw the sword slung over his back but pulled a mace from his saddle. Single blows turned charging madmen into corpses. The few surviving slaves crept up to the tree under the bellies of horses and picked up chunks of fungus from the ground. They ignored the blood and mud and scrambled for cover, stuffing their mouths as they hid.

The warriors mastered the servants, but their mounts now fought to eat of the tree. Horses reared and struck at the trunk, tearing off more of the fungus. The spongy mass went deep, and a horse's head plunged out of sight to eat and tear. The colos pushed the animal away with sweeps of their curled horns. Horses collapsed as broken bones tore internal arteries and organs ruptured. The colos turned their heads outward, seeing their riders. Warriors and mounts charged into new battle. The Keldon whip sergeant swung his mace overhand into the head of his colos, but the beast shook off the blow like a bothersome fly, sending his rider cartwheeling back. Other warriors darted in from the side, plunging long swords deep into colos sides. The blades snapped off as the mounts spun, knocking the men down. Cries sounded from the animals as they coughed up blood. Even dying in agony, they reared and trampled men and lesser animals. The living and the dead came apart under the thrashing hooves.

Jolreal felt the pain of the animals tearing at her self-control. The colos finally fell, one landing on top of a crippled slave whose limbs protruded from under the massive animal. The legs scrabbled and pushed at the ground for minutes as the trapped man slowly suffocated. The animals were nearly all dead and only a few mules remained. The heavy freight saddles broke in the fighting, and heaving withers tossed them free. A mule spun like a dancer, and two rear hooves thudded into the face of a warrior. He fell, a limp doll as his neck snapped. The expedition leader was back on his feet and charged the victorious mule. The Keldon's gray skin was suffused with blood, and he grabbed the animal's neck with two swollen arms. The beast tried to tear free, but even its strength and energetic rolling on the ground could not break the implacable grip. The crack of its spine signaled a pause in the battle. Only a few warriors and slaves survived. All fell to devouring fungus spread over the forest floor, ignoring the dead and dying as they filled their mouths. The feasting stopped as stomachs began to rebel, and the men sat in a nauseous stupor.

Jolreal mastered herself. The odor of the crushed flowers and pods filled the little depression. The fighting appeared to be over as the men groaned and rolled, their eyes glassy and unseeing. She began to get out of the water and froze. There, at the edge of the battlefield, a massive form gripped the corpse of a horse and whisked it out of sight. Jolreal put it all together. The lure of the fungus, the self-destruction of the Keldon party, the gargantuan beast—this place was a thresher beast trap, and it had caught a full load.

* * * * *

The thresher beast worked hard. The carrion under the tree was far more plentiful than ever before. Some of the prey was far bigger than the animals it usually found. The food would have to be buried fast or other scavengers would gather. The monster dug deep pits in minutes, tearing through thick tree roots to make the cache large enough. With each pit completed, it went and gathered more meat to store. Carrying the giant colos corpse was hard, and its neck muscles ached. It paused to rest, rubbing its back and neck against a tree. A new lure needed to be created, and the excitement of the huge kill tickled at the poison sacks behind its claws. It loped toward a huge tree several hundred yards away from the lure.

The thresher beast reared and set its claws into the thick bark. Several swipes were necessary to tear through a foot of bark to the inner wood. Sap oozed out as the thresher beast gouged out a fifteen-foot strip. The poison in its claws was driven into the wood and bark with every slash. The creature's venom and the tree sap would enable a certain fungus to grow, and within a year a new lure would be calling animals to their doom.

The thresher beast felt spent and sleepy. Perhaps the carrion could wait on a nap. But a faint odor wafted between the trees, banishing its tiredness. The scent of another thresher beast floated in the air. The bloody corpses were already attracting attention and must be buried for storage. The creature grew angrier as the scent of the rival slowly grew stronger. The prey might have killed themselves, but the monster would still have to fight for its meal.

* * * * *

Rayne watched the trail intently for Jolreal's return. Her aide Shalanda nervously opened and checked her saddlebags, muttering as she took inventory yet again. The other Kipamu League scout, Boyle, appeared quite at ease. The tall, lanky man sat loose in the saddle of his runner. His black-haired head turned slowly, showing a tanned and weathered face to the world. Only his blue eyes showed worry, peering rapidly over the landscape in direct contradiction to his indolent pose. He straightened suddenly. Rayne turned her attention back to the trail, and there was Jolreal coming at a run. She was soaking wet and great masses of vegetation hung around her shoulders and dragged on the ground behind her.

Rayne, Boyle, and Shalanda sent their machines toward Jolreal.

"How close are the Keldons?" Rayne demanded, swinging her mount to cover the forest with its bolt launchers.

"The Keldons aren't coming," Jolreal gasped, "but they are close by, and we need to reach them now." The odor of the plants Jolreal carried suddenly impressed itself on Rayne and the others.

"What are you carrying?" Shalanda gasped. The rest of the League scouts arrived, and Jolreal quickly told of the fight she had witnessed and the thresher beast's trap.

"It fills the mind and renders the victim unable to think clearly," Jolreal explained. "These plants fight off the effects, so I gathered as much as I could. Everyone must wear some when we get to the Keldons." Even as she spoke she made garlands and handed them out.

"I will hold the thresher beast off by magic as the rest of you round up prisoners," Jolreal ordered. "Some of the warriors know details about the Keldons' plans for an offensive strike, and we need to capture one for interrogation. The men should be unconscious, but hold your launchers ready, just in case." The scouts were all equipped with weapons holding web rounds for the capture of prisoners.

Jolreal walked back into the treeline where a dire wolf waited for her. She leaped to the creature's back and began heading back down the trail. The League scouts donned their garlands, and a fresh wave of acrid stench flowed.

"You must be joking," Boyle said, jerking his head. More vegetable pods ruptured and soaked into his clothes.

"Madness would be even less funny," Jolreal said and flipped another garland over her head. "I saw about twelve people left alive around the tree, six warriors and six slaves. Hopefully the thresher beast hasn't touched them yet, being a carrion feeder."

"How will we know which ones have information about the offensive?" Rayne asked as Jolreal started riding.

"Look for the one seven-feet tall," was the shouted response.

Rayne and the others rode up the path and reached the turnoff to the thresher beast's trap. The delicious smell Jolreal had described was smothered by the garlands, and except for watering eyes, Rayne felt totally in control. Jolreal stepped clear of the dire wolf and gathered herself, waving the rest of the party ahead as she began her spell.

The warriors and slaves under the tree were awake and watching each other. The League charge took them by surprise.

The men swung themselves up and grasped their weapons, but five launchers fired before they could do any more. Nets sailed out and spread wide, wrapping armed warriors in metallic strands that stuck to flesh and clothing. The glues surrounding the wire cables set quickly, and each movement tightened the restrictive cocoon. The free warrior and the six slaves closed in on the netted prisoners like rabid dogs.

"Try to keep them off!" yelled Boyle as he rode at the men. The runner stopped over a prisoner and flashed his wing blades in and out of their housing to cow the madmen. They only snarled and closed on another immobilized victim. Clenched fists raised knives as they fell in a stabbing frenzy over the warriors.

Rayne webbed the largest warrior when the attack first began. A screaming Keldon closed on her prisoner, and she bolted the berserker three times. The heavy projectiles left tunnels as they blew through the attacker's chest, and a bloody corpse fell onto Rayne's capture.

"Somebody help me!" Boyle screamed. He had sent his runner toward the crazed slaves and was now trapped. His runner stepped on a dead mule, driving its foot into a gaping wound. The machine dragged the thousand-pound animal around like a man with a stubborn terrier. Boyle cursed as the jolting destroyed his ability to control the machine. The six crazed slaves stopped cutting at a webbed corpse and swarmed on Boyle. The League scout jumped from his mired machine to get some fighting room. Rayne grabbed for her reloads and glanced down to ram another web round into her launcher.

Two of the other League scouts dived from their machines in an attempt to save Boyle. The runners stood impotent, their bolts deadly but unable to distinguish between Boyle and the slaves.

Boyle's rescuers used the flats of their swords at first, still thinking of the slaves as victims. A crazed slave buried a pickax in the throat of a League scout. The rest of the Kipamu League soldiers now used the edges of their swords in an attempt to save their own lives. Blood poured from the wounds they inflicted, but the injuries were ignored as their opponents showed their teeth and closed with scouts. Boyle lost his sword as he buried it in a man's side.

Two slaves fell on the dying man with the pickax wound in his larynx. Shalanda and Rayne fired as one and webbed the three into one screaming, cursing mass. Like fighting animals in a sack, they went at each other with teeth and screams until both the survivors were trapped at opposite sides of the corpse.

Rayne drove her machine forward. The academy chancellor felt nothing but rage for the death of the scout, and she triggered her runner's wings, closing with the two slaves. Rayne left a trail of blood and lopped off flesh before her machine crushed the bodies under its metal feet.

Only a screaming man with a Keldon's sword remained free, and Rayne emptied her runner's bolts into him. The dead man's hand still gripped the bloody weapon when she was through, but the arm was no longer attached to a body. Rayne shuddered as she looked at the corpse and then twisted her head to look at what remained. Jolreal still stood off to the side, locked in a trance. Rayne stepped down from her runner.

"Boyle, are you all right?" asked Rayne. The ground was

soaked with blood, and she stepped carefully. Many of the corpses were gone, and Rayne wondered how Jolreal was doing with the thresher beast. She steered clear of the webbed captives. Out of the five warriors webbed, only three survived. Two were actually stuck to the tree and the fungus that had doomed the Keldon party in the first place. Boyle was kneeling on the ground, a strip of his shirt cut free and pressed against a wound.

"I'm cut, but I'll live." He tried to smile, but Rayne could see a jolt of fresh pain hit. The adrenaline was used up, and the pain that fear and rage had buried was becoming more and more potent.

Shalanda hurried forward on foot to help with the wounded. Rayne looked at the Keldon leader. Had it been worth it? She walked back to her machine. They needed to secure the prisoners and start back for the base camp. Rayne started her machine toward Jolreal, but the sorceress suddenly fell in a seizure, her body jumping and twisting on the ground as her muscles contracted out of control.

The monster sprang to attack as Rayne shouted for Shalanda and her healing hands. It came around the tree and slammed into Rayne's machine. The beast was massively muscled with long legs. Its head was roughly canine in build but was twice the size of a great bear's. Its body was tremendous and bulbous and belied its great speed, and its skin was tight and looked to split as it roared.

"Somebody kill that thing!" Rayne shouted as she jumped free from her machine. The monster pushed the runner over and gripped the mechanical legs. It ripped a limb loose and howled with victory. Rayne ran for a riderless runner as the thresher beast ripped more parts from its metal victim. It must have tired of the metallic taste because it pursued her with leaping bounds. Then it spotted Boyle running for his trapped craft and followed him. He jumped for his runner and its weapons and started to swing himself aboard.

"Mother!" he screamed as the thresher beast's claws hooked into his calf. The muscle stripped away, and his other leg broke as his body was pulled free of the saddle. Boyle was face down but scrambling, his eyes wide and teeth clenched. The monster had run past him, and it scrapped its claws clean of Boyle's flesh as it turned to continue the attack.

Boyle was in the midst of the dead Keldon warriors, and he drew a sword from one of the fallen men. Rayne could see him sitting up and waving it in defiance as she got aboard an abandoned machine. Rayne laid the sights on the thresher beast, but the creature was upon Boyle again. The scout swung his newly acquired weapon. The sword sheared into a claw and a spray of blood and poison coated one side of his face.

Boyle looked at Rayne. "Shoot!" he screamed and then fell silent as the thresher beast continued its attack. Rayne fired a stream of bolts and felt the world drop away as Boyle's body took several hits. The thresher beast howled again. The giant beast flung itself to the side as Rayne's bolts spent themselves on a pile of slave and Keldon corpses. Its eyes locked on Rayne. Blood poured from wounds in its chest and front legs. The beast walked stiff legged, its rage obvious with every faltering move. Rayne knew she could outrun it, but she wanted it to die and readied herself to attack with the runner's wings.

A growing howl turned her attention from the monster in front of her. Another thresher beast stood over the dead slaves. The new thresher beast was smaller than the wounded beast advancing on Rayne, but it still out-massed a good-sized horse. It ignored the corpses in front of it and advanced slowly on the wounded monster. The bloody monster put its back to a tree and readied itself for battle. It glanced toward Rayne as if to promise a reckoning.

Rayne backed her machine toward Jolreal. Shalanda and the other scout were at their machines but made no move to use the bolt casters. Rayne wondered if they had enough bolts to kill the monsters. She looked quickly at Jolreal. The sorceress was beginning to tremble once again, and Rayne knew that soon there would be two monsters attacking the scouts. But then she saw her aide tense as she gathered power.

Shalanda was a healer, but it was destruction that she called up. Her head snapped back and blood poured from her nose. Rayne could hear a roar arcing through the sky, then Shalanda's wrath fell. The strike brushed against the tree trunk as it hammered the ground. A hail of splinters pierced everyone in the area. Rayne stared in shock at the chunk of wood through her side.

The monsters were alive, though spears of heartwood pierce both their hides. Jolreal lay on the ground, a victim of strain or Shalanda's attack. The monsters turned toward Rayne, and the scholar knew that her party would die as a great crack of sound broke her concentration and she looked up.

Her eyes picked up a twig falling gently to the ground. The twig grew and grew, expanding to huge dimensions. It was a log, several feet thick, and it slammed into the two thresher beasts, ending the battle in a wave of gore.

* * * * *

It was hours before Rayne and the others could leave. Shalanda aided Jolreal first at Rayne's insistence. The waves of healing energy from Shalanda's hand washed through the sorceress's body, and soon Jolreal was awake and talking. Rayne waited patiently for her aide to begin work on her wounds but pressed Jolreal for an explanation of the thresher beast's attack.

"I don't know," Jolreal stammered as she took in the blood and corpses, her eyes lingering longest on Boyle's body. "I tried to command the creatures, but when I tried to enfold it in the spirit of the forest, I was pushed away. Not only did the thresher beast resist, but also the land itself was distant. I could not draw power, and the thresher beast would not stop fighting. My body and mind stumbled under attack." She took a deep breath. "Perhaps there is a buried city or ancient Keldon battlefield nearby—something that poisons the land and drained my strength.

"After I lost the first monster, I tried to call up something to fight the first. The other thresher beast was nearby, and I could command it with some difficulty." Jolreal sighed. "I knew my command of this one was weak, but it was close by and already a danger to us. I just hoped to use it against the first beast." Shalanda returned from her examination of the prisoners and the other scouts.

"Only four of us remain, and the big Keldon webbed to the dead one survived. I collected Boyle and our other scout. There is a deep depression off to the side where we can bury them. What do we do now?" Shalanda asked.

Jolreal still seemed dazed, and Rayne answered after a few seconds' pause, "We'll bury our people, keep our prisoner tied and doped up, and ride for home."

* * * * *

The scouts rode for a week back toward camp. The prisoner said nothing, being drugged and tied upright to a pole

Rayne rigged on a runner. The smooth stride of the runner and the last of their medical supplies kept him reasonably compliant. Perhaps it was the deaths of their comrades, but even the successful capture of the Keldon officer couldn't raise the scouts' spirits. Jolreal and Shalanda felt particularly listless, and guard duty at night was an ordeal since a watch had to be kept on the prisoner at all times. Even the land seemed to reflect the mood, as Rayne noticed patches of blight in the grass and trees.

"Is that normal?" Rayne asked, pointing to withered vegetation along a ridgeline.

"I'm not sure what normal is anymore," Jolreal said tiredly. "I failed to control a beast of the forest. Perhaps it was the effects of some ancient magic or the thresher beast's lure, but I couldn't grasp it. Now everything feels off, as if a piece of that monster was caught in my head."

"I feel different too," Shalanda joined in. "I cast my power out to kill instead of heal. Now the world seems . . . sour somehow."

That two magic users should feel a change was worrisome, Rayne thought. Perhaps this wrongness was something that needed to be investigated. If only they weren't burdened by their prisoner.

At last the party reached the base camp, and Rayne felt relief as the Keldon was put in a proper stockade and she could get a full night's sleep. The next morning saw her and Shalanda inside the camp headquarters. They would discover what they had brought back to the League.

The building was dark and cramped. Rayne and the others seated themselves to the side. The room reminded the scholar of a courtroom, and Rayne wondered if she should oversee the interrogation.

Camp Commander Priget inspired no confidence in the

scholar. Small and fat, he squinted from behind a heavy desk. He was pale, and Rayne wondered if Priget ever went outside. The night before he had listened to Jolreal giving her account of the scouting expedition in obvious disbelief. Only the sight of the drugged warrior outside his office had silenced his snorts of incredulity. The commander had taken the prisoner, and Jolreal had been too exhausted to argue.

Priget sat on a dais on one side of the room, flags and apparent battle trophies ranked behind him. A low table rested on the floor. On it were instruments of torture. Thumbscrews, skewers, and knives lay arrayed. Next to it sat an unlit camp stove with branding irons leaning against its side.

The Keldon warrior was herded into the room like an animal. Four men with poles controlled rope nooses over the prisoner's neck. The chair they chained him in was short, and his knees rose nearly to his chest. The guards dropped their poles and withdrew.

"You are called to explain your crimes," Priget announced. "Any attempt to deceive this court will be punished." The commander gestured to the tools of pain. Rayne hoped that the prisoner was fluent in the languages of the League, because Priget hadn't thought to use an interpreter.

"I am Couric, war leader and blood letter." The warrior paused to spit on the floor. "You mean nothing to me."

"Such behavior will result in punishment," Priget warned, waving a sergeant to stand by the table.

"You haven't even heated the irons," Couric said with contempt. "The League knows nothing of terror." He ignored Priget and turned his head to glare at the rest of the room. "You are weak, and we will sweep over your armies. Even now our forces march into position to start the final attack.

"We will pour from the north, and your men shall fall

under our swords. Our barges will bull their way through your flimsy cities. The screams of your fallen comrades will announce our coming. We will own you all." The Keldon's voice filled the room, overriding Priget's weak tenor.

"The lands of our ancestors will be ours again. We shall walk in the footsteps of the Heroes and kick aside the trash that has settled the land." Couric spit again, the saliva carrying to the shoes of a guard.

"You all will be whipped and beaten into service. Your women," Couric jutted his chin to Rayne and her aide, "will go into the cradle houses and bear warriors for the greater glory of Keld!" His body heaved with each shout, and the chains scraped against the wood of the chair.

"Our ships will carry a river of captives to the north, and the League will cease to be anything but a story whispered by slaves!" Couric bellowed. The big Keldon stared at Priget with eyes full of hatred and disgust. "The winds of Twilight are upon us. The witch kings will ascend from the grave, and all of you will be judged by Keldon steel."

"Silence him," Priget shouted, and the sergeant moved toward Couric, a bludgeon held high to shut off the torrent of words.

Couric strained, the chains pulling against the structure of the chair, and he began shouting words from memory.

"The first wind of ascension is Forger, burning away impurity," he growled. A burst of flame exploded below the prisoner, and the arms and legs separated from the chair. Couric stood free, glowering at the sergeant, his arms still manacled to scraps of charred wood that used to be the arms of the chair. The angry Keldon warrior looked around the room, challenging the guards and magic users with his eyes. The guards hesitated at first, taking the Keldon's measure, then charged him en masse.

"The second wind of ascension is Reaver, slaying the unworthy." Couric was heavily muscled, and the Keldon scythed down the charging men with the broken wood still attached to his arms.

More guards poured into the room, trying to subdue the prisoner, but Couric surged back, ripping the handles from several poles at once.

"The third wind of ascension is Eliminator, clearing Keld's path to victory." One pole was in the Keldon's hand, and he stabbed it at the faces of the circling guards. Teeth and bones broke, and the victims fell to the floor, constricting the room even more as the captured warrior moved toward the door.

"Somebody get a webcaster!" Rayne called, and she moved closer to Priget, hoping to use his huge desk as cover.

Shalanda, who was nearer that door than Rayne, forced her way through the stream of oncoming guards to find something she could use to subdue the Keldon.

Couric was hemmed in, but he was holding his own and making ground. The dead bodies of the first round of guards littered the floor, and while the new soldiers carried stabbing spears, they were wary of the massive Keldon, not wanting to be another of his victims.

"Kill him!" Priget ordered. The commander was trapped but was ready to hide beneath the heavy desk if fighting moved any closer.

Couric gasped as a blade punctured his side. He struck at the attacker, but the League soldier retreated into the ring of spears. Priget rose from behind the desk to watch his troops dispatch the Keldon officer. Rayne stood beside him, feeling powerless in the interrogation room with no weapons.

"The fourth wind of ascension is Anointer, defying the

worthy," the Keldon bellowed, and spinning to face the camp commander and the Tolarian scholar, the mammoth warrior threw himself at the dais. Priget retreated toward the wall. Couric shouted at his retreating face, ignoring everything in the room now except the man who had given his death order and the woman who had captured him.

Shalanda rushed through the door, a blue-robed figure in tow.

"The fifth wind of ascension is Exalter, fulfilling Keld's destiny." The warrior raised his hands for a mighty blow.

Spears sank into Couric's back, and the blood coated his clothes. He slammed into the heavy desk, and the bolts securing it to the dais sheared under his weight. Blinding blue-white energy arced from the doorframe toward the desk and the charging warrior. The Keldon seemed to slow in mid-attack, his cries of rage sounding deeper as his words stretched out. Another blast of arcane light burst from the blue-robed figure—this one targeted at Rayne.

Shalanda had returned with Barrin, and the ancient wizard now acted to save his wife from being crushed by the rampaging Keldon. The spell wrapped itself around her frame like a giant gloved hand, and it pulled her away from the sliding desk. Barrin's first casting had given him the time to save Rayne's life, but the camp commander wasn't so lucky. Hundreds of pounds of hardwood and Keldon forced Priget against the paneled wall. The commander was pinned at the chest, and Rayne could hear bones breaking, tearing into Priget's internal organs. Couric sprawled over the desk, bled out and nearly dead as he looked into the eyes of the crushed commander.

"Even a chained Keldon can kill one such as you,"

Couric whispered as angry soldiers stabbed him again and again with spears. The Keldon warrior died smiling under the dead gaze of his final victim.

CHAPTER 11

The afternoon sun beat down as Barrin and Yarbo flew over the League army camp. The sun glinted from the arrays of war machines. Technicians labored over their charges, looking more insectlike from the height than the weapons they serviced. Cavalry and corrals of horses lay at the ends of the camps with formations of infantry conducting maneuvers in open fields. The combined forces of Kinymu and Arsenal City had gathered to drive the invaders back, and Barrin hoped it would be enough. Yarbo flared his craft's wings, and the ornithopter began a slow circling descent to the landing circle and a waiting committee. Soldiers came to attention as the craft settled, and Barrin stepped outside. For the first time since coming to Jamuraa, Barrin could not smell the sea.

An officer stepped forward. He was a very large Jamuraan man, as big as many of the Keldons Barrin had seen, but this man's features were more majestic and dignified—not as harsh or severe as those of the invaders. He wore an animal hide around his waist that covered him from mid-belly to toes, and his exposed upper body and face were swathed in a white chalky substance—presumably war paint. His hair was hidden beneath a great helm, but it was his green eyes that caught Barrin's attention. They seemed to measure everything, and the slight tension in the officer's figure signaled a readiness for action. This was the sort of officer who led his troops from the front lines.

"I am General Mageta, Lord Barrin. My enemies call me the Lion for my fierceness in battle. I will be your guide if you wish to view the army before your consultations with the war council."

"Let's start with the combat troops, General," Barrin said and started walking toward the groups of war machines that he had seen from the air. Mageta hurried to catch up as Barrin departed for the tour. The general gamely began describing the war machines as Barrin walked closer to their ranks.

"All League war machines have been constructed for decades at Arsenal City. The machines here are found throughout the League and have been standardized for many years. Reinforcements will therefore fold right into the formations we see." Mageta spoke with pride, but Barrin wondered if the system he described hadn't stifled advancement.

"These are called steel ants." The general gestured to groups of small war machines being serviced by technicians.

Each machine was waist high with six legs. The head was oversized, and Barrin thought it crowded with sensors and a set of bladed mandibles and saws. "They are the smallest war machines that the League fields. They are quite fast, and when directed they close and dismember the enemy."

"Do they carry anything with a longer bite?" Barrin asked.

"That is something we are particularly proud of," Mageta said, pointing to the oversized head. "A modular weapon bay sits inside that can take three bolts or a light war rocket. The modular weapons bay design is included in all our machines, though you can't trade modules between classes."

"They are limited, but they are fast, cheap, and rugged for their size. The Keldons fighting them hand to hand will be very impressed when these machines charge their lines," the general maintained stoutly. "If it's heavier machines you want, then perhaps the crabs will do."

Mageta quickly led Barrin past the tents of the mechanics to another group of war machines. These were large, nearly topping six feet. They were slightly wider than they were long and stood crablike on six legs. Two huge jointed arms were held high, but instead of claws, each arm ended in a massive metal bludgeon.

"These are the center of the battle," the general said. "The arms can swing down amazingly fast, and a blow can topple small trees. Lest you think these also lack a long-range bite, the wide body enables us to have three double-sized weapons bays. A module can take six bolts, two rockets, or an oversized web round. A force charging them would dissolve in quick order."

"Very impressive," said Barrin. "But I notice that there are far more steel ants than these crabs. They also appear to be less mobile than their smaller cousins. How fast do they travel?" He was certainly more impressed by these than the steel ants, but he was wondering how the different types of machines would work together.

"I confess they are somewhat slow and therefore usually anchor the center of an attack. But we *are* discussing barbarians after all. Perhaps they have overpowered eastern outposts, but I doubt they'll offer much of a challenge to two city armies." Mageta was speaking with pride, but Barrin suspected it was ignorance.

"We only have a few examples of the last type of war machine," Mageta confessed. "It was originally developed to fight in closer quarters and smaller groups than the ants or crabs." He pointed to a set of twenty machines. They stood nearly seven feet tall and were painted in an array of bright, angry colors. "The mantis is somewhat of a compromise beast. Its head shares several common systems with the ant and will take the same weapons modules. The body is narrower and faster than the crab but can carry only one double-size module to the crab's three." Mageta finally pointed to the massive jointed arms that gave the mantis its name. "Each of the interior sides are razor sharp, and if a blow does not dismember the target, it's hauled up to the cutting jaws of the head." Barrin liked the statement the mantises made in their bright color schemes and detailing. The artwork showed pride and perhaps bravado that had a place on the battlefield.

"How are the machines usually employed?" Barrin asked. "Can they act on their own without constant supervision? I have never seen them unaccompanied in battle."

"They are directed against the enemy and then attack until the enemy forces are disabled," Mageta explained.

"What do you mean by disabled?" Barrin responded.

"You must understand that for years in Northern Jamuraa

wars were waged by machines fighting machines. A machine is disabled if it's smashed, dismembered, or gutted by an attack. The Keldons will not take more damage than that, I trust."

Barrin only grunted. "And what about the human troops? May I see them next?" Barrin was satisfied with his preliminary look at the war machines, but how the human troops looked would be more important. The production of war machines was limited due to the shortage of powerstones. The longer the war lasted, the more human troops would be serving in the field, if for no other reason than to allow dispersed war machines to be amassed on active fronts.

"You saw the human troops—the mechanics and technicians behind the crabs," Mageta said with a straight face.

"I mean the combat troops, the ones who will actually be fighting on the line of battle."

Mageta's long silence told Barrin that he wouldn't like the answer.

* * * * *

"You mean there are no combat troops here whatsoever?" Yarbo asked incredulously that night. "Surely there must be in two cities of this size."

"Yes, they have soldiers, but they serve as watchmen, ceremonial guards, and maintenance workers on the city defenses," Barrin explained. "Infantry, cavalry, and people trained to fight as an army are far out on the frontier. Close to the cities, the war machines have taken over the combat role as fighting was ritualized and limited. Why maintain a large army when you buy war machines that will last for decades, require only a small force of technicians, and don't draw wages?"

"But they've had Keldons raiding the League for years now," Yarbo replied. "And if they have no soldiers, who are all those people out in the fields outside the city walls? We saw infantry and cavalry!"

"Those are new recruits," Barrin said shortly. "Most of them without any armor except what they could scrounge from an attic, and perhaps they carry an old spear or sword. If I had a couple of blimps or dirigibles for cargo, I'd haul a load of League launchers here." Barrin waved his hand toward the camp. "Maybe one out of ten of the men have a launcher."

"The coastal cities have fought off raids," Yarbo argued. "It must be possible for city militias to fight effectively."

"They were marines, not militias that fought on the coast, and usually the Jamuraans had greater numbers," Barrin said tiredly as he thought about what tomorrow might bring. "We better pray that my guide was right and their machines kill the Keldons, because I don't see any way they can use the rest of the army."

* * * * *

Morning brought some good news. Teferi diverted a pair of Kashan blimps to help with reconnaissance. The aircraft observed the Keldon camp and perhaps sixty land barges altogether. The estimate of the approaching army was under four thousand, an indeterminate number of them slaves. While Barrin did not think the number meant an easy fight, he believed the numbers pointed to a League victory. As the Keldons broke camp, he heard distress calls from the scouting blimps. "Evasive action!" resounded through the communications room. Barrin waited, opening his senses for any other messages. Then one of the craft reported.

"Tell Barrin we're sorry, but he'll get no more close views of the enemy. They have skipping fire launchers down there. They just took out the *Moonrise*. Unless a Mushan with long-range glide bombs gets diverted up here, we'll keep our distance from any and all barges." Barrin knew the crew was all volunteers, but he still cursed and regretted their deaths.

"I'll fly," said Barrin. "I need to see the enemy, get a feel for what they might throw. I wish the army had more experience in large scale maneuvers." A general who had been listening to the blimp reports spoke candidly as Barrin called for Yarbo to ready the ornithopter.

"Our soldiers are untrained, ill-armed, and afraid," the officer said. "But chances are very high that we can beat the Keldons during this particular battle. If we avoid battle, it would be more corrosive to morale and feed the Keldon legend of invincibility. Better to take casualties in achieving the victory and focus on training later."

Barrin agreed with the sentiments but thought the acceptance, even eagerness, for fatalities repugnant after the losses already seen. A vision of Urza floated before him. The ruthlessness that Barrin so admonished in the planeswalker was a quality he would have to cultivate as the war continued.

Barrin and Yarbo took off as the League army began to march. Barrin could see Tolarian runners fanning out along the axis of the attack. Yarbo took the craft toward the last Keldon position.

"Be sure everything is secured," the pilot said to Barrin. "There may be some sudden maneuvering."

The wings beat faster, and the craft accelerated toward the Keldon army. Barrin opened his mind and tasted the air over the camp. The sky was filled with traces of magic, and the wizard could feel the Keldon magic users below. The weapons and concentrations of power were coals burning on the plain. Then it was as if naphtha was thrown in a furnace as arcs of fire sprang into the sky. The pilot sent the ornithopter racing under the balls and streamers of flame. Barrin gripped his seat while the machine screamed in a dive that sent them whipping over the warriors below. The craft tilted as Yarbo sent it in a new direction. Barrin looked down on the camp. The launchers were firing. The weapons were mounted on smaller versions of the Keldon land barges. The major difference between these and the ones the old wizard had already seen was that the heavy upper wooden shell was completely removed to accommodate the launchers.

Barrin could feel a pulse of power, and he watched a ball of sulfurous flame launched straight at them. Only Yarbo's dropping turn generated a miss. Barrin heard his bones creak as the pilot snapped his wings level and began climbing beyond the camp.

"We need to make another pass," the wizard announced. "I thought I felt something new when we flew over." The pilot turned the ship and sent it racing toward the ground.

"I hope you find what you need this time, because I'm not doing this again," Yarbo hissed.

The ornithopter dodged close to the ground to avoid fire while Barrin sent his senses out once more. The wizard massed power for attack as the ornithopter came closer to the Keldon army. Their craft was so low that Barrin feared a collision with the warriors and slaves scrambling for cover. The ancient magic user could feel stores of energy quiescent in the land barges—not hot like the magic that he had detected before. Waves of fire and attack spells prevented Barrin from looking further.

Keldon air defense crews ignored the danger of creating

casualties and fired on Barrin's craft. Streams of flame dug into the ground and incinerated warriors in the Keldon camp as anti-air fire missed. Barrin directed a slap of power against a fire barge racing for a better position. The enemy craft exploded in flame, and the ornithopter jinked around the rising cloud of flame and smoke, pulling for altitude behind the screen of fiery destruction. Streamers still filled the air, but the pilot let out a long breath of relief as the range opened and the ornithopter sped away from the camp.

"I hope you got what you needed," Yarbo said as he rose to a high altitude.

"There is definitely something in those barges," Barrin replied distractedly. "It's more than the magic propelling them. There is some surprise cargo carried here for battle."

"Well you're about to find out," said the pilot. "The League is attacking."

The Keldons were near the bottom of a long rise and pulled back a hundred yards to deploy. Barrin could see the League massing its forces on the lip of the rise. War machines lined up, settling into place like restive horses at the start of a race. The infantry formed behind. Spears glinted as squares of soldiers prepared to kill or die. The cavalry was two irregular masses on the wings of the force.

"Don't attack now!" Barrin shouted, his voice reverberating in the cabin. Below him the first wave of League machines poured into battle.

The steel ants raced down the slope, quickly pulling ahead of the other machines and men. Barrin could see the Keldon lines contracting, tensing like a spring, then a flare of energy burst from the Keldon anti-air unit. It was a clear shot over the lines, hitting the face of the rise. War machines were smashed as they advanced down to the enemy warriors. Fire barges broke up the League units, and the ants hit the fighters awaiting them in disorganized driblets. The bludgeoning crabs, the center of the attack, started down the rise with infantry close behind. The fire barges would boot them all over the landscape. Barrin's head threatened to explode as he raised power over the hostile enemy force. A continuous bolt of lightning flashed from the ornithopter to the ground.

"Go slower," Barrin said through tensed lips, and the pilot cut speed to almost a standstill.

The lightning advanced at a brisk walk, leaving a narrow trail of fused soil. The arc bumped into a fire barge and played over the vehicle for long seconds as slaves and mages threw themselves onto the ground and away from pending disaster. The vehicle did not explode, but fires broke out and engulfed it, roasting the crew who were too slow to abandon their charge. Some fire barges surged into motion to escape the lightning's path. Others ceased firing on the League army and concentrated on Barrin. The pilot swooped like an escaping thrush, and Barrin let loose a second stream of lightning on a fire barge. The Keldons cooked and died, and the craft turned circles with the helmsman steaming on the deck.

The ants bunched up against Keldon warriors, and Barrin threw his senses over the fight. The men fighting the machines were large, garbed in heavy leather and swinging swords that bit into their metal opponents. Blood showed on steel mandibles, but more and more machines went down. The Keldons attacked joints, and those with axes and clubs pounded machines to pieces.

The second wave of League forces arrived at the base of the rise. Crabs advanced with infantry close behind. Enemy warriors started breaking from the lines for the land barges in the rear. Barrin dared hoped they were running, but only a thin stream of men withdrew from the formations. For each warrior that entered the barges, several armored figures came out. Barrin could feel a swelling of magic power as the Keldon army grew larger and larger. The swords and axes lifted against the League were wielded not by men but by simulations of warriors. Manikins—hollow warriors—pulsed with energy that mimicked fighters leading them from the barges. Warriors led squads to reinforce the lines as the League crabs arrived, each set of false men in sync with a living leader.

The Keldons chanted, and the line tensed, becoming rock hard as the crabs hit. Crab bludgeons rose and fell, each blow smashing men and manikins alike to the ground. Barrin could see misshapen corpses falling as bones shattered into mush.

League officers screamed orders as they ran to the line, and the crabs unleashed flurries of bolts into the Keldons. Men fell as blood and gore exploded from projectile wounds, but the hollow warriors soaked up the fire without wavering. A few of the false men dropped, but even the heaviest League blow couldn't crack the line. More and more swords flowed from the barges, and the Keldons started to advance. League machines attacked as individuals, but mixtures of manikins and warriors acted as unified squads. Manikins threw themselves onto war machines while axes severed mechanical limbs.

The infantry lagged behind its steel allies, hesitant to add merely human strength to the destruction the war machines inflicted. Now the League constructions were falling. Chanting madmen swung bloody swords. Here and there near-giants inspired twisting maelstroms of slaughter. Some Keldons were in heavy armor, steel enclosures on the shoulders and chest holding burning coals and brands. Waves of smoke poured over the League lines. Soldiers coughed and felt a spreading terror. The war manikins threw themselves on infantry spears and broke the League units into clumps of panicking men. The crabs were consumed, and more and more soldiers abandoned all hope. Many began to run away from the battles, streaming back to camp or into Keldon territory, fleeing the fighting without regard for direction.

A few units held firm. The single section of mantises advanced into the Keldon line, their arms flickering in attacks that yanked warriors into range of their cutting jaws. The infantry with the mantises supported the machines, protecting their flanks, but the rest of the League was melting away. Even the elite soldiers retreated. In the midst of the fighting withdrawal, Barrin could see General Mageta directing men equipped with launchers. The unit fired light rockets into the warriors and manikins. Dozens flew apart in explosions, but the Keldons charged, some jumping over the remains of their comrades. Mageta and other soldiers moved forward with swords and shields while their comrades reloaded.

The Kipamu League cavalry had swung wide and fell on the left wing of the Keldon army. Bolts bled Keldon warriors, and the League riders taunted them out of position, pretending to retreat and then turning on the strung-out warriors chasing them. The horsemen turned to attack again, but now the barges moved to the flanks. Ballista bolts and fireballs left wounded horses screaming in the dirt. Young warriors finished off dismounted cavalrymen.

The Keldons were charging up the slope after the retreating Jamuraan army. Barrin could feel the force of the enemy magic fading. The air-protection units were walking up the slope to provide cover.

"Wing down along the slope," Barrin told the pilot.

"The battle's lost, sir," Yarbo said. "The army has come apart, and you can't put it back together."

"I can't salvage the day, but I can save the army," Barrin growled. "Now do as I say." Reluctantly, the pilot nosed the ornithopter down as he had been ordered.

Barrin had held back, hoping that the League generals knew what they were doing. The reversal had been so sudden that the wizard couldn't hope to turn the battle. But he was damned if he would just fly away with the Keldons utterly victorious. Barrin pulled energy from the land harder than ever, his rage and disgust growing as he came closer and closer to the Keldon forces. Fire streamers began to fly again, and the ornithopter dodged. Barrin compressed his wrath until it beat against his control like a maddened beast, then he released it. A narrow spike of energy burst from the ornithopter. It entered the ground like an awl. Huge amounts of energy flowed through a narrow channel, filling the ground with power.

An explosion erupted deep in the hill, and Barrin was spent as he flew away, his mind barely aware of what was happening. The slope was not deep, and the landslide was more of a slump than a cataclysm, but barges tumbled and buried themselves in the dirt as the ground trembled and lost cohesion. Warriors who feared no man screamed as they were buried alive. Only a small part of the Keldon army was covered, but all pursuit stopped as warriors and slaves desperately dug at the turned soil, hoping to bring living men up from the dirt instead of corpses.

"Take us to where the army is rallying," Barrin whispered to Yarbo. The wizard felt drained, disconnected as the ornithopter climbed away from the battlefield.

CHAPTER 12

Haddad dreamed. He fell through space. Through the still air he could see the clouds rushing up. Then, a cloud surrounded him, and there was no movement. His hands and feet knocked on wood as he turned. He was in the stasis box! The smoke forced itself down his throat, trying to strangle him. He jumped up and ran. Everything was covered. It was fog, and he ran slower and slower as the chill of it drained the heat from his body. No matter which direction he ran, he was still lost. He began to stumble and trip over uneven ground. Was that water he waded through? The fog was clearing, and now he could see. He was on a battlefield. Torn and mangled bodies stretched toward the horizon, many submerged in bloody pools of stagnant water. They were his comrades he had trained with. He stumbled from corpse to corpse, looking into dead eyes as he tried to find a survivor. Now he found childhood friends, schoolmates from years before, neighbors from his youth, and members of his family. He screamed in grief, and his voice swept everything away. He cried alone on an empty plain. Then someone walked toward him. It was Latulla! The artificer stood before him, her arms open wide and a smile on her face. He ran at her, his fists clenched so tightly that blood leaked from them. She showed no fear and waved him on. He struck her, and her arms shattered at the blows. But it was Lord Druik who fell at his feet. The warlord's limbs and face were gone, eaten away by the jelly, so only a torso and head lay writhing. Then Druik was on a table, and Haddad attached new limbs and forced machine parts into the Keldon. Finally, Druik had arms and legs, and Haddad lay weapons at the hands and feet of his creation. Just the head remained to be done, a fleshy skull without eyes. Someone handed him a mask to place over the head. As Haddad screwed the metal to bone, the eyes of the mask opened and stared at him in pain. Haddad awoke.

The former League soldier lay on an actual bed. It was narrow and creaked loudly as he tried to raise his head. He finally managed to sit up. Haddad's mouth seemed full of cotton, and he staggered toward the door. A table with a bucket of water on top diverted his path. He checked to make sure it was not the chamber pot and drank using his hand as a cup. Haddad blinked as he considered the room. Light leaked through a shutter and provided a dim illumination. In a corner his gear lay in a pile, and except for the bed and the table, there was no furniture. A candle sat on the table, and he could see a chamber pot under the bed. For an inn it seemed inadequate, but for a prison it was surprisingly comfortable. Haddad tried the door, but as he expected, it was firmly locked. The window opposite the door was not locked and neither was it barred. Haddad threw the shutters wide and blinked away tears as the light assaulted his eyes. Eventually his vision cleared, and he looked out over a cluster of buildings.

In the distance were bare hills, a low wall of weathered rock hemming in the sky. There were scattered, massive structures of stone and timber. There were no real streets, just beaten paths between buildings and a road that lead off to the hills. The shadows were long and covered the ground under his window. Everything was quiet, and Haddad wondered at the silence. Now he could see warriors and slaves walking between buildings, but the scene seemed nearly deserted. A gust of wind made him shiver, and he grabbed the blanket from the bed as he looked out.

Those were women walking, he now thought. The groups were organized around a core of large richly dressed figures with smaller women orbiting around them. Haddad watched and noticed there were no children visible. In every city he knew at least a child or two played in the streets or was carried by its mother. He watched a warrior walk below him. The sound of his footsteps was muffled, and he left footprints in the ground that slowly vanished from the thick coating of moss.

Haddad was up several stories, and he wondered if he was in a building like the others before him, all high peaked and very large. Windows for light broke the walls, and on the roofs were skylights and light wells. There were smaller buildings scattered around, and Haddad recognized animal corrals, though few beasts moved within them.

Haddad listened carefully and heard the voices of children off to the side. He leaned forward and looked left and down into the corner of a walled compound. The wall enclosed acres, and children played and ran in the open field. Behind them loomed a complex of buildings with figures moving in great numbers. Haddad looked at the children near the wall as a circle formed, and a free-for-all erupted. A larger boy moved through the fight, dealing out blows that left youths gasping for air. On the opposite side of the battle several girls moved as a group, setting upon fighters who came too close. The fighting died down as the victorious boy slowly circled the girls, and then the children started back toward the complex of buildings.

"Perhaps it's a school," Haddad muttered to himself and then turned as the door opened behind him.

It was a Keldon female. Her gray skin was weathered and her hair was sprinkled with white. She wore a dress of deep blue with several panels of brown leather. Her feet were booted, and a belt with dagger and wallet completed her wardrobe. She was slighter than Latulla but looked hard.

"You're awake then," she said. "I am Iola, the steward of this house. Please follow me so you may commence your duties." She paused slightly before turning to lead the way from the room. "Now I suggest you hurry and finish dressing."

Haddad had woken dressed except for boots, which he found sitting under the bed behind the chamber pot. He jammed his feet into them and patted himself down quickly. He paused. Something was on his left arm. He quickly rolled up his sleeve and discovered a metal band, which covered his upper arm. It was a dull bronze, and Latulla's sigil circled it in a repeating pattern. He tried to locate the catch or seam by which he could remove it but found nothing. How could he have not noticed it before? It was tight enough that he could not slip a fingernail under its edge. He began to dig into the skin around it when Iola interrupted him.

"You can scratch your itch later," she said. "Follow me now." Her voice contained the warning signs that Haddad learned from Latulla, and he stood up at once. He stepped quickly to follow her as she proceeded onto a staircase, and he closed the door after him, noting the sigil on the door. It was a stylized rodent, and Haddad wondered if the carving reflected his status in the house.

"May I ask questions, my lady?" Haddad knew flattery never hurt. "Where are we?"

"You stand on Keld, first among nations," she replied as they walked down the stairs and through a series of rooms. Haddad peered uncertainly as his eyes adapted to the interior lighting. They arrived at a great hall. He looked up and could see the shafts of light from light wells falling to the floors. Metal reflectors threw a spray of light into the corners. Haddad could see a raised dais, but the hall was mainly empty.

Haddad and Iola walked along a series of balconies and smaller rooms.

"These chambers are for meetings and guests of Latulla. Stay out of them except when on errands," commanded the house steward.

"Is Latulla important here?" Haddad asked.

"Important?" Iola scoffed. "She holds the house. When she was barely out of the cradle house she expelled the former master and took it for her own." She spoke with obvious pride at what Haddad considered little more than a great theft. "But her travels and work meant the house suffered, so she took me as a second and placed it in my hands."

"Is she here now?" Haddad asked, wondering if they were going to report to her. He could see more clearly now, and carvings seemed to jump out of the walls. Every panel, every railing, had a design. Haddad thought the wall he passed showed a story rather than just an ornamental pattern.

"She had business among the great lords and is not expected for quite some time," Iola answered. Then she turned a corner and walked away from the interior hall. The light grew dimmer, and the carvings were less ornate. Iola pointed out the firewood room and other storage areas and then went down to the next floor. The narrow staircase was black, and Haddad felt his way down the steps as Iola waited impatiently at the bottom. He could feel carving on the railing and the walls as his hands guided him down. He turned a corner, and there was more light. Haddad and Iola were in a kitchen, and he looked at the men and a few women preparing food. The air was hot, and Haddad perspired as he passed the cooking fires. Panting dogs ran in work-wheels, turning spits of meat. The cook and the principal workers in the kitchen were women and showed the gray skin of Keldons, while the men were all subject races. Humans, dwarves, elves, and a few races that Haddad could only guess at were stirring pots and making bread.

"You have access at all hours and may freely take what you need as long as you do not interfere with the others' duties," Iola continued as she headed toward the pantries.

Iola and Haddad passed many slaves, but none were introduced, and all ducked their eyes at their passage. Iola opened the door to the yard and stepped outside. She was walking toward a network of outbuildings almost exactly like the workshops Latulla had constructed back on Haddad's home continent. Iola waved for him to stay where he was and yelled for a slave to stop. The man fell to his knees as Iola approached.

Haddad turned and looked at the exterior of the house. It was the size of a palace! Haddad would have thought a king or great family lived there, and he wondered how even Latulla, strong as she was, had been able to evict the previous tenants.

Haddad heard the sound of a blow being landed but only saw Iola walking toward him as the slave staggered away. Iola continued as if nothing had happened.

"You will be working in the farthest workshop, the one next to the cradle house." She waved toward the wall behind which Haddad had watched the children battle.

"Is the cradle house a school then?" Haddad queried. If Latulla came from that particular institution, Haddad had no wish to meet the rest of the graduating class.

"Of course the cradle house is a school. It is also a hospital and nursery. All Keldons are born and raised in a cradle house." Iola shook her head at his ignorance. "You foreign slaves ask the most bizarre questions."

They stopped before the workshop where Haddad would be working. It was a high-peaked structure of at least two stories.

A staircase ran along the exterior of the building, and Iola started up the steps. Haddad followed, looking into the windows of the first story. He could see little beyond shadows and covered tables. A large lock closed the door at the top of the stairs, and Iola took a ring of keys from her wallet and sorted through them. She extracted one and opened the door.

Haddad entered the room first. It was still dim even with the door open, and Iola proceeded to open the shutters, letting in more light. Haddad noticed that these windows were barred. On the floor lay a collection of crates with Latulla's mark, and a series of League technical manuals sat on a nearby table. Iola gestured toward the piled supplies.

"Latulla commands you to reconstruct one of your war machines from the materials provided. She will expect it completed at her return. You will work on it except when you are resting at the main house." Iola handed him the key to the door. "You will be responsible for securing your work. Let no other slave enter, and say nothing about your work. Meals are your own responsibility." And with that, she left.

Haddad was alone and free from observation. He locked the door from the inside and stretched with unaccustomed freedom. If he had been given some liberty, he wanted to put it to good use. He began inspecting his work area. There were a plethora of tools that he could use as weapons—chisels, hammers, bar stock, metal shears, and more. He put aside an awl and some wire for construction of weapons. Then, thinking that he might be questioned by Iola, he opened the crates. They did indeed contain parts for a steel ant, several in fact. The problem was that every casing had been pried open and examined. Gears and cabling were missing. Many of the parts showed what must be combat damage. Worse, there were no powerstones to move and control the device once it was constructed. Haddad was trained in quick field repairs using modular parts to replace damaged subsystems. Building an ant would be much more difficult than it had first appeared. Haddad rubbed the metal band on his arm as he considered what would be necessary to fulfill his commission from his Keldon masters. His arm itched, and he wondered what it signified. He wondered how long it would itch and turned back to work with a promise that he would ask about the armband. He emptied the crates and considered how to proceed.

It was growing late when Haddad finally prepared to leave. The workshop lacked lamps or candles, and twilight was ruining Haddad's vision. He was starving, and he promised himself that in the future he would bring food and drink with him. He sat at a table, looking at his hands and thinking about the next day. His hands were colored with oil and grease from the parts he inspected. As he cleaned them on a cloth, he noticed how the stains had set in quickly and already looked several days old.

He was in front of a window facing the cradle house. The rise of the workshop and a dip under the enclosure wall allowed him to look within the compound. Children were being called inside, and Keldon boys raced each other. Pregnant women rose from chairs and walked into the buildings within the compound. None of the women appeared gray skinned, and Haddad wondered where the Keldon mothers sat.

It wasn't until he was outside that he realized almost the entire day had passed without thoughts of escape. Access to all those tools, and he made no weapon nor had he appropriated a tool for his private use. All he was carrying was a League manual and some writing supplies.

He promised himself that at the very least he would write down his observations and any information he thought the League might want. His current freedom was an illusion that might end at any time. He must start planning for an escape.

Only a few seconds after starting toward Latulla's house he heard the creak of a gate behind him. He turned to see a hidden door opening in the cradle house's enclosure wall. Several figures stepped through before it closed. Even after seeing it open, Haddad was unsure of the gate's position on the unmarked wall. Remembering the respect toward cradle women and midwives demonstrated by the Keldon warriors back in the military colony, Haddad stopped and lowered his head in respect as the party passed. The leader of the party was cloaked, but her companions were not Keldon—

the first women of other races that he had seen close up for longer than he cared to remember. He forgot to duck his head and stared as they passed him, but no answering glance was sent his way. He waited a few seconds and followed them, wondering where they would lead.

Iola greeted the party at the door. "Erissa, what a pleasure to see you. Latulla will be so upset that she has missed you." The steward fairly fawned over the unexpected guest.

Erissa uncloaked and threw her outerwear to one of the women accompanying her. She was shorter than anyone else in the party and heavy. Time seemed to have compressed her to a stump compared to her taller companions.

"I doubt that very much. Plans are not going well, and Latulla and her supporters are a source of constant disappointment," Erissa said. She and Iola walked toward one of the rooms that Haddad had been forbidden from entering. He followed the rest of the group, holding the manual up as if in explanation to anyone who might question him.

"Latulla knows that the invasion is necessary, Erissa," Iola said. "It's just forcing the members of the ruling council to acknowledge that fact. There are other clans and houses fighting to bring down the League after all."

"But the bulk of them stay here or waste their time sailing and raiding for mere booty," Erissa spat. "Pursuing folly while our heritage and eventual victory is stolen by the Kipamu League. Even the women you have captured from that country have not reversed the birthing trends."

The human women accompanying the two Keldons stopped and seated themselves on the furniture and chairs while their principal withdrew into a farther room. Haddad cursed the luck and took a seat as well. In response to their questioning looks, he brandished the manual and bared his arm with its metal band. The women only shrugged and began dividing up the foods on the table. At the sight of the bread and dried fruit, Haddad's stomach loudly announced its currently empty state. One of the women smiled and offered the plate to Haddad. He took it as an invitation for conversation even as he grabbed several slices of dried apple.

There were four women regarding Haddad. Two of them were blonde. One was very muscular, her neck and forearms sharply defined. Her eyes were dark blue but hard as she stared at him. Her blonde companion was slender and her features almost ethereal. Her ears appeared somewhat pointed under her hair, and Haddad wondered if she had elf blood.

"So what is life like in the cradle house?" he asked. The women looked at each other while considering their answers. The other two shifted their seats to face Haddad more fully. One woman was dark haired, and her eyes were green. Her face was odd to Haddad. The skin was tight against her skull as if blown back by a wind. Her mouth seemed small, but her teeth were sharp and perhaps filed. The final woman was dark, perhaps from the southern kingdoms in Jamuraa. Her hair was tightly braided against her skull, and intricate networks of scars framed her face, drawing Haddad's gaze to her brown eyes.

"It's good enough for some," the brunette replied through sharp teeth. "Once they adapt to certain realities."

All the women nodded in agreement. Haddad looked at them. All were in good health and on the backside of thirty, and all of them exuded confidence and power. Any of them should have appealed to his senses, but he felt numbed by their presence.

"What realities are we speaking of?" he asked. The response was stunning.

"The hardest for some is giving up their children. Even though they know the babies will receive good care, some can't overcome their feelings. No matter how firmly one tries, some breeders won't adjust," the muscular blonde explained. Haddad wondered what sort of people considered loss of a child something to ignore.

"One woman from down south, who shares your coloring," the brunette interjected, "wouldn't stop crying after her first child went into the nursery. Even though there was a good chance that it might become a war leader."

"And at least hers didn't die like so many others have done of late," the slender blonde added. Something about this comment set the others staring at her. Haddad now saw the women as they saw themselves, hard and indifferent. They had closed off their empathy and been rewarded with positions of authority inside the cradle house. Haddad heard the Keldon women returning, and he withdrew as the others stood. He went to his room to consider what he had learned.

That night he wrote notes regarding all his experiences and what he had observed. He dared not keep it in his room and decided that he would hide it somewhere in Latulla's workshop where it was unlikely to be discovered. He blew out the candle and went to sleep.

* * * * *

Haddad dreamed. He was inside the walls of the cradle house, and instead of buildings, there was only a small basket in the middle of the yard. The women he had met stood at either side, and a long line of new mothers stretched out into the distance. As the line moved forward, each baby was ripped away and thrown down into the wicker container. As each child disappeared, the basket swelled and grew until the women were throwing children high into the air. Each was gulped down, and then something broke out of the cradle house and fell upon every living thing.

Dawn woke Haddad, and he rose from bed with a will. He stuffed the papers that he worked on the night before into his wallet. Best to get to the workshop as early as possible and let Iola find him toiling away like a good little slave. This time he thought to stop by the kitchen after freshening up.

The baker and her assistants were just putting out the bread from the pre-dawn baking, and Haddad snared a loaf. He ignored the baker's indignant utterance and snatched a sack of ale that he spotted lying unattended. He stepped outside into the crisp air. Despite a touch of frost, Haddad found he was warm in the clothes he had selected from his gear. If the workshop was too cold, he would check the small stove to see if he could start a fire. He remembered that a load of wood was stacked to the side. The door opened easily to the workshop, and he locked it behind him.

Hours passed as he worked on the parts for the steel ant. Perhaps by cannibalizing several machines he would be able to create a fighter for himself. He certainly would trust the loyalty of a mechanical construct over the other house slaves. Haddad remembered the advice two nameless men had provided him. Seek to escape and trust no one.

He lost himself in sorting through a box of gears, looking for a replacement he could use in a leg assembly. The day passed quickly with no interruptions. Haddad considered the assembly project against the parts he had available. He could finish it if only he had enough time. The most difficult part would be closing and filling the modular sections that were picked apart. The League machine was near perfect in its performance, but it depended on the high quality control of the sealed modules. A steel ant might go months without maintenance, barring battle damage. If he could contrive some plan of escape, the ant might be the key. In addition, just completing the repair would boost his confidence in a time when he needed some small victory. He wasn't even sure where Keld was, much less how he would get home. Finding the information he needed would take time.

He grew increasingly drowsy as he tried to plan his escape. Who could he talk to? How to keep from raising suspicions? Who to bribe and how? All questions that needed to be answered and soon.

He rested his head against his arm, the metal armband cool and soothing against his skin. When he awoke it was growing dark. He didn't know how he could have dozed off. Perhaps the ale he had drunk was far stronger than he realized. He thought no one had checked up on him the night before, but he couldn't be sure. It was possible that he had already missed the bed check or closing of the house doors. He needed to get back to his room. He reached into his wallet for the shop key and found the notes he had written still inside. Carrying them back to the house seemed incredibly foolhardy to him now. He needed a place to hide them, but while he had identified which cabinets and tool chests saw frequent use, there was no guarantee if he hid the papers in one seldom used they might not be discovered.

He needed a hiding place where no one would look. Haddad fell to the floor looking for a loose board, a crack under a table, anyplace to hide the incriminating words. He was back among strange tools and books he could not read when he found what he was looking for. His hand brushed a board, and it rocked. He gripped it, and to his surprise, it lifted completely free. The gap it left was approximately six inches by eighteen inches. Haddad wondered what purpose the cutout had served. The pattern of rust and signs of brackets told Haddad that a tank had been removed in the past. The cutout must have allowed hoses to carry liquid up and down from the floor below.

On his knees, he peered through the hole. There was a small ledge along the wall, but it was almost impossible to see anything in the floor below. Haddad thought a moment then walked to his tool kit. Yes, there were several metallic mirrors for examining inside war machines. He selected the largest and maneuvered it, scanning the space below. The second floor was reinforced with extra large beams. There was a gap between a beam and the floor plank right by the cutout. The removal of the tank had allowed the flooring to rise. Haddad could just shove the papers into the gap. Let someone try to find them now, he thought.

It was the creak of an opening door that made him freeze. He could not conceive of a more suspicious situation to be caught in. He breathed a sigh of relief as he realized the noise was coming from the first story. He heard the sound of rustling fabric.

"Make sure that the curtains completely seal the windows," whispered a voice. Haddad could make out light footfalls as someone complied.

"They are all closed, Erissa." The voice was the high piping of a child, and Haddad wondered what was going on. He was sure that it would be suicidal to call down and ask. A candle was lit, and Erissa and a young Keldon boy were revealed in the mirror. A cloak covered the woman, and she leaned against a crate as the boy hurried through the room, closing shutters and pulling curtains. His figure went in and out of Haddad's field of view as the League technician remained frozen, staring in the mirror.

"Now Greel," Erissa said, "let us talk of your journey south to Jamuraa." The child seemed petulant as he kicked at the floor with his heel. He appeared a sturdy boy of eight in well-made clothes.

Perhaps he's family, Haddad thought. *I wonder why they are talking here?*

"I don't know why I need to head south," Greel groused. "I am happy here. There will be no children for me to play with. Surely Latulla needs no watcher over her."

Erissa punched him sharply, her rings tearing flesh. No blood seeped forth, and Haddad watched the gashes begin to close, hoping that it was a trick of the candlelight—but knowing it wasn't—as the flesh healed.

"Latulla's plan for reviving the witch kings will fail, but she will command in the south. Even with all the aid and spells I've provided her, I still don't trust our grip. If she were tied to the altar, I would treat it as an ambush," she hissed. Erissa took a deep breath and looked at Greel. "It's time to put your childhood behind you. You will find new playmates among the League and our less fervent supporters. Now I have a treat for you." Erissa opened her cloak and revealed a sleeping babe in a sling. She unstrapped the child and laid it down.

What in the nine hells is she doing? Haddad wondered. He knew something was dreadfully wrong, and as he watched, Greel struck.

The boy—or whatever it was—leaped up and balanced on the side of a crate. It inhaled and then crouched down, its mouth open wide as it began to exhale. Wider and wider the jaws opened, like a snake swallowing an egg.

Haddad tried to move but couldn't. Greel was a nexus of

despair and death, and he drained every bit of Haddad's energy. The candle seemed to dim and flicker as if going out. Erissa seemed unaffected, and she moved, blocking Haddad's view of what was going on. The workshop seemed colder and colder, Haddad's armband bit into his flesh as it began to frost. Would his body be discovered in the morning? Haddad wondered. Then, the cold began to abate, and the room returned to normal.

The creature seemed a boy once more, panting as if a race had just ended. He was larger now, and his features were more mature, more rugged. Greel stretched, and his mouth gaped wide as he breathed. The babe was still, and Haddad knew it wasn't sleeping.

"I will need more sustenance, Erissa," Greel said as he wiped his brow. His voice was deeper now. "We need to find an eating place within the cradle house. I will be a warrior's size soon."

"The curse of the final days is upon us," Erissa laughed. "A few more dead children will surprise no one." She moved to the window and blew out the candles.

Haddad heard the curtains being opened and then the creak of the door. Who could he tell? A slave's word against a cradle mistress's? Any hint of what he had seen would mean his death. He knelt on the floor a long time before he replaced the cutout and found his way to his room.

CHAPTER 13

Haddad's work on the steel ant continued. Each day found him carefully repairing parts, recreating linkages, and reconnecting cables, but he no longer imagined that he would miraculously escape once he completed it. A single ant wouldn't carry him from Keld, and he couldn't have it following him around like a pet.

He found it harder to concentrate. The murder committed in the shop below him preyed on his mind. He saw Erissa and her entourage several times through the window as they went back and forth from the cradle house to visit Latulla's house. The cradle mistress was accompanied by a number of young boys, each bigger than the last. Greel was growing fast. Haddad also watched several funeral processions slowly wind from the gates of the cradle house toward the mountains. Haddad knew that the small shrouded forms were the result of the monster's appetite. How could Erissa and her creature kill within the compound and not be discovered? In any League town, one often saw children's funerals, but to have so many in just a few days? Haddad also remembered the cold comments of the cradle women. The death of children was common in the cradle house but had increased of late. Just what dark sorcery did Erissa practice?

Haddad resolved to learn more. He requisitioned some pure alcohol to clean parts of the ant's mechanism and ordered several times what he needed, using the extra to spike a sack of wine.

"Come join me," Haddad called to a stockman the next day. The League technician sat inside a stable with two cups and his wine. Latulla had several separate enclosures for beasts, and one was nearly abandoned as many of the mounts were with Latulla's party. A lone servant was cleaning and repairing tack for the missing animals. The slave was returning from the main house with a chunk of bread from the kitchen. Haddad knew that the man often ate separate from the other servants.

"Some wine will wash your meal down better than water from the trough," Haddad offered as he filled a cup. The liquor was far stronger with the addition of the cleaning alcohol, but the slave gulped it down without a word of appreciation. The stockman only held out his empty cup for more.

"I am Haddad from the southern continent. I know very little about the other servants or about Keld," Haddad explained as he filled the man's cup once again. "Perhaps you might instruct me."

The stableman's response was to drain his cup again, this time in slow swallows. The man was big, but smaller than the Keldon warriors. His clothes stank of dung and sweat. His brown hair was long and greasy, and his face was nearly hidden by a snarled beard. A series of tattoos swirled around his eyes, and a broad expanse of scalp hinted at his previous hairline.

"I do not gossip like an old woman. Talk to others if you would know more." The stableman threw the dregs of his cup against the wall, leaving a stain. Haddad spoke quickly before the slave could leave.

"I would speak to the old women, but there are none to be found. I know women have been stolen from my own country, but I haven't seen any female slaves except from the cradle house. Where do they all go?" Haddad asked hurriedly. The stableman paused.

"As you said. All women go into the cradle house. They bear Keldon children or help care for them. Perhaps other places in Keld allow human females to be outside the cradle house walls but not here," he said slowly.

"But if only slaves bear Keldon children, where do the Keldon women give birth?" Haddad was trying to get a firm grip on the facts.

"They don't," was the reply. "Here all warriors spring from slave mothers." The slave continued, "The Keldon females *can* bear children, but almost all choose not to."

"Why?" Haddad asked. A race that replenished itself by stealing women to bear its warriors? A race with little or no pregnancy by accident? The Keldons seemed beyond understanding.

"Males and females do not have sex except to bear children. The mother would bear most of the burden alone after the male left. It is much easier to have slaves do the hard work of bearing children while the Keldon women concentrate on other things," he finished. "Now I must work." He staggered as he got up but set a course for the tack room and walked fairly straight.

Haddad looked at the deflated sack of wine and considered the information he had just received. The Keldons raided for tufa, but a race that depended on slaves to replenish itself had an endless appetite for subject peoples. Haddad wondered if the League could beat off an invasion by such a race.

* * * * *

The following morning Iola called upon him in the workshop. "I am checking to see what progress you have made in completing the ant," she said as she swept through the door. Haddad had continued working, but the machine was still primarily parts scattered over the table. Iola turned to him with a severe expression.

"Latulla will be arriving in several days for the Festival of Passage. I suggest you have the device completed by then, or your screams will sound throughout the night when the mistress arrives," she warned.

Haddad knew that no excuses would be acceptable, and Iola left before he could get a more precise timetable. The next days were spent entirely in the workshop. Haddad soon realized that testing would consume more of his time than he had planned. Without a powerstone to show if the parts were working, Haddad had to go through laborious exercises and makeshifts to see. Finally he realized that until he had a powerstone, he would never know if his repairs worked. He locked the workshop a final time and went for his room. The sheaf of notes he had written on his experiences in Keld he left in the rafters of the first floor, but he took with him a wire garrote sewn into his clothing and a small knife hidden in his wallet. They were small prizes compared to the wealth of tools he left behind, but perhaps it was better to travel light when one has a long way to go.

The Festival of Passage commenced, and a bizarre sense of gaiety could be felt throughout the household. The Keldons observed a holiday to commemorate the beginning of change for the approaching year. The festival celebrated the completion of the flight from their enemy in ancient times. Even the slaves were happy, for by custom, punishments for everything except serious crimes were waived or delayed. Not that the slaves ran wild with freedom, for the Keldons had a long memory and were always ready to punish when the festival was over. But for a few days, the slaves were free of the heavy hands of their masters.

Warriors competed in fights with blunted and padded weapons, their aggression channeled against each other as it was inside the cradle house. Winners of the contest gained the attention of the commanders and perhaps a chance to advance on the next mission. Slaves aped their masters with feats of strength, and Haddad watched the stableman win the wrestling matches. Other slaves gave the victor trinkets, but no overseer took any notice. Haddad could see the fights inside the cradle house enclosure grow more and more vicious as children sought dominance. More and more he saw single males mastering their fellows while the girls bonded together into separate groups. Everyone was locked in contests for position but Haddad. The struggles seemed irrelevant as he worked on the steel ant. Each day saw him closer to completing it, but his work furthered his enemies' plans. Each part fixed and oiled felt like a betrayal.

Haddad tried to appear content under the eyes of Iola, but he could not. So far his living conditions were comparatively pleasant when contrasted with his earlier captivity, but at least at the colony the illusion of escape or the more improbable rescue by Kipamu League forces kept his spirits up. Despite the run of the kitchen and the respect he received from the other servants as an arm-banded slave, Haddad felt impotent.

His mood did not improve as a round of guests appeared from the cradle house. Erissa was accompanied by a new set of female followers. They were well groomed, and the male servants took advantage of an opportunity they hardly ever had—the chance to talk to a woman of their own race. The cradle women were soon surrounded by as many admirers as any socialite beauty at a League ball. Haddad had no desire to speak with them. Each one collaborated in the enslavement and controlled breeding of humanity. Whole nations might flow under the hands of the cradle mistress and midwife, but only Keldons marched away as their slave mothers bore more Keldon children.

Erissa was talking quietly with Iola. Stooped and eating a small cake and tea, the cradle woman reminded him of an elderly maiden aunt. Then he saw the young warrior standing behind her. The youth was near his full growth and clad in fine clothes, a sword at his side. His stance and alertness unnerved the technical officer, but he had no idea why. Then the soldier turned, and he got a glimpse of the extra-wide mouth. It was Erissa's demonic servant grown large—either that or a close sibling. Haddad was unable to say which would be worse. He began moving as far away as possible. Then an announcement rang through the hall.

"All gather for Sirk, the storyteller." All present flowed to the side of the room and stopped a respectful distance from an old warrior. The man was scarred and infirm though not missing any limbs as many other older Keldons.

His clothing and weapons were of fine quality but jarring in the clash of color and styles. It wasn't until after Sirk walked to stand before the crowd and bumped into a table with a searching hand that Haddad realized the man was blind.

More warriors and women poured in from other parts of the house and the grounds. A large crowd began to push each other for better viewing positions. Haddad moved to the rear of the room and could catch only glimpses of the storyteller, but once the Keldon spoke, his voice filled the space.

"Not all great tales are finished. Listen to the prophecies of the final days," Sirk said, and he gestured grandly in a style of speaking that Haddad was unfamiliar with. "Keld was created from the blood of heroes, drifting from our ancient shores until we landed north. At first these children were timid, holding only enough land to live and selfishly thinking of themselves before the people. In time the blood ran thin, and the spirit of the people gasped for relief and for the taste of battle they had left behind. On that day the first Keldon Witch King was born." Sirk paused to wet his throat with wine.

"He towered over the north as giants loom over normal men. 'A great destiny awaits me,' were his words when soon out of the womb. 'I shall bring forth a nation to cleanse the world from all darkness.' The king lay down with the women of his enemies and brought forth sons and daughters to swell his army. At last he stood upon the mountain and called forth, 'I am ready for the darkness, let my enemy stand forth and the final battle begin.' But the servants of evil were cowards and hid from the witch king, plotting his death. Many times they tried to pull him down but always failed. Still they refused battle, denying the witch king his rightful victory. At last the king called to his people. 'I am growing old, and a new leader must follow and claim my victory.' With that, the king passed the crown and went to the Necropolis, falling into a sleeping death. Each king has followed him into his palace as the millennia have passed. Each waits for the enemy to reveal himself, for the final days to begin the final battle. And on that day, all the witch kings interred in the palace will arise from their slumber, and a great host shall march and crack the world." Sirk finished his recitation with a flourish.

"But the final days are upon us," rang out a warrior's voice. One of Latulla's guards climbed on a table and began speaking to the crowd. "Death is spreading throughout the land. Children die in the cradle houses as the enemy seeks to choke our numbers! We must awaken the witch kings and take the battle to the enemy!"

"And where shall we march?" argued a gate guard. "The enemy hides as he has always hidden. Until he reveals himself, we cannot raise the kings!"

"Blasphemy!" cried yet another warrior. "The kings shall rise when they are ready, and you imperil the final victory by your talk of disturbing them." A multitude of voices broke out as every Keldon forgot their usual deference to their superiors and tried to shout each other down. The respect and awe that all Keldons felt for those of greater strength fled as religious fever drove each to define what was right and true.

Swords were drawn, and cries of pain began to sound in the hall as steel punctuated arguments. The cradle women and the slaves were caught up as well, and Haddad wondered how many would die before the fight ended.

"*Enough!*" The shout was punctuated by the chandeliers and candles throughout the room flaring and then exploding in blasts of boiling wax. Arguments were forgotten as all present squinted their eyes and desperately wiped off the fiery debris. Latulla had returned home.

Iola ran through the crowd to explain to the artificer but was waved silent before she could reach the mistress of the house.

"Dogs baying in the night!" Latulla said intently. "Arguments that have been said a hundred times and solved nothing! I came to celebrate passage, but it appears that you are stuck in my way." She drew herself up and looked over the crowd. "The festival is over. A new passage has begun." She pointed off to the side. "We travel for the Necropolis tomorrow, and the witch kings will awaken, or we will drag them into the light of day."

Latulla stalked away, leaving a confused babble behind her.

CHAPTER 14

The next morning Haddad hurried out to the workshop to present his work to Latulla. She had looked less controlled than usual the night before, and he was determined to appear his best. Latulla's travels would be far more conducive to escape than his current imprisonment deep in the Keldon interior. Crawling a little would be worth it if it got him moving again.

The workshop was open on both levels when he arrived. The first floor was being emptied into cargo wagons. The draft horses were uneasy, shifting in their traces. He could hear Latulla giving orders and talking as he looked through the double doors blocked by the wagon.

Iola was taking notes while Erissa sat to the side. Haddad was relieved to see her free of her attendants, both mortal and magical. Latulla knelt by the steel ant that Haddad had reconstructed. In her hands was a powerstone. She placed the crystal in the machine and closed the hatch. The ant came alive, and Haddad knew that she must have already designated herself as its controller.

"Go forward. Go left. Go right. Back up." Each command was given in a clear voice, and the ant promptly complied. Latulla noticed him and looked over his shoulder. A large dog was crossing the yard, one that the stockmen used to herd cattle.

"The four-legged animal one hundred yards out." The ant seemed to nod as Latulla spoke. "Kill it!"

The ant brushed Haddad as it raced out the door. The impact spun him around, and his hand smashed into the side of the wagon he was standing next to. The cart-horses whinnied in fear as the machine went past them, accelerating to maximum speed in only a few seconds. The ant hit the dog at a run and nipped off two legs in passing. The machine skidded along the grass as it stopped, and then it turned to hit the howling dog. Soon there was nothing but a pile of canine parts.

"Excellent," Latulla said, looking on with a maternal pride as the machine came back. "I'll have to get more of these." Then she added pensively, "Though they kill awfully fast. There must be some way to stretch out the process." She turned to Haddad, and he thought he saw what could have been mistaken as a smile.

Iola looked puzzled as she looked at the dead dog. A guard to the side had a faint air of disgust as he regarded the dead animal, and Haddad saw him mouthing "waste" to another warrior beside him. Haddad snapped his attention back to Latulla as the artificer came toward the door.

"The ant performs up to my expectations," Latulla said as the machine came trotting back. Haddad saw her considering the rings on her hand and concentrating. The burst of pain that struck him was totally unexpected. He could feel the agony radiating from his left arm in waves. Was he having a heart attack? Haddad's muscles along the left side of his body contracted, and he fell to the floor in writhing agony. The artificer was silent until Haddad put his eyes back on her face.

"However," Latulla continued, "Iola informs me that it was necessary to prod you into completing your work. In the future, I expect you to finish quickly with no prompting."

Haddad couldn't even nod, the pain drew him so tight. Then it started to fade. Erissa watched it all with a bright, lively interest, while Iola kept her countenance completely neutral.

"Are you sure that we can't lower the cost of that armband and spell?" Latulla asked Erissa. "It is so useful. I would like to equip my entire household with it."

"Alas no, Latulla," the cradle mistress replied. "I myself band only a select few, and the extra control you gain just doesn't pay for the amount of time you have to take establishing the bond."

"A pity." Latulla turned back to Haddad. "Go up to the second floor and pack the red banded tools and what you used for the ant."

Haddad tried to get up but was slow. He could hardly gasp for air, and she was telling him to bounce up and continue the tasks she ordered?

"Do you need another nudge then?" Latulla taunted.

Haddad crawled out past the horses and slowly up the exterior staircase. He felt as if he had strained all the muscles in his chest, and he went through the open door and collapsed by his workbench. The bottle of alcohol was there, and Haddad took a drink before remembering just how strong the stuff was. It burned a track down his throat, and he gasped for air again.

How had she been able to do that? Haddad undid his shirt and lifted it free of his torso. A deep flush flowed across the left side of his body. It all spread from the band. He looked at his arm for quite a while. How could something have such control of his body and leave him unaware of his vulnerability? Haddad also wondered why he had never cut the band off. He decided many times that he wanted it gone but always came up with a rationale for retaining it. Could more than just his body be vulnerable? Could the device be affecting his mind as well?

Haddad crawled to the cutout that he had observed Erissa through. This immediate act of defiance so soon after Latulla's lesson convinced him that his mind was still his own. He lifted the block out very carefully.

"That's all for now, Iola," he heard Latulla say. Iola withdrew.

"That was a very impressive display last night," said Erissa. "I almost believed it was real rage fueling that outburst."

"After all the work I put into having the religious firebrands show up?" Latulla replied cynically. "It took quite a lot of time and mood drugs in the refreshments to provoke that riot. It was all I could do not to laugh at the fools."

Erissa did laugh. "Now we will arrive with news of last night chasing us and a personal reason to call for a decision on the witch kings and the invasion." Erissa's voice became more thoughtful. "The women of an entire continent to fill the cradles of Keld."

"I will have an additional reason to dangle before the council. Lord Druik has survived the round of experiments," Latulla announced triumphantly.

"I hope my assistant Greel was useful in your endeavor," Erissa said.

"His aid was important to the project," Latulla admitted. "I was surprised that you found a boy with such skill. It was a shame that he could not stay with me full-time while working on the war leader."

"I am afraid that I have important tasks that only he could can perform to my satisfaction," Erissa explained.

"I am surprised that you haven't banded him, even if he is a Keldon," Latulla observed.

"My grip on him is sure enough," Erissa said. "I performed a few simple ceremonies to anchor my fist in his soul. Perhaps after the invasion I can introduce them to you."

Haddad would be just as glad if he never saw Greel again. He toyed very briefly with the idea of revealing some of what he knew to Latulla. That fantasy he shook off immediately. Even if she believed him, there was no guarantee that she wouldn't embrace it. He certainly thought her heart black enough for the deed.

"Well I must be going," Erissa announced. "If I am to speak to all of the cradle mistresses before your meeting with the council, I must be off at once. I will see you again at the Necropolis." Erissa stood, and Haddad could hear her cane tapping as she exited the building. Realizing that silence would only gain him pain if Latulla did not hear him working, he quickly replaced the cutout and began gathering tools.

Haddad managed to follow Latulla till mid-afternoon, carrying out orders, relaying messages, and not provoking another lesson in pain. It was something of a personal best. Soon it was time for Latulla and household to depart for the Necropolis. There were seven heavy wagons of just her personal baggage, and Haddad found it an interesting contrast to Latulla's voyage without a single personal servant when coming back to Keld.

At last the wagons and warriors were arrayed in a line, and Latulla inspected each wagon and soldier. The warriors stood ready with swords and spears at hand, but the commanders and common soldiers looked disturbed as Latulla stopped and minutely inspected weapons and armor.

"She acts a warlord," a Keldon soldier whispered to another as Haddad lagged behind Latulla. There was a general atmosphere of confusion, and Latulla seemed to sense it, for she jumped on top of a wagon to look across her servants and warriors.

"Today is the start of a new era," she called. "The witch kings sleep until Keld can call them forth. We will call them forth! The wagons hold the means to raise the kings, and I know it is time to awaken them. We are the first units of an army that will sweep the world under our feet as the witch kings lead us to victory." She raised her arms and shouted, "*To the Necropolis!*" She jumped down and ran to her colos steed. The convoy moved out of the gate with Latulla leading. Haddad wondered at the mood of the soldiers. There had been only a half-hearted cheer, and every gray face seemed lost in thought as Latulla's crusade began.

* * * * *

Another party joined Latulla's on the road, and Haddad had his first pleasant surprise in quite some time. He overheard two guards talking.

"The warlord killed a sea beast that devoured everything," one warrior said. "Though crippled by his injuries and old wounds, he turned the tide of the battle."

"He was a great captain years ago against the giants.

Perhaps these new victories will propel Druik and his retainers to glory and command once again."

At the mention of Druik, Haddad hurried toward the new arrivals. The wagons did bear Lord Druik's sigils, though the lord traveled in an enclosed wagon surrounded by guards. Haddad wondered how much of the lord survived the trip to Keld, but his wondering turned to merriment when he spotted an old friend traveling well back in the party.

"Fumash!" he yelled.

The small slave quickly glanced to see who might be calling. A smile lit his face as Haddad approached. It was strange to see Fumash's teeth the same yellow as the other slaves rather than the rich black Haddad remembered. The former customs inspector had a long scar on one side of his face, hooking from the eye to his mouth. He looked altogether more dangerous than before.

"Haddad, I thought you long dead or lost here in the north," Fumash said. An overseer came hurrying toward the pair, and Haddad lifted his sleeve to show the bronze armlet.

"I see you have moved up in the world while I have moved down," Fumash commented, his smile vanishing as he saw Haddad's symbol of special status.

"What do you mean? Don't you still serve Lord Druik?" Haddad asked.

"I have not seen Druik since he was sealed up in stasis. When I was decanted in Keld, Latulla had taken him to some remote place to recuperate. I was left to the welcoming arms of Yacuta, Druik's female business manager, social secretary, and other wifely equivalents." Fumash shook his head and continued, "In Jamuraa my skills were valuable, but in Keld where women already form an educated class, I was considered only as valuable as the physical labor I could perform." Fumash looked stronger, but he was still a small man, and Haddad nodded his head in sympathy.

"Now perhaps my luck is turning because it is rumored Druik will be returning to Jamuraa, and a literate and organized slave will be valuable once again." Fumash looked at his friend. "What happened to you, Haddad?"

"I awakened only a few weeks ago in Latulla's house," Haddad said. "I had to build a steel ant for her," he confessed, his shame showing on his face. "I thought to use it somehow to escape, but she has already frozen its controls to respond to her. I think she wanted an attack dog at her beck and call."

"Wait a moment," Fumash said, interrupting Haddad's recollections. "You awakened only a few weeks ago?" He looked intently at the technical officer.

"At most. To be honest, I haven't kept very good track of time." Haddad was wry as he confessed his failing.

"Haddad, it has been months since the ship came in, not weeks," Fumash spoke with intensity. "The Keldons waken everyone when they have landfall. Druik was still in stasis, but he was a special case. Why would you be kept in stasis?"

Haddad tried to think of a reason that he would have been left in storage. He had assumed that waking off the ship was a normal experience. Now it was unusual, and the former League soldier didn't like the vulnerability that he felt.

"The first thing I remember is waking up in a bed, fully dressed, in a private room in Latulla's house. The housekeeper came in while I was up and put me straight to work building Latulla's ant." It did sound strange now that he related it aloud.

"From what I experienced and from what others have told me, waking up out of stasis is not something you forget. You gasp for air as the smoke fills your lungs. And as for dressing you in new clothes, a man in stasis is as solidly unbending as rock. None of this makes sense," Fumash said emphatically.

Haddad leaned a little closer and spoke in a whisper, not caring how suspicious it looked to whoever might be watching. He tapped the metal circling his arm.

"The band inflicts pain, my friend. When Latulla wishes, I writhe and wish for death." Haddad paused. "Perhaps I was kept in stasis until she could attach this leash." He struck the armband hard and then shook his hand to ease the pain in his fingers.

"It is possible," Fumash conceded. "The other possibility is that you were awake earlier but have somehow forgotten everything that occurred." Fumash glanced over his shoulder and stepped away. "My mistress approaches."

Yacuta rode forward on a colos to see who the strange slave was. When she saw the armband with Latulla's mark, she rode no closer but stared at Fumash and Haddad with lidded eyes. Realizing that an extended conversation would lead to an equally extended interrogation for Fumash, Haddad cut their talk short and walked quickly back to the wagon containing his gear.

How could he find out what happened? No matter what, one thing was sure. If he was awakened earlier than he thought, then Latulla and Iola had conspired to keep him ignorant.

* * * * *

The convoy made good mileage that day. Latulla arranged accommodations by taking the wagons to the largest house in the area and expelling the owners and their chattel. The country was rocky, and each great house stood alone or far from its neighbors. Haddad was seeing a land without the cities and towns or even villages that he had expected.

Every day brought another brooding, massive peaked house into view as Latulla settled in for the night. She took the lord's rooms and sent servants scuttling out of the way. In the hinterlands, no one dared refuse her, so a series of houses were abandoned to her use. Soon they drew near the Necropolis, and the land and people began to change. Now the houses were closer together, and Haddad began to see signs of trade on the road. Latulla now picked the smaller houses, instead of the largest ones, to occupy. Warlords watched and drilled their soldiers as Latulla passed their dwellings. Latulla's reputation as a sudden guest made her few allies, but no one openly opposed the column's passage.

As the march continued, Haddad was able to speak to Fumash several more times. The two friends wandered far to the left of the column and paralleled the main party. Fumash seemed particularly despondent, and Haddad asked him to explain the march, hoping the role of instructor might improve his friend's mood.

"Latulla and her supporters believe that the death of the Witch King Kreig marked the end of the Second Cycle of Blood and the beginning of a new cycle," Fumash said, looking toward the column and then back to Haddad. "The first cycle was the mixing of ancient warrior races in the time of the Heroes. Tribes and nations congealed to form the early Keldons. Then the second cycle marked the forging of the witch kings. The final years of the cycle birthed the greatest of the witch kings through training and breeding. Kreig was the result of generations, and many Keldons believe that the enemies of the Second Cycle attacked Keld to stop Kreig and the emergence of a perfect people."

Haddad laughed. Perfect was not a word that he would apply to such bloodthirsty barbarians.

"Remember," Fumash said, "this is what Latulla and her faction professes. They believe that Kreig was the ultimate warrior, and when he fell, the Second Cycle ended. The Third Cycle is the creation of an army to conquer the world. Now every man is a warrior, and the females have the responsibility of running the nation. The cradle houses arose to allow the expansion of Keld through careful breeding with captured women of spirit and ability. It allowed the Keldon women to run the rest of the society while Keldons were pulled from the wombs of captured women. Now more and more warriors swell the Keldon ranks every year, and many believe Keld should march and conquer the globe. Every cycle to date has ended in a sea of blood, and Latulla and her allies are desperate for a war. They believe that an enemy will pull Keld down once more, and generations might pass before the nation will rise again. They want the war now while they are strong."

"But why this march to the Necropolis?" Haddad asked. "They are already fighting throughout the world. This call for battle seems superfluous."

"In recent months there have been outbreaks of disease among the cradle women and poor harvests in some of the holdings. Latulla has seized on this as a sign that the final battle is approaching, and she acts to take advantage. But the closer we get to the Necropolis, the fewer supporters she has. Yacuta right now rides to houses to find supporters for Latulla in Druik's name. She finds very few, and her temper grows more foul by the day." Even as Fumash spoke, Haddad could see Yacuta returning. His companion immediately turned and walked toward the column. Haddad followed behind, wondering at this sudden turn.

"It is best not to be noticed in bad times," Fumash said as he rejoined the outriders of Druik's party. "Remember Haddad, we are nearing the heart of the enemy, and nothing is more dangerous than drawing attention."

* * * * *

It was growing dark under a cloudy sky. For the first time, Latulla's party had not received use of a house. Scouts had returned to the column with news that no housing would be made available to the artificer. Haddad believed that only the proximity of the Necropolis and the need not to alienate possible supporters prevented Latulla from falling upon a house and slaughtering the inhabitants for shelter. Warriors circled fires as slaves hunted for ground to sleep on. Blankets and extra clothing were pulled from the wagons as many prepared for the night. Latulla's slaves were fairly close to a circle of young warriors. The League technician's eyes locked on one of the figures seated around the fire.

Haddad watched Greel. The familiar had grown more. He towered over many of the slaves and was as tall as many of the warriors. He was slender and his face was narrow. A predatory smile showed on his face as he looked from warrior to warrior. As Haddad passed, Greel winked at the League officer and laid his hand on the warrior next to him. The warrior started coughing, and Haddad could see Greel squeezing the warrior's arm in apparent concern. To Haddad, Greel was checking the quality of the meat. As the coughing increased, Greel showed a small expression of disgust, as if the meat was slightly off. Haddad crowded into the group of sleeping slaves rather than staying apart as his custom. He pulled his hidden knife from his wallet and tried to sleep. He could see Greel's smile behind his closed eyelids, and he didn't get any rest.

How long Haddad lay with his eyes open he could not say, but he was wide-awake when sudden motion caught the edge of his vision. Two men stood not ten yards away. A wave of ice seemed to sweep over him as he recognized a face.

Greel held his hand over his companion's mouth. The Keldon warrior was taller and heavier than the familiar but looked as helpless as a rabbit. The fighter tossed his head and tried to scream, but no sound issued. An absolute stillness covered the camp, and Haddad could barely grip his knife as he watched the Keldon's legs churning the ground. He could hear nothing, and the rest of the slaves slept on, oblivious. Haddad was frozen with more than fear. He could not even blink or avert his eyes. Like a dream, the attack continued, and no one could see it except Haddad. Greel pulled the warrior closer and began to sink down. The warrior's back arched, and the sudden stillness of his legs signaled the breaking of his back. In silence, the victim's arms flailed. The struggles grew more frenetic as Greel gripped the man's shoulders and squeezed. The warrior's mouth was open in scream, but still nothing could be heard. Then Greel crouched over the still body, and Haddad blinked. The sounds of the camp returned like a sudden clap of thunder. Haddad could hear the horses and colos at the edge of the camp. A few of the sleeping slaves around him groaned and turned over. Greel stood, shaking out his cloak and then hauling the cooling corpse up and draping a shattered arm over his shoulder. His eyes lifted from his victim and stared at Haddad. For a long moment Greel looked at the technician and then smiled. He backed away, the corpse dragging at his side.

The morning saw many of the slaves complaining of aching joints and tiredness. Greel was nowhere to be seen. There was no outcry over the missing warrior, and Haddad wondered if Latulla was covering for the monster. Several of the livestock had died as well during the night, and Haddad thought it amusing that the death of the animals was marked with swearing and questions while the disappearance of a man was ignored. Haddad wondered if Greel was connected with the animal deaths as well.

For several days they had been drawing closer to a cluster of hills surrounding a mountain. As they came closer, Haddad noticed that the mountain was surprisingly regular. Finally, he realized that the mountain was the Keldon Necropolis, city of the witch kings.

Latulla was marching on the center of religious, political, and military power of the Keldon nation. Each great building that they passed was merely a gatehouse to galleries under the earth. They passed an empty sealed barrack that waited for the witch king's armies. It reminded Haddad of the badlands. It lacked life, and the column's presence seemed an intrusion. The landscape dwarfed mortal men, and Latulla's supporters grew fewer the closer they came to the Warlords' Council. At last the entrance to the Council Hall appeared. A mighty fortress with walls thirty feet high, great towers supported the corners of the wall, and the gatehouse sat at the bottom of a steep ramp leading to the central keep. The heart of the fortress jutted directly out of the mountain rock, as if the mountain had half swallowed the building. Latulla stopped. No one was visible, and the gates were closed. She advanced, looking for someone to announce her.

"I seek an audience with the council!" she yelled, and her voice echoed, the sound mocking.

Slowly, a sally port opened and out stepped a woman. She wore a gray cloak with the hood thrown back, her dress a faded red. At her breast was the sign of a cradle mistress that Haddad could see as she moved forward. An iron-shod staff was in her hands, its haft covered in runes. Her face appeared unlined, and only her voice hinted at her age as she spoke.

"I, Gorsha, greet you. As a servant to the Witch King Council, I await your reasons for intruding."

Latulla's servants and allies drew away, leaving her isolated.

"These are the final days," Latulla declared as all eyes locked on her. "Keld is failing! The warriors who should carry on our legacy die in the cradle houses. The armies and navies of lesser nations thwart us. The legacy of heroes is being stolen, and we are locked in futile argument! My own house is torn with fights over when the hour of the final days will occur."

There was a long pause. Gorsha showed nothing except a slight frown.

"It is time to march! Time to take control of our destiny and wake the witch kings of old!"

Latulla's supporters began shouting. "Wake the kings! Wake the kings!"

Gorsha raised her staff and brought it down on the stone cobbles. The resulting noise screamed right across the mind and sanity. Haddad could almost hear his bones wincing at the sound.

"Very impressive," was Gorsha's measured response to Latulla's oration. "But shouts will not wake the kings, or they would have risen long ago. The final days cannot occur until the witch kings rise. The council finds you unpersuasive and foolish." She shook her head from side to side as if chiding a child.

"Then you shall have proof that I can do what I have promised," Latulla answered. "Many of the witch kings are shattered in body and must be healed before they can rise. I present Lord Druik to prove that such miracles are possible."

Druik's brave actions in saving the ship on its way to Keld had expanded until he was a mighty hero in many Keldon eyes. The fact that he suffered grievous wounds only increased his stature. All held their breath as the covers on Druik's wagon lifted, and the giant walked out.

The war leader wore heavy armor and surveyed the crowd. Haddad wondered what trick was being played as Druik came closer. He heard the light whisper of sliding cables as the warlord turned, sweeping the Keldons with his gaze. Druik was as crippled as ever, but somehow Latulla had created a set of armor that he could pilot. Haddad's eyes focused on a raised blister on the armor's breast. Haddad knew where the powerstone was, and more details on Druik's armor flooded into his mind. Haddad knew now that he had woken and helped Latulla construct the armor. Glimpses of weeks working on Druik played through his mind. Latulla had crushed his memories, and only now did Haddad realize how deep her control over him ran.

Gorsha stepped away from the gate and approached Latulla. An uneasy muttering broke out, and Haddad wondered if this signaled some break in tradition. Each step she took raised the tension, and he could see Latulla bracing herself for battle. Gorsha stopped, and when she spoke, only the closest could hear her.

"A masterful performance, but I am not impressed by

your puppet," Gorsha said coldly. "I will not allow you to pass, and if you force your way through, the council will destroy you and your allies."

"I will not back down," Latulla said softly. "The kings will rise under my hands." Her eyes shone at the idea.

Gorsha's distasteful grimace told Haddad that Latulla's quest was hopeless. The council servant stepped back and called to the crowd.

"Latulla's demands are rejected!" Gorsha cried. "Her mad schemes are to be opposed by all true sons and daughters of Keld. I challenge her now." Gorsha spoke more quietly. "Win and the council might hear your plea, but lose and your cause falls with you. Your supporters will depart, and never again will a crowd cry to 'wake the kings.' "

"I accept!" Latulla yelled. "Let the strongest prevail!"

Though the day was drawing to a close, the entire party turned and followed the two matriarchs as the pair walked down the path. Still there was no sign of the council, and more warriors and women were leaving Latulla's entourage. Haddad could see his master growing more and more angry at each defection. Fumash won free of Yacuta and hurried over to Haddad.

"It is a contest of magical strength," he told Haddad. "When they find a large enough space the combat will begin. I have heard other slaves describing the fights."

"You think there would be a ring or formal arena," Haddad said as the company turned toward an open area.

"Too much damage for it to survive," Fumash answered and then stopped. The rest of the crowd stood still while Latulla and Gorsha continued on. Mages and wizards who followed Latulla began chanting and focusing their power to protect the crowd. Gorsha had no seconds, and Haddad wondered if she was a fool. Could Keldon honor be so powerful that cheating was impossible? Who would enforce the rules of the duel?

Latulla struck while the pair was still walking. A bolt of flame flared from her hand and enveloped Gorsha. The council servant was hidden from view, and Haddad could hear the rocks around her pop as they heated. Then the flames guttered and contracted, shrinking into tiny wavelets of flame that danced along Gorsha's staff.

Latulla retreated, her arms raised and her cloak billowing as she opened the distance between herself and her opponent. Haddad crowded into the front lines with Keldons pushing and shoving their way forward for a better view.

Gorsha's staff swallowed the last of the flame, and as she gestured, it vomited great gouts of smoke. The vapors collected around the council servant until she was lost in a roiling cloud. Latulla threw more bolts of fire, each blast vanishing into the smoke. Latulla's hands dripped flames as she tried to find Gorsha. The cloud was still expanding and shapes began to appear. Birds and gargoyles formed from the smoke, and they swooped through the air, diving at Latulla. The artificer scrambled away as vaporous appendages swatted at her face. More and more attackers flew, and Haddad thought Latulla would die as smoke tried to force its way into her lungs.

Fire once again burned on the dueling ground as a long streamer of flame danced from Latulla's fingertips, playing over the smoke creatures trying to smother her. With each touch of the fiery ribbon, the shapes burst into flame. Within seconds, an army of burning vapors rose into the air and then turned to fall on Gorsha. Each creation exploded as it entered her magical shield, and Gorsha's protective covering was tattered as each traitorous offspring returned to its former master.

Latulla cast flames into the ground, and a blaze sprang up. It mounted higher, and then like a prairie fire, it raced toward Gorsha's smoke. Haddad viciously elbowed a warrior, crowding him as Latulla closed with her opponent.

Gorsha's smoke thickened and began falling as a dense ash, smothering Latulla's flames under a growing blanket. Latulla pressed the attack harder. She created a long sword of brilliant blue fire and chopped at the thinning smoke, cutting through Gorsha's protection.

Gorsha stepped out of the cloud suddenly, and Haddad waited for the magical counterstrike. Instead Gorsha stepped inside Latulla's swing and hammered Latulla's temple with a closed fist. The artificer's sword of flame flickered out as Gorsha continued to deal out physical blows, each punch distracting Latulla, preventing her from mustering her forces. Soon Latulla was on the ground.

An incoherent roar broke Haddad's fascinated gaze as Druik charged into the field. Haddad could hear bones breaking as Druik smashed into the warriors nearby. Lord Druik was running down the mountain to aid Latulla, each stride coming faster. Gorsha was stepping back to swing her staff when Druik arrived in a long slide, separating the combatants. Rocks thrown up by Druik left bloody bruises on both combatants, and the warrior turned to face Gorsha. The steel ant broke free from the wagons and arrived at a run. The council servant parried strikes from its mandibles as it attacked her. The crowd around Haddad gasped at the interruptions, but no one interfered as Gorsha continued to avoid the war machine's attacks. Whether by design or accident, Latulla's creations protected their mistress.

Gorsha stopped retreating, and now her parries cracked the ant's armor in magically enhanced blows that pealed like thunder. The legs shattered, and Gorsha seemed to laugh as she turned the machine into a pile of scrap after several heavy blows. But Druik still stood guard over Latulla, and the artificer rose, her bloody face snarled as she cast a magical attack.

Gorsha's cloak and dress began to ripple and then smolder as Latulla directed her hatred at her opponent. The council servant's hair stood out from her head, and Haddad could see her image wavering as the air heated as well.

"Enough!" Gorsha shouted and raised her staff high over her head, plunging it into the earth. The ground trembled under Haddad's feet as soil and stone shattered and fountained high into the sky. Rising, it blocked the sight of the sun and hung as a mountain over Latulla and Druik. Both retreated to avoid being swallowed by the pit growing before them, but they could do nothing about the attack building over their heads. The pyroclastic cloud collapsed. The superheated vapor and particles of rock hit as a tidal wave. All vegetation and animals within hundreds of yards were burned, crushed, and suffocated. A great groan sounded from the Keldon magic users protecting the crowd from the attack. All of them united were barely able to stay Gorsha's anger.

Eventually the cloud settled and dispersed. The landscape was different, sculpted into bizarre shapes in seconds by the mighty spell. Gorsha stood at the edge of a great pit. On the other side were two bodies encased in stone. Magic users poured power to cool the ground so the crowd might descend to view the aftermath.

When Haddad and Fumash reached the scene, Gorsha was standing tall again. Druik's armor and limbs had been blown free, and at Gorsha's nod, Latulla's former allies threw the body into the pit. Latulla was encased, and Gorsha's supporters moved to throw her down as well.

"Hold!" Gorsha called. "She lives yet." The midwife surveyed the destruction and gave her orders.

"She has failed. Let her and her servants die and wither in far off lands. Let her never leave Jamuraa as long as I draw breath." Gorsha considered the crowd. "The strongest has prevailed, and the witch kings shall not be disturbed again by any in this company."

Warriors rounded up Latulla's servants and her closest allies. Fumash was dragged away by Yacuta before Haddad could say a word. As Haddad was kicked back toward the wagons he felt hope rekindle in his heart. Sentenced to Jamuraa, another chance to escape for home, he laughed as he was crowded together with the losers of Latulla's bid for power.

CHAPTER 15

"We can win this war, Teferi," Barrin said, looking over the defensive works going up around the city. "But if we lose here then the League is finished."

The defensive works appeared to be on schedule. A series of trenches and traps grew under Barrin's orders. Technically, General Mageta was in charge. Barrin had been surprised to see him alive. The landslides unleashed by the wizard's covering attack for the retreating army had buried the general, but he had dug himself out and fought his way through Keldon excavation teams to rejoin the League forces. When the army withdrew west to Arsenal City, it was Mageta who commanded on the ground.

"The core of the League weapons development is here, and it's next in the path of the Keldons," Teferi said resignedly. "If only it were farther away."

Arsenal City was in a flat valley near the coast. The surrounding hills were thick with mines. Metals and tufa flowed down to the city for industrial use. For generations small factories turned out war machines for the Kipamu League cities. The steel ants, crabs, and mantises were all manufactured there. A network of roads and a canal connected the factories to the rest of the League and the ocean port, but it was still isolated. Men and supplies took weeks to arrive.

"Will you be able to hold the walls with the men you have?" Teferi asked. The wall enclosing the city was only twenty feet high, and years of maintenance and repair had been missed. A few sections had been raided for building material. Men under Barrin's orders tore down houses inside the city to reclaim stones for the defensive works.

"We'll fight in the earthworks outside the walls," Barrin replied. "We need the fighting room, and the factories inside the city can't produce with soldiers filling the streets." Even as the two friends looked out into the valley, a stream of fighting machines and weapons were being produced behind them. Technicians trembled with fatigue, and warehouses emptied as the factories squeezed out every last ounce of production.

"I'll have a few words with the war machine builders before I go," Teferi said. "I'll bring back supplies and the men we need. Is your glide bomb project any closer to success?"

"Nearly," Barrin replied. "With the new Keldon fire barges out there, blimps just can't survive long enough to drop bombs. If we can work out a few production headaches, we'll have a weapon we can use from airships."

"I'm surprised Rayne is not working on the problem," Teferi said. "I hear she is scouting outside the city." Teferi was stuffing the notes and maps he had brought into a travel case. Barrin looked out toward the horizon.

"Rayne returned to check on a pattern of blight in the northwest. She thinks it might be related to the Keldon attacks," Barrin said distractedly. "She thinks it might signal some new Keldon weapon or destructive spell. She thinks that it's important to find out what's affecting the land."

Teferi waited a moment then shook his head. He left the wizard lost in thought and staring out over the defensive works growing slowly as scared soldiers wielded their shovels.

* * * * *

"Are they inside yet?" Rayne asked. The scout shook his head. Rayne looked to either side of her. Ten runners crouched in the bottom of the ditch. A few hundred yards away a small Keldon land barge was stopped in front of an abandoned farmhouse. Hopefully the Keldon riders would dismount and search the farmhouse for food, giving Rayne and her group the opportunity to attack.

"Are you sure that barge contains the blight?" Rayne pressed.

Shalanda was haggard from days in the field and the strain of trying to find the source of the disease showing throughout the central forests. Finally, the healer found a trace to follow, and it led to the farmhouse. But the Keldon barge had proved an unpleasant surprise. Rayne was searching for signs of a plant contagion, not looking for combat. The scouts had withdrawn into a shallow gully and knelt their machines. Then her aide gave her more bad news.

"I am sure there is a concentration of blight onboard that vehicle. Maybe we can identify the source and find out where it comes from," Shalanda said.

Rayne shook her head and glanced at the scout watching the disembarking Keldons. If only Jolreal were still here. The women had expected to find a particularly thick or heavy concentration of disease, not a vehicle filled with armed men. Jolreal and the rest of the scouts were strung out toward the east. Rayne did have a group of steel ants attached to one of the scouts. The League was experimenting with long-range raiding parties, and the scout was evaluating how well the war machines kept up with the Tolarian runners. Combat was something to avoid, but now a key piece of the puzzle might lie only yards away. There was no choice. Rayne needed to capture the barge.

"I think they're all outside the vehicle," the scout whispered down. "They're starting to search the outbuildings now. They won't be there much longer." Rayne knew it was time to attack.

"Shalanda, stay alert for any sign of magic. Worry about the wounded after we've won," Rayne admonished her aide. Then she waved and brought her runner up out of the gully. The line of runners crested the lip of the depression in a ragged line and silently charged the Keldons. Halfway to the farmhouse a warrior saw the scouts and bellowed a warning.

The barge was small, and the upper wooden shield was open. Eight of the runners unleashed a barrage of bolts into the interior, killing whatever crew remained inside. Boxes of cargo shattered as the runners' projectiles smashed through the vehicle and impacted against the walls of the house. Four scouts dismounted, drawing weapons and throwing themselves into the barge to secure it. Rayne and the scout commanding the ants swept around the Keldon vehicle.

The enemy warriors converged on the stone and timber

farmhouse, diving through the door as Rayne unleashed her bolts. Retreating warriors sprawled in sliding falls as they died at a full run. The League scout drove his steel ants before him like a pack of hounds. The war machines piled onto the warriors, mandibles tearing at limbs and weapons. A Keldon held off an ant as his fellows struck off its limbs. The ant had its revenge as it amputated the man's arm. Two ants worried at a warrior like dogs with a toy, leaving a trail of blood and gore as they grappled with the corpse. Rayne and another scout brought their runners into the melee, triggering metal wings. The blades cut through armor and flesh as the Tolarian machines circled. The Keldons outside were dead, but their sacrifice allowed their companions to complete their retreat into the house.

The door slammed shut, and the sounds of furniture being piled in a barricade could be heard. The ants shifted in front of the building, and a few circled around the sides, searching for access. The house appeared stout, and Rayne could see movement through a few narrow windows. She rode back to the Keldon vehicle.

The rest of her party surrounded the small land barge. They had captured the craft with no losses, and Shalanda examined the interior and its cargo. The other scouts had remounted and stood ready to continue the attack. Rayne considered what to do. She had achieved her primary objective, but there was still a party of armed enemy warriors to deal with. Storming the house seemed a bad idea as sounds of barricade building continued.

"Can you move the barge farther back from the house?" Rayne called to Shalanda.

"I don't think so," she replied. "The Keldons have turned off the motivating force. This isn't going to move an inch without their cooperation."

A crossbow bolt shot from the house and imbedded itself in the upper shell supports. Shalanda hopped out of the vehicle and crouched behind the barge's legs. Another shot skimmed along the ground and rebounded off a runner's leg.

"Apparently, they aren't going to cooperate," Rayne said as she signaled the other scouts to crowd against the barge and crouch their machines so the Keldon vehicle blocked shots. "Call back your ants," Rayne ordered the ant handler.

The steel ants still circled the house and dug at the walls, but the scout called them back with a whistle. They came at good speed, but one collected a bolt that crippled its rear legs. It dragged the dead limbs as it continued on the other four.

"We need to see if the Keldons are exiting the rear of the house," Rayne said and pointed to a League soldier. "Circle around and check if our reluctant friends are doing anything. Keep your eyes open for enemy reinforcements." The scout looked apprehensive as he turned and raced away. He stopped and began riding in a circle to stay out of range of the crossbows.

"Reload weapons," Rayne ordered. The scouts paired off. Leaning far to the side, a rider could just feed fresh bolts to another person's runner while keeping behind cover. Rayne guided her machine to her aide who was popping her head up to look inside the barge in quick glances. "What do you think?" she asked.

"I need only a few more minutes to examine the barge," Shalanda replied. "There are crates of vegetation and a few sealed boxes that seem related to the blight but somehow different. If only I could open the crates. Perhaps if I am quick enough?"

Rayne shook her head. "Without heavy shielding it's just too dangerous," the scholar said. "If we can't move the barge, we'll have to clear out the house."

"If I lie on the floor of the barge I should be safe enough," Shalanda insisted.

"Eventually the Keldons are going to realize that we want the barge and its contents," Rayne said. "I expect a barrage of burning crossbow bolts will soon follow. We need to move now. Save your energy for healing and investigating the barge. I don't know how soon Keldon reinforcements might arrive."

Rayne turned her machine toward the other scouts who gathered around her. They crouched lower as another crossbow bolt sailed through the barge and off into the distance. A scout began feeding bolts into Rayne's machine.

"We need a plan of attack," she said.

"We could send in the ants to open up the walls," offered one scout. "It would take time, but we could drive them out." The ants could chew through heavy walls, but it was slow.

"We need to end this fast so Shalanda can finish examining the cargo," Rayne replied.

The ant handler reached into a saddlebag and drew out a metal cylinder.

"If I could get some covering fire, I could burn them out." The scout was carefully taking the container apart. A fragile pottery vessel lay inside. "The other scouting parties captured a fire barge last week. I and a few others decided to test some of the munitions. This should start a fire without Shalanda expending herself."

"Everyone go around the right side of the barge and fire your bolts into the windows facing us," Rayne ordered and then pointed to the handler. "Go around the right side of the machine and run up to the right-hand corner of the house. Stay clear of the front windows or you might be shot."

The scouts quickly jockeyed for position, and then Rayne gave the signal.

Eight runners darted out and unleashed a steady barrage of bolts. Two crossbow bolts came from the house, one sinking into a scout's arm. Blood spurted out of a cut artery, and the man sent his machine back behind the barge. Shalanda pulled him out of the saddle and in seconds was locked in a healing trance.

Meanwhile, the ant handler's machine reached the house. One ant followed, like a dog after a horse, trying to keep up. The scout paused at the corner and threw the captured Keldon munitions onto the building. The pottery broke, and a thick, oozing molasseslike liquid slowly coated the wall. The scout and the accompanying ant raced back for cover.

"Back behind the barge!" Rayne called, and the scouts retreated. The ant handler dismounted and crawled onto the deck of the barge. He creeped forward, dragging his launcher behind him. Then he sat up and fired a light rocket toward the house, aiming at the liquid soaked into the timber and coating the stone base. The projectile blew a hole only a hand's breadth wide, but it ignited the fluid. Within seconds the fire caught and spread over the house. The hole left by the rocket seemed to suck the fire inside, and Rayne could hear Keldons screaming inside. Smoke poured from around the barricaded door and windows. Warriors threw shutters open and tried to breathe and then crawl through the small openings.

The handler rolled to the backside of the barge and whistled the ants to him. The war machines milled below, and then, at his direction, ran toward the burning building. The warriors inside forced open the door, kicking the remnants of the barricade into the yard. They exited coughing and crawling. Each warrior must have been nearly blind from the smoke and many waved swords wildly against attackers they could not see. Like helpless kittens they died under the implacable jaws of the war machines. Ants hauled the bodies away, tearing at the dead flesh.

"Circle and pick off anyone on the other side," Rayne ordered. "Keep an eye out for that crossbow." She sent her machine toward the house, swinging wide to see around the building. The ant handler remounted and accompanied her. Shalanda was already searching through the crates.

Rayne watched the house burn. The smoke poured out so thickly it was hard to see the building. A Keldon and servant tore out a window frame and stumbled clear, coughing and teary-eyed but both carrying loaded crossbows. The ant handler bolted them, and they dropped, twisting as they fell so they lay against the wall.

"They came a long way to die," Rayne said. Burning pieces of the shutters fell onto the bodies, igniting their clothes.

"Well, I didn't invite them," the handler replied. The building was totally engulfed in flames, and the roof collapsed into the building's interior. The handler whistled the steel ants together and headed back to the captured barge. Rayne smelled the roasting flesh and wondered how many more lives would be destroyed in the war. At last, she turned her machine and started for her aide to see just what they had captured.

"I found the source of what I sensed earlier," Shalanda said. She kicked open a crate, and out poured dead ground squirrels. Each tiny corpse had been covered with a layer of preservative, and the bodies stuck together like melted hard candy. "The animals all died without a mark. The other special crates contain other species of dead animals and samples of dead vegetation."

"So animals are being targeted now as well as plants," Rayne said. "How are they spreading the disease?"

"I can't tell without doing more research. I can use these samples to complete my own investigation." She looked at the crates with a more speculative eye. "Rayne, they may not be spreading the blight at all."

"There is a connection," Rayne said. "They are driving people off the land, and the war is destroying what's left." Rayne looked to the burned-out shell of the farmhouse. "They are a disease that is killing this land."

CHAPTER 16

"An army on the march is a terrible sight to behold," Barrin said. He peered through the glass at the mass of Keldon barges slowly advancing toward Arsenal City. The Kashan blimp he rode was high and miles from the Keldons. The fire barges accompanying the enemy force provided an umbrella of protection that he dared not violate. He could see the huge transport barges, some of which must have been just constructed, judging from their simple decorations and the almost pristine superstructures.

"I see targets, not an army," Alexi said as she watched the forces snaking along the hills. "If it wasn't for those cursed fire barges, I'd be killing Keldons right now." She pointed, and Barrin focused his sight back through the glass. The barge was low slung and trailed smoke from secured braziers. The craft scuttled forward rapidly and then froze in a new position to provide cover to the column. Other fire barges could be seen dashing forward as the troop transports continued their advance.

"If we could, I'd have you fighting now, but the new bombs aren't ready and won't be for weeks," Barrin said as he looked for the Kipamu League scouts who lay in ambush. "The design was finalized last week, but we are only starting construction. I don't know how long till we can get you the ordnance you need." A blimp swung out of a cloud ahead of them high in the sky. "Maybe that Mushan will have some luck."

A dozen bombs began falling toward the ground. Every fire barge in the line cast flame upward in balls and streamers. The more distant vehicles sent skipping streamers as the Mushan dumped ballast to soar out of range. When Barrin reached out with his senses he could feel gas generators on full bore as the ship tried to generate extra lift.

"He has blowers on, and the fire suppression is off," Barrin said with disbelief.

Smoke clouds and particles of fire rose from the barges, and bombs fell into a space that cleared as the barges flowed away from the impact zone. One small barge was close to the drop site and shuddered to a halt before continuing after a few moments pause. Alexi turned back to Barrin.

"If you drop from that high the Keldon mages will simply push your bombs off target. He should have dropped from a lower altitude." Alexi didn't condemn the Mushan pilot for taking a chance; she only thought him too cautious.

"Alexi, you're not thinking of a low altitude run?" Barrin demanded.

The Jamuraan mage only laughed. "Things will have to get a lot worse before I can talk the rest of the crew into a suicide run," she said and then sobered and considered the forces converging on Arsenal City. "I believe that by next week I will be ordered to do so if the city falls."

A group of Tolarian runners and steel ants rushed from cover at a fire barge. The ants unleashed their rocket attacks en masse on the vehicle. The light loads that the ants carried didn't do much damage individually, but their collective damage shattered the vehicle's legs and smashed the catapult in the open interior. The secondary blast as the barge blew only knocked a few ants down as the League forces retreated at high speed.

"Not much of a return for the risks they took," Alexi said as their blimp began to turn and fly at maximum speed toward Arsenal City.

"No, but the fire barges are moving closer to the transports." Barrin was looking back at the Keldon forces. "If we can keep them bunched up so they can't dodge, maybe a high altitude attack will work before they reach the city. The other benefit is in making them angry. We need them to attack the army immediately."

Alexi only nodded sadly, accepting the fact that whatever the result of the coming battle, the flying navy would only deal with the aftermath. The army would have to fight on its own.

The city and its defensive works appeared before them, and Barrin got into a transport chair. The seat was a board on a sling and was attached to a rope dangling a few hundred feet under the blimp. Ground troops grabbed the rope to steady it as Barrin slid down. When he disconnected, the blimp jumped up, and its fans were shrill as it climbed. Mageta and Shalanda were among the ground crew.

"How does it look?" General Mageta demanded.

"The scouts are attacking the stragglers and going after the catapults," Barrin explained, waving Shalanda toward him as he saw her walking through the camp. "If the scouts obey orders and continue their hit and run tactics, the Keldons should perform as expected and attack immediately."

Armorers set additional reloads outside the perimeter to load returning scouts and the steel ants. The marines were loading mantises with the heavy war rockets that filled their main weapons module. Barrin planned for the machines to cripple the transport barges while they were unloading. The men servicing the war machines seemed confident, but the infantrymen were nervous. Crates of rockets were moved out of supply dumps as the battle approached.

"Shalanda, any sign of the contagion spreading from the eastern forests?" Barrin asked. If things went badly and there was a siege, illness could destroy the League army as brutally as a Keldon attack.

"There seem to be just a few small pockets of influenza but no mass kills of animals or infection in the fields," Shalanda replied. "I've isolated the flu carriers and those who may have been exposed. Hopefully there won't be any problems." Rayne's aide still looked troubled.

Barrin pressed further. "Can you do anything if there is a flare-up of disease?" the wizard asked.

"We've curbed outbreaks of disease before, but I'm still uncertain about this one's true nature, and I can't pinpoint its source," Shalanda said candidly. "The blight and death of wildlife could strip the League as surely as the Keldon army." Barrin waved for her to withdraw, focusing on the problems of fighting the immediate enemy and allowing others to deal with the blight and wildlife deaths. Mageta moved closer as Shalanda made for the runner depot.

"How many do you make the attackers?" Mageta asked. The general seemed filled with nervous energy, and Barrin wondered if it was fear or anticipation that fueled Mageta's emotions.

"I would estimate the numbers of Keldons and war manikins at between ten and twenty thousand." Mageta's face fell as Barrin stated the size of the attacking army. The wizard tried to curb the blow.

"We knew that we would be outnumbered. That's why we decided to dig in and engage the enemy here." He pointed out to the defenses that did not look quite so substantial now. "Make them assault fixed positions and prevent them from surrounding us piecemeal. And we've learned that the hollow warriors can be deployed for only a short time. We will win if we hold fast and force them to exhaust themselves." Mageta only nodded and ran to oversee the issuing of additional ammunition. The Kipamu League would be outnumbered at least four to one, and the infantry's lack of experience might be a blessing. Perhaps most of the men did not realize how truly desperate things had become.

Barrin went to talk to his wife. Following in Shalanda's footsteps, he neared the runner depot where Rayne readied her runner for the press of battle. The runner was being carefully reloaded, the normal complement of war-bolts replaced by enhanced models that would do more damage at the sacrifice of range.

Rayne was part of the regular army now. She had more experience than most of the current riders in using the machines. Jolreal and Shalanda still tracked the extent of the blight and the animal kills, but Rayne convinced Barrin that her skill at maintaining and managing the runners would be better employed in combat.

"I still wish that you could stay within the walls," Barrin said to his wife. She finished securing loads for her personal weapon, so they would be at hand during the coming fight.

"The light runners and the steel ants that we use are speed machines. Fighting in fixed positions would limit the damage we can do. Besides, this city is a trap if you don't win the initial battle. Out there I can reform and retreat far faster than the enemy can follow. I know your plan is based on exhausting the Keldons, but I would rather have room to maneuver."

"You're right, of course, but I still can't help how I feel," Barrin explained. "If things go badly, I want you to withdraw west at your best speed. The other coastal and river cities have raised massive armies and are slowly working their way east. I think if we can just hold the city against this attack, the League will be able to fight for the conquered lands instead of waiting for attacks." Barrin gripped her shoulders and drew her into an embrace.

"Your troops will be at the heart of any actions east." He paused for a moment. "You must be willing to accept our defeat if it comes to a choice between preserving your forces and saving the city."

Rayne kissed him and mounted up. Her mixture of Tolarian and League soldiers followed her out of the defensive works to link up with the hordes of ants stationed in hidden depots far from the city. Barrin hoped that he and the city would survive the day but felt better that his wife was sure to survive.

It was only minutes later that the first barges began to become visible. The Keldons deployed well back from Barrin's works. The invaders were far enough away that they could retreat or activate their hollow warriors before his heavy war machines could cover the distance. The Keldons gathered, and while there was no evidence of a clear and organized attack, a lot of gray-skinned warriors were leaving their vehicles. The wizard sent a runner back to the communications room to convey the information to Teferi. Barrin considered the growing ranks of warriors and then hurried to the command post.

Mageta's bunker was heavily reinforced and provided an excellent view. Communication runs and trenches converged on it. As Barrin ducked inside, he saw Mageta donning armor with the help of his aide. The metal seemed to shine even in the indirect light, and a golden lion was riveted high over the general's heart. Mageta grimaced as an aide finished wiping the device.

"I am supposed to inspire confidence and awe in the men," the general said. "As if a fancy set of armor will turn the course of the battle."

"At least the men will be able to pick you out of a crowd," Barrin replied diplomatically.

"I know a better way to capture their attention," Mageta said, gripping his sword with a free hand. The sword was ordinary and worn, the scabbard of dirty leather. "I dug myself out of the grave with this sword, and I rallied my men by slaying the enemy. Deeds are what the men need to see, not fancy armor."

Barrin only nodded his head. "A reputation can be a weapon more valuable than a sword. It drains the heart of your enemies and gives strength to your men. That armor may seem foolish now, but after the battle it will be part of your persona. It will be expected by your men and feared by your foes." A messenger entered the bunker, his cheeks flushed from running.

"The enemy is readying themselves for the attack, General," the soldier reported. "The main thrust could happen within the hour."

"Tell the marine squads and their mantises to start their

attack," Mageta ordered. The soldier and Mageta's aide left at a run. Barrin stood to the side as the men went by. In only a few minutes the League would execute the attack plan that Barrin and the commanders had developed. General Mageta lifted a tankard of beer from the table and drank deeply, emptying it and then slamming it down.

"I leave the command to you, Barrin," Mageta said as he pulled on a helmet and picked up a shield. "I can do the most good up in the front works."

Barrin followed the general outside. The sun was shining brightly, and Mageta breathed deeply.

"Remember that you and the other magicians are the final reserve." Mageta glanced back toward the city. The magic users were forming a circle on a balcony looking out over the battlefield. "Commit them if the army falls. We need a victory of arms rather than magic if we ever hope to take the battle to the Keldons." He nodded and started down through the connecting trenches, calling to the men he came across. Barrin was left alone with only a few runners waiting to carry additional orders.

"He must not fall," Barrin said, calling magic to send his senses over the coming battlefield. The Keldon camp was a pool of naphtha waiting to explode as he tasted the quiescent magic driving the alien artifacts. The circle of magicians in Arsenal City was a circle of chanting children trying to raise power. Finally, the League trenches and earthworks appeared—a field of gopher holes that Barrin sensed among the scattered war machines. Even as his senses tried to focus on Mageta, the attack commenced. The League made the first move.

The marine mantises had been concealed in trenches at the front lines. At the prompting of their handlers, each lifted out of its hole and walked silently onto the field. Less than two hundred of the machines had been constructed by the overworked factories. The mantises advanced with a few lightly armed marines jogging alongside. They approached the enemy without fanfare. The machines and men in small groups looked helpless against the opposing army.

The Keldon barges were in a line surrounded by soldiers putting on their armor and stoking braziers as the mantises came closer. The warriors emptied smoking coals and shaved colos horn into receptacles on their armor. A haze of smoke rose, and a light breeze blew the fumes toward Arsenal City. Barrin could see the soldiers becoming more fearful as the smoke increased. The wizard detected a surge of energy as the warriors walked into barges and powered war manikins. The Keldons began chanting as they prepared to charge, promising death to the League soldiers waiting for them. Warriors shouted derisively at the few war machines standing before them. The mantises raised their arms and lowered their hindquarters as if in response. Then with a roar, each machine fired a heavy rocket at the Keldon barges.

A few rockets detonated on launch, and mantises exploded, cutting down the surrounding machines and men. The first League deaths of the battle were self-inflicted, but the remaining rockets arced and fell onto the barges. The crafts' heavy protective shells shattered in huge sprays of splinters. Secondary explosions bloomed like flowers as Heroes' Blood ignited and incinerated barges, leaving climbing balls of flames. The League soldiers behind the trenches heard the angry moans of the enemy as frantic barge crews ran into the remaining vehicles and drove them away from burning piles of wreckage. Delayed detonations sent huge pieces of machinery flying in all directions, killing warriors and shearing through other barges. A cheer went up as the mantises turned sharply and retreated back to their hiding places. Barrin could see marine technical troops digging out new loads of heavy rockets for a second wave of bombardment.

General Mageta stood outside a trench with sword held high. His armor caught the eyes of the troops and they began chanting "Lion! Lion!" as his golden emblem flashed on his chest. The fear that the Keldons inspired was momentarily gone, and Barrin counted it a victory. Then he felt the swell of magic as the enemy finished animating their hollow warriors and charged the League earthworks.

The mantises were nearly inside the trench lines when their heads turned one hundred and eighty degrees. Each launched a small rocket, lashing into the ranks of enemy soldiers. Manikins and men sundered in sharp explosions. The Keldons screamed in rage as the mantises jumped out of sight into the trenches.

The enemy was a sea coming to sweep the League away when crabs reared up and fired. Hundreds of them had been buried during the night. The machines fired only light rockets, but each crab carried six of them. The leading ranks of the charge dissolved into gouts of bloody foam as the machines fired in a massive coordinated blow. Warriors floundered in the remnants of their comrades, and the charge stumbled to a stunned halt.

"Fire!" Mageta called as he rose once more from the trenches, holding a launcher. The general discharged a war bolt that vanished into the milling crowd of the enemy. Barrin couldn't tell if anyone fell, but the infantry in the trenches began firing in a sporadic barrage. There was a serious shortage of launchers and war-bolts, but the fire was a light rain on a pile of sand. The Keldons were dissolving away under the attack. Barrin could see the League technicians loading the weapons modules of the mantises and crabs. For a moment the wizard hoped the enemy might break, but then warlords in fantastic armor forced their way to stand in front of the Keldon lines. Barrin could hear their shouts as they exhorted the warriors.

"Do you think victory and glory are free?" an armored giant of a man bellowed. "A great people are known by the strength of their enemies! Kill for the glory of Keld! The final days are upon us! Kill the thieves, kill them . . ."

Even as they shouted, Mageta was leading men and machines from the trenches, gambling on breaking the enemies' spirits. Barrin wondered at the boldness, but knowing how outnumbered the League forces were, he acted to make the blow as strong as possible.

"Attack the rear!" The call echoed through the aether as the wizard drew power and called to the light forces beyond the battlefield. Rayne's troop of fast runners and ants was out of sight, but he knew that they charged at his call.

The crabs from the trenches slowly advanced. Each few yards a fusillade of bolts poured from their weapon bays. Some of the supporting infantry knelt and fired launchers while the rest advanced with swords and spears jabbing into the air for blood. Mageta was just behind a crab trotting forward, signaling the advance with every step. The Keldons started forward, but they came at the League in a string of disorganized driblets instead of the unified front that the warlords desired.

More bolts and rockets flew toward the enemy, but the Keldons were implacable now, advancing in a silent rage. Mageta halted and dressed his line of men and machines. Clumps of spears faced the enemy and formed small arcs of soldiers anchored by crabs. The heavy war machines launched all their weapons at point-blank range, and then the forces met. The soldiers with spears funneled Keldons and hollow warriors to the crabs. Massive metal arms rose and fell. Manikins and men almost exploded as they died under the relentless pounding clubs. The bodies mounded up into piles, and the crabs inched back as warriors mounted the shattered bodies to continue the attack.

Now League soldiers were within range of Keldon swords, and infantry dropped screaming as gray-skinned warriors shattered bones and parted flesh. The soldiers carrying launchers drew swords. Mageta shouted and mounted the back of a crab, a spear in his hands. He yelled and signaled for the League troop to back toward their earthworks. The crabs slowly stepped away from their mounds of victims and began rebuilding their fleshy barricade with new corpses. Mageta was covered in blood and poorly balanced on the back of the crab but remained there as he directed the withdrawal, needing the extra height to be seen. Axes and spears flew toward him, but the crab deflected them, smashing them out of the air.

Barrin raised more power, and his senses flew toward the general. He enveloped Mageta in a web of power. The wizard could feel crossbow bolts burning to ash as Keldons finally began sniping at the general. Mageta threw his arms wide in defiance of the enemy, trusting in the magic that surrounded him. The League withdrawal slowed as the general's actions brought fresh heart to his men. The wizard could hear Mageta whispering through the surrounding magic.

"I really hope you can keep this up, Barrin. Otherwise, I'm dead."

More weapons flew past the waving arms of the crab to burn up in the wizard's shielding spell, and Barrin drew more power, waiting for the Keldon mages to enter the fray. Then cheering rose from the retreating troops. Hordes of steel ants came swooping from the distant flanks, falling upon the enemy.

"Your wife is coming to save me from myself, Barrin," General Mageta said to the wind.

Rayne and Shalanda on their runners fired groups of bolts into the Keldons, tearing at them like rabid dogs. Wing blades scissored as they cut apart groups of warriors. Steel ants nipped at the enemy, leaving wounded who stumbled and crawled through the ranks. Rayne had directed the ants around her to wound rather than destroy. Barrin had protested the inhumanity of the tactic, but Rayne insisted that wounded warriors were more trouble to the enemy than dead ones. Additionally, the ants were less vulnerable if they didn't linger over their kills. Hundreds of voices screamed and tore at the will of the Keldons, confirming her tactics.

"Send the mantises against the Keldon transports," Barrin ordered.

A runner tore his eyes from the battle and ran to relay the command. Mageta was holding the line and retreating at a crawl that allowed more Keldon warriors to reach the crabs. Here and there a machine went down as axes and swords sheared legs free, and a crab collapsed. One huge Keldon used a crab arm as a giant club, leaving a trail of smashed League soldiers dead among the field of crushed enemy warriors. Mageta shouted orders and then led several swordsmen against the champion. The general dodged an overhand strike, and his sword cut the tendons on the warrior's arm. The Keldon grabbed Mageta with his free arm, and the general battered the warrior's face with blows from his helmet until a League soldier cut him free.

The steel ants still lashed the peripheries of the enemy as the Keldon center advanced into oblivion under the hammering metal arms of the crabs. Now Barrin saw the mantises charging the left wing of the enemy army. The colorful machines broke through the thinning lines, their long arms slicing through flesh and manikin with equal ease. Then the marines and their charges were through with the barges only a few hundred yards away. The machines ran forward as their handlers ordered them to engage at point-blank range with their reloaded rockets.

Then Barrin sensed magic from the Keldon barges like a sea of fire burning. Slaves and barge crew rushed out of their craft in a panicky mass, and flocks of birds issued forth. They circled and rose high over the battlefield then fell onto the League forces. As each small body smashed into a soldier or machine, it disintegrated in a sharp explosion. Barrin could see the center melting away, the bludgeoning crabs chewed to pieces by the attack. The surrounding infantry died as men fell with sudden ghastly wounds. Mageta struck out at a diving bird, and the resulting explosion tore at his arm and knocked the general to the ground. More bomblets dived from the orbiting flock, now striking at the steel ants that had feasted on the flanks of the enemy. Shalanda went down as her runner was struck, and Rayne attacked the Keldon warriors who rushed to kill her aide. The mantises fired rockets, but many had already fallen or were crippled, and only a few barges exploded.

More of the tiny bombs launched into the air, and Barrin knew that only magic could save the day.

"Throw fire and lightning!" he called to the magical reserves.

A long stream of power leaped from Barrin up into the

sky. Explosions rippled through the flock, disrupting its structure and sending many of the birds spiraling to the ground. The League and the Keldons suffered equally as men died and huddled for shelter. From the circle of magic behind him, a diffuse cloud of flame moved toward the birds. The birds began to detonate as the outskirts of the flock flew within the League spell. Barrin sent energy to shield the friendly forces, but the battlefield was too large. He concentrated on shielding Rayne and Shalanda as the rest of the fire-swallows fell out of the sky. Finally the rain of death stopped, but the League center was down, and Keldons rushed into the defensive works.

However, Barrin felt rising hope. The warriors and manikins moved slower and stumbled even as they tried to exploit the breach. Barrin could feel the Keldons stopping as some began to fall in exhaustion or even death as their fighting machines sucked the last energy from their frames. The wizard's heart lifted even more as he saw Rayne and Shalanda back up. The scouts and their runners had survived, and handlers directed their ants to attack once more. The outskirts of the enemy army could only beat weakly at the small machines as war manikins stopped in mid-swing and warriors collapsed.

"We need to reinforce the center!" Barrin ordered. "Everyone will advance and engage the enemy." Runners ran to order technicians, cooks, and quartermasters to charge the enemy. Barrin walked forward, raising power as he prepared to sluice the trenches clean of invading warriors.

Then he was stunned by a surge of new magical energy from Arsenal City. The magic users had not recognized the Keldons' weakness. Magic that Barrin hoped to direct against the enemy was instead expended in a wordless ringing call. His senses seared by the wave, it took him precious seconds to regain his equilibrium. During that time, Teferi appeared on the battlefield.

The planeswalker jumped into the defensive works, and Barrin could hear him calling. Teferi's magic touched him, but only Barrin's momentary injury communicated itself to the planeswalker. Surrounded by enemy warriors and dead League soldiers, Teferi cast a mighty spell.

Energy rippled out in a huge wave through the ground. Even those with almost no magical talent could feel the surge. The ground began to liquefy, flowing into the trenches and burying Keldon warriors and the League dead. Out on the battlefield, huge sinkholes appeared and sucked down the enemy corpses. The land barges tossed and bucked as the land danced under them. The Keldons retreated in confusion and fear as the ground itself showed allegiance to the League. The soldiers who had been around the crabs climbed to their feet and reformed as the retreating enemy flowed back to the barges. The center was saved, but the effects of Teferi's spell continued to spread as Barrin watched.

Steel ants bogged down as thousands of small pits opened up. Marine mantises almost in firing range of the Keldon barges were shoulder deep in the ground, their arms tearing furrows as they tried to slash themselves free. More Keldons retreated, struggling through the mud holes appearing everywhere. Barrin could see the land barges advancing into the muck as Teferi's attack waned. The huge craft moved slowly but were able to reach the core of their army.

Mageta was up but nearly unrecognizable. "Cowards!" he yelled and struggled forward. Covered in mud and blood, only the device on the general's helmet identified him. He slogged a few steps, his injured arm hanging limply at his side, before falling down once more as he passed out.

* * * * *

"We survived. That's the most important thing," Rayne whispered into Barrin's ear as the couple clasped each other tightly. Rayne's runner had finally battled its way through the uncertain ground and the dead as the wizard struggled through the earthworks to find her.

"It was a chance to destroy the Keldon forces, and now they've withdrawn." Barrin looked east in anger. "Our first chance to crush the enemy on land, and we missed it."

Teferi and the support troops were bringing the wounded and the war machines into the city. Here and there a Keldon warrior was found alive, and troops converged to capture them.

Rayne only nodded noncommittally. She stepped past him and knelt to inspect a fire-swallow. It had started life as a bird but at some point was transformed into a weapon. The eyes were stitched shut, and the feathers were glossy with some sort of coating. Barrin sniffed the air and could smell the refined tufa liquid draining and soaking into the dirt.

"Those were an unpleasant surprise," Barrin said as he looked at it. "The battle was in our favor before they launched."

Someone clearing her throat interrupted the couple. Shalanda stood thick with mud. She had been inspecting the battlefield and the casualties. She had just come from healing some of the wounded, and she breathed heavily as she recharged her strength to try again.

"Seventy percent of the wounded should be ready for

duty in two weeks, Barrin. But we might have a problem. That flu has cropped up again among some of the wounded and the personnel helping clear the battlefield. It may be a few weeks before the illness burns itself out," she declared.

"That's fine," Barrin replied. "It will be a few months before we can concentrate enough forces to march east." He straightened, and his lips thinned. "I think we've turned a corner in this war. From now on, we take the fight to the enemy."

CHAPTER 17

Haddad woke at sea, his lungs burning as he breathed smoke from the censer swinging above his head. He thrashed and threw his hands over the sides of the stasis box. Haddad moaned in pain as his muscles shook with tremors and cramps. The crash of waves could be clearly heard in the hold as the former League officer gripped his head and coughed up the dust from his lungs.

Lanterns swung from beams, and he tried to orient himself by their light. Latulla and her entire party had been interred in stasis boxes within minutes of the artificer's defeat. Slowly the party was being revived. They must be at or near Jamuraa.

Iola knelt beside a stasis box, and Haddad could see Latulla's features in the changing light. She awoke almost gently, her eyes opening and the look of confusion fading in seconds. Haddad felt a surge of envy and wondered how Iola had spared Latulla pain.

"We are just outside the colony, mistress," Iola said. "The council has exiled you here for life." She paused, and Haddad could hear the despair in her voice as she continued. "All your holdings are forfeit, and your retainers were expelled with you." Haddad remembered Iola's pride in managing Latulla's house and felt a little pity.

"Why were we awakened at sea?" Latulla demanded as she levered herself up from the erstwhile coffin. No word or expression showed awareness of her servants' loss. "We should have been awakened after we safely docked."

Latulla was in full regalia, and she tested the strength of her cane with a few sharp blows against the stasis boxes of her servants. She ignored the groans that issued as the human slaves clawed their way to consciousness. One slave uttered a curse, and Latulla tested her cane on flesh.

"The League has attacked ships near the port," Iola answered, wringing her hands in worry. "The captain thought all passengers should be awake in case the ship was hit."

Even though Haddad was in immediate danger, he felt a tremendous surge of hope at the news. The League was finally operating around the colony. Not only was his nation fighting back, but also escape might be easier with local forces in the area.

"Everyone up on deck," Latulla ordered as she strode to the stair and forced her way up into the wind. The others followed her, still staggering as they recovered from stasis, but weakness was no excuse in Latulla's service.

It was midday and the sun sent rays down through the clouds. Haddad wondered why the sea was so rough. Then he turned from viewing the coast and looked seaward. The clouds of a storm were piled high and dark. The captain nervously considered the storm as the ship sailed closer to the protected bay.

"Captain, what's the problem?" Latulla demanded. The captain was a massive Keldon with a peg leg, which he pivoted on when Latulla spoke.

"We had word from a warship that the League is trying to sink ships in port and block access to the piers," he explained. "I am waiting for an armed escort vessel to follow us in."

"I will provide all the cover you need," Latulla said. She rapped the captain smartly on his wooden leg. "Take the ship in, and I will watch for League patrols."

The captain opened his mouth to argue but decided to keep silent at Latulla's angry look. Haddad saw that the artificer wanted to show her strength after her defeat at Gorsha's hands.

"Take her in," the captain ordered the helmsman. The sailor swallowed nervously and turned the ship's wheel to take them into the channel. Latulla sent Iola down into the hold to inventory what the council had allowed the artificer to bring with her. Haddad looked at the approaching coastline.

How long had it been since he saw Jamuraa? He couldn't know. He didn't even know if this was the first time he was awake. Keld had made him doubt himself on many levels. He looked at the shore and wondered if he could ever go home again.

The ship was inside the channel and moving into protected waters. The storm that loomed behind began to break up as the ship pulled closer to the dock. Latulla and all her supporters were back on deck, arranging themselves in lines and trying to appear impressive. Latulla sent crewmen and slaves from their regular duty stations into the ship's cargo areas to find additional clothes and weapons.

The ship was docking, and Haddad could feel the tone of the propulsion spells changing as they moved the ship closer to the pier. A crowd was gathered, and freight handlers stood ready to empty the ship at a moment's notice. As the ship was tied off, Latulla walked to the gangplank.

"I have returned to you with news that Keld is no more!" she shouted. There was a general air of confusion among the crowd and the ship's complement. "Keld has given up and rejected the prophecy that you have all accepted—that this land is the home of heroes and must be reclaimed from the weak and corrupt League to the west."

A few Keldons began cheering because they did believe that their birthright was being stolen. Other warriors and some slaves cheered because glory required a great cause. The rest cheered as Haddad cheered, because it was expected of them.

Haddad considered the Keldon exiles as Latulla continued her exhortations. "You are Keld! All that Keld has been. The defeat of our enemies, the conquest of new lands, the construction of the future! You are the children of all who have gone before. It is time to pick up the prize left by the Heroes from whom we sprang!"

Haddad's eyes locked on a familiar figure. It was Greel, Erissa's demonic assistant. Latulla had brought more than rhetoric from the land of her ancestors. How long would it take this cancer to grow in a new land? Haddad promised himself that his first act upon escaping would be to reveal Greel's nature. The children of Jamuraa would not lie in graves to feed the monster's appetite.

"I bring you the future," Latulla said, spreading her arms

wide. Haddad turned from the scene and considered the sea. Then he saw the nose of a blimp poke itself out of the stormy clouds that hung offshore.

For a few seconds he was alone as the others concentrated on Latulla and her speech. It was not until the bombs fell that shouts drowned out Latulla's voice. The blimp was huge, and it withdrew back into the clouds as each bomb sprouted wings. The weapons' trajectories flattened, and their velocity increased. Shouts sounded as almost every slave ran for cover, with a few curling up on the ground and trying to shut out the world. Haddad saw them trampled by the running crowd, their flesh torn by shoes and boots. Warriors drew weapons and shouted challenges, but the airship was gone, and only the bombs remained to hear the futile cries. The weapons neared the water and came straight at the ship.

"Why aren't the fire barges shooting?" shouted a warrior who had accompanied Latulla into exile. The bombs skimmed over the ships and detonated among the dockside warehouses. Splinters and fiery debris rained down everywhere. Chunks of wreckage draped across the rigging over Haddad's head, and he joined a rush to clear the ship. Latulla was almost trampled in the stampede, and Haddad hid a smile as he swirled past her livid face. The ropes began to burn, and sections of the dock were covered in flame. Weapons stored in the warehouses shattered and released waves of flammable liquid. Haddad could hear the collapse of burning floors and the hiss as timbers dropped among the dock pilings and extinguished in the sea. The captured League soldier flattened against the side of a building as more people rushed past him. He could see Latulla running up the gangplank to fight the fire on the ship. Her hands moved, and the flames shrank back like a frightened pet.

She waved for the crowds to return even as she calmed the fire. Now magic users from the colony were running up to the docks, and the destruction Haddad had cheered began to be controlled. Slowly the fires flickered out. The warriors began to chant Latulla's name, and she directed the final efforts of the impromptu fire brigades. The League had interrupted Latulla's speech, but she rallied the colony to her cause because of it.

* * * * *

It was nearing dark when Latulla and the rest of the household straggled to their quarters. The fires destroyed one warehouse completely, though all ships were saved. Lord Urit sat within the house, and Latulla moved to confront him. Haddad stayed in the outer room and looked through the door.

The curtains were drawn and the lights low as defensive measures against air attacks. Latulla appeared incensed that the League would dare attack the colony.

"Where were the fire casters and magic users? Why were we left so exposed?" she demanded.

Lord Urit answered her. The former swamp overseer was in charge of the colony slaves and had become an important figure.

"The western expedition did not go as planned. We had to retreat," Urit confessed shamefacedly, and Latulla reined in her temper with visible difficulty.

"A temporary state of affairs. We will rebuild and crush them like we have always done." She spoke confidently.

Urit shook his head. "Their armies do not wait for the blow. Now they seek to fight." He looked up and seemed to stare through the roof. "Their airships range over the west looking for detachments to kill. Almost all fire barges are protecting the armies and our new holdings. In fact, their airships seek battle relentlessly with any barge they can find."

"They may be using their blimps, but we can destroy their bases as we did before," Latulla said. "There will be more forces arriving from Keld regardless of what the fools on the council believe."

"We can barely keep our forward bases intact while new classes of airships drop bombs on our home ground. We will have to recall forces and concentrate our warriors," Urit insisted.

"I will hear from you later, Urit," Latulla commanded. "Leave me now, so I might rest."

Urit said nothing but bowed and withdrew, his face stony at his dismissal. Haddad kept still as the major domo, Briach, bowed and entered. The chief slave appeared calm and content as he waited to hear Latulla.

"What has happened here, Briach?" Latulla asked.

"The first expeditions went well, and many slaves were taken for the glory of Keld. There are shiploads winding their way to cradle houses in the north. Cities fell, and the artificers control mines and refineries for the Heroes' Blood. Huge stores await only shipment back home to build you an army," Briach explained.

Latulla smashed his hand with her cane. "This is home now. Keld would not have me, and now they will live with their decision. Suspend all shipments north until further notice. Start construction of factories and a cradle house. The midwives and female slaves are to report to me from now on."

Briach whitened at the blow but remained still as Latulla stood and began to pace.

"What happened to the second expedition?" Latulla questioned.

Haddad saw Briach consider his words carefully. Latulla collaborated with the military commanders before leaving and would not brook even implied criticism from a slave, however favored he might be.

"The attack, from all reports, went well, but the League machines proved more lethal than previously believed. Their weapons were heavier, and our war manikins could not overwhelm them. But the battle was still in our favor until the planeswalker appeared on the field and unleashed a great spell. He turned the ground of the ancestors against their descendants."

"How many died under Teferi's hand?" demanded Latulla.

"Almost none, but the warriors had powered the hollow warriors a long time, and many fell from exhaustion," Briach answered. "The leaders called for retreat."

"So they were not defeated—they gave up!" Latulla said angrily. "At the heart of enemy war production they retired because they couldn't beat the League with the first blows." Latulla threw herself back into her chair and drummed her fingers on the side table.

"How do the warriors feel about their loss?" Latulla spoke slowly as she considered her plans.

"Many of them cannot accept that they did lose," Briach said. "The sailors have lost to the League before, but the army has not suffered a serious setback since it landed. Many of the warriors are angry, striking out at slaves and each other. The number of fights between warriors has soared despite the best efforts of the war leaders to curb dominance battles."

Latulla nodded to herself in satisfaction. "Of course they're angry. They should be enraged. The leaders betrayed them by withdrawing from the field too soon. Had the army stayed, they would have conquered the enemy," she said intently. "We must act quickly to isolate those who would lead us to defeat."

Briach nodded but with some confusion. "Mistress, I am sure that you know best, but I do not know how you can displace the war leaders," Briach stated.

Latulla only threw her cane at his head for daring to question her decisions.

"Of course I can't take direct control of the army, but there are always subordinates whose ambitions can be fired and directed to my benefit. Other voices will say the commands in battle, but the orders will be mine. Call my supporters to me when dawn comes."

Latulla went to her bed, and Haddad crept away as well. The artificer had been expelled from Keld in disgrace. Awake for one day, she was already setting up a personal empire.

Haddad shook his head in reluctant admiration and went to his room. There he dreamed of a kingdom of puppets with Latulla pulling the strings. He sank into a deeper sleep as he appeared in the dream—a marionette dancing to Latulla's commands.

* * * * *

Haddad carried another set of invitations to captains of barge crews and commanders of small companies. Latulla had thrown parties and private dinners all week. She was still imperious and cold, but many of the lesser war leaders received assurances of support for their ambitions. Latulla cast her net wide, and Haddad hit every section of the camp. But he was not her only emissary, and he shuddered as Greel stepped from a tent ahead of him. The monster was smiling and laughing as he left a group of drunken comrades.

"Haddad!" he called and walked over. The League technician wanted to run but could not. Haddad felt a cold sweat as he realized that Greel called him by name.

"What are you holding, slave?" Greel asked. He smiled broadly at Haddad, and that alone signaled he was not a Keldon.

"Invitations to another of Latulla's dinners, master." Perhaps if he was obsequious enough, Greel would be bored and go away.

"Let me see those." Greel reached and took the envelopes from Haddad's fingers. He flipped through them quickly. Many of the passersby looked at Greel. A Keldon male appearing to read was unusual. Haddad usually read the message aloud or handed it to a literate slave when he found the addressee.

"Many of these are my friends," Greel slurred. "I will deliver them if I see them." Greel appeared drunk, but Haddad knew it was an act. Failure to deliver the invitations would mean a severe beating for Haddad.

"I would not have expected you to find friends so soon," Haddad said as he reached for the invitations. It was broad daylight, and Haddad was growing tired of fear. Greel gave back the invitations but still smiled.

"I have many friends, old and new, in this land." He tapped the bronze armband concealed under Haddad's clothes. "You could be my friend since you bear this."

Haddad could not stop from shying away. Greel's face lost its pleasant expression, twisting into a snarl. It almost seemed to glow, and for a moment Haddad thought Greel's true form would burst forth. The fiery light sprang not from inside the monster but from streams of fireballs rising into the sky. Haddad and Greel looked toward the heavens and saw the Keldon weapons converging on an apparently empty space. Then sheets of flame outlined a camouflaged blimp and its defensive fields. Haddad wondered if more than color hid it as his eyes refused to lock on. Suddenly a rack of bombs rained down, and the blimp disappeared. The launchers shot at the falling weapons, and one exploded in a green disk of fire that enveloped the other bombs. The weapons did not fratricide but instead diverged wildly, corkscrewing through the air.

Haddad was rooted to the spot as Greel gripped his arm tightly. The familiar's hand did not even tremor as Haddad tried to pull free. Explosions sounded throughout the camp, but Haddad saw only one. The flash was brilliant white, and the League technician was hurled to the ground as Greel keened in pain. Haddad's eyes cleared, and he saw that the bomb had hurled ropes of fire. The material clung to everything as it burned. Slaves near one building dumped water on a strand stuck to an exterior wall. The water just drained away, and the slaves tried desperately to scrape the fire off as the wood burned fiercely.

Greel crouched in gasping agony. Haddad could see channels of burnt flesh across his chest and neck. The skin bubbled as Greel knelt, oblivious to the world. Haddad ran as magic users closed to extinguish the fires. In the sky, the blimp had vanished, though fire-streamers still shot into the air searching for the craft. After a few more seconds the fire barges stopped, the fires extinguished as the might of the Keldon mages turned to ending the fires.

Greel rose to his feet as a group of slaves came to help him. His features were burned away, and bone showed through the charred meat. One of the slaves vomited at the sight. The monster's fists crushed skulls and caved in chests as he tore through the crowd around him. He ran toward the edge of the colony, pulling a screaming slave behind him like a child's rag doll. Haddad hoped that a mage would burn Greel down before he could feed, but he doubted the monster would be caught. Haddad hurried to deliver the last of the letters, hoping that he could escape soon.

* * * * *

Haddad shifted at the back of the crowd. Latulla had been closeted with her circle all night, and Haddad was dismissed before he could learn much of their plans. He did know that Greel was an instrumental part of those plans, and that was reason enough for worry. A platform had been raised in the field with the stock pens in the background. Latulla chose the spot because it was the largest open space, but Haddad smiled slightly as the morning breeze wafted over the crowd. Latulla's words would smell like manure to the listening masses.

There was a stir as the artificer came into view. The stage was low and there was no bunting or color. Latulla did not warm up the crowd as Haddad half-expected. Instead she launched directly into the heart of her speech.

"You have lost everything!" she screamed to the crowd. Mutters rose as they absorbed her words. "You left Keld and the battles of the north. Many of you were shipped in stasis, powerless to affect your destiny. There are no cradle houses in this land, the slaves are arrogant, and there is the tedium and trouble of working without female partners. Why would anyone come here?" Latulla paused and looked at the crowd.

"Because there is a land to conquer!" she shouted, and her supporters cheered her with a few of the crowd joining in. "These lands were the home of your forebears. Heroes and gods roamed these hills and contested with each other. But an evil force swept over the land, killing and slaying in the dark of night. The widows and babes of your ancestors fled north to escape destruction."

Latulla lifted her hands, as if in benediction, over the crowd. "But you have grown strong and have come to take your birthright back. You have arrived in the land from which Keld sprang and found what?

"You have found a race of weaklings who hold what is yours." She whipped a cover off something on the stage. A steel ant lay revealed. "A race so cowardly that it constructs a machine to fight while its soldiers stay behind." She pointed up into the sky. "A race that attacks your camps from the air for fear of your strength."

Finally she whipped the last tarp off the stage. Five dead Keldons lay revealed, none with an obvious wound. "An enemy who, when he failed to kill you, has resorted to the spread of corruption and disease." Haddad had heard of some dying from illness but found it unsurprising in a camp of this size. "The League has shown by its every action that it is the successor of the evil that battled our forebears. Will you let them win again, or will you break the world and remake it in your image?" Cheers erupted again, and Latulla seemed to swell as they rolled over her.

"The final days are upon us, and the final battle awaits in the west. Who will follow me into glory and victory?" Even Haddad cheered and chanted her name—not because he wanted the Keldons to win, but because this expedition west might constitute his last chance to escape. He cheered the fulfillment of his own plans and cursed the Keldons silently.

* * * * *

"Pig slop!" Alexi exclaimed as the deck surged up, a gust of wind grappling with the blimp. "Keep it steady!" she yelled up the cabin to the pilot. A muttered obscenity wafted back, but she ignored it as she tried to keep her stomach under control. When would this ride be over? she wondered silently.

The *Hunter* and the *Eagle* were hovering beside a storm. The two Mushan blimps had spent three days tossed by winds as Teferi worked the storm. Jumping from ship to ship, he herded it toward the coast even as he wove his spells into its structure. The planeswalker was ready to expunge the Keldon colony from Jamuraa, and now his moment neared. Far out to sea, a fleet of surface warships waited to land marines and supplies, but Teferi had put the attack on hold. Through magic he observed a huge exodus of the colony's warriors and fire barges the day before.

The surge of power as Teferi appeared in the cabin surprised Alexi. The planeswalker dripped water from his sodden clothes onto the deck, and a puff of ozone and magic assaulted Alexi's nose. Teferi worked inside the storm now.

"Signal the fleet to start coming in," he ordered in a tired voice. "I am going to force the storm onshore. The marines should be able to make an unopposed landing. You will report any problems to the fleet." He looked exhausted.

Alexi spoke quietly. "Can't you stay aboard and rest just a little?" she asked. "At least direct the storm from here instead of jumping into its winds."

Teferi shook his head. "It's already starting to tear apart," he explained. "We need to act now. Call the fleet in, and be prepared for communications interference from now on. In a few minutes I will start a series of spells on the other blimp to smother Keldon calls for help. The enemy reinforcements marching west can't be allowed to know what has happened. I must go." Teferi closed his eyes and jumped. Alexi spun and stared angrily at the communications mage.

"You heard him," she said. "Call in the fleet now while we still have the opportunity." The man dropped into a trance as Alexi moved forward toward the pilot. "We will be moving inland with the storm." The pilot looked at the edge of the turbulent cloud and then his hands flashed to his throttles and rammed them forward. Teferi had begun.

The air seemed rough to Alexi, but seeing the torn mists and rain swirling inside Teferi's attack she knew that the *Hunter* flew in relative calm. The clouds seemed to draw away.

"Faster!" she ordered.

"We're the same distance away," the pilot said irritably. "The storm's getting smaller."

Alexi could see it now. The clouds were drawing near to the coast, and they grew even blacker. Like a hunkered giant, the storm crept into the bay. The clouds dropped lower and lower, touching the water. The high winds tore into the violent seas, and water began to pile up. The waves mounted higher and higher. Huge black-green hills of water raced from the storm to the docks. The bay narrowed, concentrating the attack.

The first wave hit. All small boats turned to kindling, the planks and oars flung up onto the docks as the larger ships surged up against the pier. The second set of waves arrived. The large ships listed heavily as the sea gripped and turned them. Masts hammered down on a warehouse as ships rolled nearly ninety degrees. Most ships capsized. Looking through a set of magical lenses, Alexi saw a few sailors flung from the wreckage to break against the pier pilings. The storm seemed to submerge as another giant wave raced forth. Fire rose over the bay as Keldon mages realized it was a magical attack, but their spells were matches flung into a stream as water raced toward docks.

In the colony, Alexi could see figures boiling out of houses and tents. Some went for higher ground as a wave over thirty feet tall hit the piers. Warehouses were shoved off their foundations and struck houses and workshops like battering rams. More and more people ran inland as Teferi began to push the storm toward the colony once more. It crept up the bay, sending a constant stream of fifteen-foot waves forward. Each wall of water picked up debris and threw it farther from the sea. Houses were bludgeoned by water and fragments of wood as the water level rose higher and higher. Like a cupped hand, Teferi's spell tried to empty the bay onto the town, and destruction mounted with every passing moment.

The waves crashed far from the bay as the stables and corrals were destroyed. Here and there barges raced for cover. Now water surrounded one and rose a few inches per second. The barge began to lose traction as it floated. Men swarmed over it. More and more crowded aboard, and Alexi could see swords hewing into slaves and warriors as the crew tried to preserve their craft. It was a hopeless battle and under the mass of screaming humanity, the barge capsized as it lost all traction.

No structure still stood in the town, and Teferi's spell dissipated as the last of it submerged in the muddy water. Deprived of the storm surge, water cascaded back toward the bay. Like a draining bathtub, the water left a thick coating of mud as it withdrew. Corpses and debris mixed with mud appeared as the land drained. A few living men struggled to stand, the water abandoning them in its race back to the sea. Alexi could see hundreds of corpses and wondered if anyone could know how many had died in the previous minutes. Teferi appeared in the cabin. His eyes looked tired.

"Tell the fleet to land outside of the bay," he croaked. "They'll never be able to get through the mess down there. Warn them that there are still warriors inland who may attack as messengers reach them with news of this disaster."

"Surely you can relay that information faster than we can," Alexi said.

"No!" Teferi exclaimed and shook his head. "I must remain here. I destroyed the warriors and barges stationed here, but I killed the slaves as well." Deep tremors began to shake his frame. "I have to stay here and begin rescue operations. I will scout for survivors and work with the marines when they land." He sounded lost and despairing.

"We'll stay and help you, Teferi," Alexi offered.

"I have killed thousands today," Teferi whispered. "If it is to mean anything this war must end soon. You will fly west and tell Barrin what has happened here. I will maintain the communications interference so the Keldon armies in the west know nothing of this. Destroy them, Alexi. Kill them and end this war." Teferi jumped without warning, leaving Alexi to carry word of the massacre to the League.

CHAPTER 18

The League army marched east, kicking up dust as men and war machines pursued the Keldons fleeing toward their home territories. Barrin and General Mageta rode on runners side by side as they went from column to column. The armies and war machines of the western League cities had finally arrived. With news of Teferi's victory, Barrin knew the Keldon cause was finished. The only question now was how much damage they would do before the army was destroyed. The Keldons were massing in the interior, and if he hoped to defeat them in detail he must catch them soon.

"Rayne," Barrin called as he saw his wife leaving the lines on her runner. "Where are you going?"

Rayne looked calm as Barrin and Mageta moved closer. The general sat stiffly on his runner, his wounds still bothering him despite repeated sessions with Shalanda.

"There are reports from the forward scouts of dead and dying wildlife around the water holes," Rayne replied. "Shalanda is investigating, and I'm hauling some more equipment out to her." She patted bulging saddlebags on the back of her machine.

"Damn," Mageta said. "We'll never catch the enemy if we have to divert to find good water."

Barrin shook his head in agreement. Though the war machines did not require water, the marching soldiers did. More importantly, so did the draft animals hauling the supply wagons. The attack on watering holes was an unexpected tactic from the Keldons. Barrin hadn't expected them to use the land against the League.

A set of scouts came in from patrol. Blood leaked down from the gaskets and spotted the mechanical legs. The blades that swung out from the sides cleaned and sharpened themselves whenever they retracted.

"Run into the Keldons?" Mageta demanded before they could make a report.

"No, sir," their leader replied. "Just groups of highly aggressive parea. We have orders to kill them before they come close to the column." He spoke matter-of-factly about the "tigers of the plains."

"I know supplies are tight, but I believe that the army can afford you shooting them from a distance," Barrin said with gallows humor. The scouts laughed.

"Soon we will have proper targets," Mageta said. He massaged his arm and looked east.

* * * * *

Haddad sat at the side of the barge and watched the miles roll past. After all the dreams and plans for escape, he was finally going toward his homeland. Latulla's speech gave her the support to demand an immediate attack. Messengers had set a rendezvous point with the Keldon troops pulling back from the League advance. Latulla and Greel drafted several of the remaining land barges and loaded crates of cargo on each. The boxes were doubly sealed with both Latulla and Erissa's sigils. Haddad wondered what deviltry waited to be used against the League. He was supposedly part of a ballista crew, but in reality he was focused on when to abandon the barge.

A small scouting barge came alongside at high speed. The Keldon cavalry had been bled dry by counter raiders along the League border, and only the small barges were available to make up the lack.

"The League is advancing on the rendezvous point! At the current speed, they will engage our forward elements at least an hour before you and the main body arrive!" the captain of the barge shouted. Latulla glared as if he were personally responsible for the bad news.

"Signal all barges to advance at maximum speed," she commanded. The pilot on their barge relayed the order. The craft seemed to lower as the speed rose. Haddad could hear significantly more noise from the legs of craft, and the joints seemed to hum under the higher power load.

"Artificer, this power demand will exhaust the reservoirs in short order," the pilot said, and then he pointed at two barge slaves. "See them draining and refilling the reservoirs around the seals? Many of the craft are not carrying enough refined Heroes' Blood."

Haddad snorted. Heroes' Blood indeed. Whatever the source of tufa, he doubted it sprang from the veins of Keldons.

"Blood is blood, and with Greel's aid I can supplement the power for the craft." Latulla was matter-of-fact, but Haddad swore that her eyes rested on him. He began watching more carefully for a place to disembark.

The scouting barge thrust a batch of dispatches at the end of a long pole to Latulla's vessel, then it accelerated to the supposed military commander's craft. The fact that it stopped to inform Latulla first and obeyed the orders for high speed showed where the true power in the army lay.

Latulla was reviewing the dispatches and paused as she came across one particular report.

"The scouts have spotted numerous dead animals, particularly around waterholes." She thought for a moment and then chuckled. "They really are trying to use poison and disease."

Greel overheard her. "That would explain the deaths we have been enduring in the camp. If the League is using such methods, then it must be much weaker than you supposed." Greel sounded earnest even to Haddad's suspicious ears.

"If that is true, then their attack will be hollow." Latulla grabbed a slave from the crew and turned back toward Greel. "We will need to increase speed. I know you helped Erissa in her experiments. Do you know any way we can use this to increase speed?"

Haddad could see Greel's customary smile broaden. "I am sure that we'll think of something."

Within minutes the barges were going faster, but the League technician was appalled at the cost.

"More power," Latulla moaned, and her hands were palsied as she reached for another unwilling slave. The next victim moaned in fright, but made no other movement as Greel pushed him into Latulla's grasp. He hugged them both, and the air seemed colder as the slave sprawled down comatose, barely breathing. There were more slaves waiting their turn, and Haddad edged slightly closer to the side with each falling body.

Latulla had stopped briefly and taken on as many slaves as possible in a window of a few minutes. The other Keldon magic users now drew on her power to enhance land barge performance. Like the war manikin spell, it drained away the strength of the caster to power the machine—the difference being that a warrior in combat could power a group of manikins for tens of minutes, and already this spell was leaving a trail of bodies.

Greel assisted Latulla with the ritual, holding down the slaves as Latulla sucked the life out of them. Haddad saw that each death seemed to increase Greel's energy, and the technician knew the monster was feasting on lives once more.

Latulla shook, and another flare of energy was sent out to the fleet. The artificer became aware once more and laughed.

"So much easier than calling the power on your own," she said. "You must show me how to initiate the sacrifice without you, Greel. There is a corner of the ceremony that I can't quite see."

Greel was frowning with disappointment. He had another slave held in his arms in preparation for continuing the ceremony. He quickly schooled his face and put the slave back in the line of waiting victims. He did it with the care of a glutton saving a favorite snack for later.

Haddad was thumped on the head and spun wildly. Another scouting barge had drawn alongside, and the poled sack of dispatches had hit him. He grabbed the sack and felt great satisfaction as the warrior at the other end of the pole almost fell.

Latulla grabbed the messages with only a blow to acknowledge Haddad's aid. She searched through it hurriedly, reading each quickly before throwing it aside. Slaves gathered them up with startled lunges as some started to float overboard.

"Blimps have been sighted far ahead," she said worriedly. Despite Latulla's contempt for the League, the attacks on the colony had given her a healthy respect for League airships. "Command all magic users to start a deceptive haze." Servants quickly broke out chips for the brazier, racing each other to show they were more than fuel. Latulla looked at Greel. "Perhaps someday we can learn to use that spell for other things. For now, smoke is needed to hide us until we can engage the enemy. They won't drop bombs if they can't see us." Greel laughed as Latulla talked of deception. Smoke began to billow, and Haddad could see less and less as the haze thickened.

* * * * *

"Where are they?" Barrin hissed in frustration. The scouts could not tell him the position of the second column. They must be only minutes away, but the reinforcements had temporarily disappeared. He and Mageta exchanged glances.

"It's time," they both said.

Mageta called for battle preparations, and the men and machines began to line up. There was a rolling series of crashes as supplies were cut free from the crabs' backs, and boxes of reloads for weapons were smashed open. Ants and mantises formed into fighting blocks, and the fast runners and scout ants circled nervously in their loose formations.

"Communicator," Barrin called, as he dismounted and

walked quickly to the mage set up in a wagon. "Get me Alexi immediately." The officer didn't salute but fell immediately to work.

Soon Alexi's voice sounded. "Is there finally a target to hit?"

Barrin could hear the frustration Alexi battled all day as she waited for the enemy.

"Yes there is," he responded sharply. "The group that we've been chasing. I want you to unload half of your bombs on their column immediately. We've lost the other group, and we can't afford to have them link up. Smash them, and keep your eyes open for the incoming column."

"You've finally made me a happy woman, Barrin." Alexi left to commence the attack, and Barrin could see the blimps turning as they prepared to drop the new weapons.

Rayne rode up to Barrin. Her launcher was loaded and ready, and her flushed face momentarily entranced Barrin.

"What news of the enemy?" she demanded, eager to start the fight and perhaps finish the war. Barrin merely held his finger to his lips and then pointed to the blimps in advance of the League army.

There were nearly sixty blimps at high altitude. They had been silently following for so long that most of the army had forgotten they were there. Kashan and Mushan blimps floated lightly in the air accompanied by a huge dark airship. The *Storm Cloud* was the first Negria class to fly, and it was a bull in a field of sheep. Bombs poured from the blimps and raced for the horizon. The Keldon forces the League chased were not visible to Barrin, but he could see fireballs and streamers being thrown into the air in a vain attempt at vengeance or interception.

The bombs dropped out of sight. Even over the noise of the preparing troops, Barrin could hear the long ripping roar of explosions as each bomb laid a clutch of bomblets before settling down to roost at the collection point. He could not see them hit, but he did see the smoke from burning barges.

"Alexi, how much damage?" he demanded. The reply was hard to make out over the cheers on the other end.

"Nearly a clean sweep," Alexi replied. "Probably ninety percent of the big barges were hit and perhaps fifty percent of the small ones. They're not destroyed, but that group will be a while conducting repairs. If you want to be sure let me drop the other bays."

"No," Barrin scolded. "Find the other column. They must be close by." Time was running out, and Barrin couldn't say all that needed to be said to his wife.

"Here," he said, and took a crystal from his wallet. "I'll pulse it twice when I am going to have Alexi dump her load on the enemy. It will pulse just once to signal a flank attack." Rayne caught it as he tossed it to her. "I love you," he cried as she went back to the scouts and ant swarms. She may have said something in reply, but Barrin couldn't hear in the confusion.

Barrin's ears picked up the quickening beat of an ornithopter's wings and turned to see his private craft coming in for a landing. He rushed toward the craft, furious that Yarbo should be on the ground while an entire enemy column was missing. Shalanda dismounted and met him before he could begin yelling.

"Barrin, it's not poison, it's plague!" Shalanda cried as he nearly ran into her.

"What?" He had no idea what she was talking about. Didn't she realize a battle was about to start?

"The dead animals around the water holes were killed by disease, not poison," Shalanda explained. "When I inspected the carcasses and the water I realized that it was a disease." She took a deep breath. "I think it might be a more advanced form of the flu we spotted during the attack on Arsenal City. The League is starting to report hundreds of cases over the naval channels. It's jumping from animals to men."

"I can't believe the Keldons would do this. Don't they realize they are vulnerable too?" Barrin was enraged at the idea of disease being spread to kill whoever might be exposed.

"I don't think the Keldons are responsible," Shalanda said. "It looks far too advanced to be something of their making. The spores appear to be part organic material and part machine!"

Barrin had no time to digest this new information because the sky seemed to clear, and the missing enemy column appeared less than a mile away.

* * * * *

"Deploy the warriors and the war manikins." Urit issued the order but at Latulla's direction.

The League forces were fairly close, and Haddad wondered if he would be killed by friendly fire. Latulla had screamed murderously and pounded a slave to death at the news of the other Keldons' destruction. Her curses against the League were interspersed with promises of terrible punishment for the commanders stupid enough to be killed by the blimp attacks. A small barge brought them the news along with one of the weapons responsible. Latulla wasted no time in cracking it open, and Haddad closed his eyes in prayer, waiting for the blast the madwoman was sure to unleash. Instead the artificer dissected an almost empty shell. Haddad thought he grasped how it worked, but it was the powerstone and the command set that fascinated Latulla. She calmed almost instantly and called Greel and Iola to her for a quick conference. Whatever the result, Latulla wasted no time in calling for an attack. Once the order was relayed, she called the captain of the barge to her side.

"We need to be closer to the front of the battle to activate the weapon. Prepare to move us up with the assault forces," she directed.

"We are going nowhere until I can beg some Heroes' Blood from another barge. We have completely exhausted our supply." The captain pointed to the slaves working on the scals and reservoirs. Haddad knew what Latulla's preferred solution would be and said his good-byes to slavery.

Slipping over the side was easy. Latulla's barge had stopped sooner than the other barges, and all watchful eyes were toward the enemy. Even if he were spotted, a warrior would not throw away the battle to chase an escaped slave. He would get away and circle back to the League lines. In his excitement, he forgot that he was not escaping from a Keldon warrior but from Latulla. The pain was an ax in his side as her rage tore into him through the bracelet.

He was on the ground and a very small child could have captured him in those first moments of pain. He could smell the crushed grass he writhed in. The pain seemed to peak and then subside slightly. He moved his legs, turning his body until he could see the Keldon position. There was a growing crowd of warriors and war manikins.

Latulla's barge was almost leisurely moving toward the front of the lines. A single figure left it and began walking back toward Haddad. Had Latulla sent a slave back to retrieve her toy? It was Greel, and Haddad recognized the smile before any other features were visible.

"Thought you would take a walk, did you?" The voice was almost bantering as a boot nudged Haddad's side. "You should have known that Latulla never lets anything go once she owns it." Greel knelt and lightly slapped Haddad's arm. The prone man choked as a bolt of pain stopped him from breathing.

"I think that you know who I am," Greel said. "I think you've seen me when I am more myself." Another playful slap rocked Haddad's head.

"I must be going, but as soon as I come back, we can tell each other all about ourselves. You are Latulla's gift to me, and I always play with my presents." Greel raised his hand to slap the bracelet, and Haddad couldn't help cringing. "I'll give you a pat when I get back."

The familiar walked back, and as soon as Haddad could, he rose to his hands and knees and crawled back to the Keldon lines and the oncoming Kipamu League forces. Maybe a Keldon warrior would kill him or a League bolt would skewer him, but he was not going to remain alone in the grass waiting for that monster to return.

* * * * *

General Mageta ordered the attack to commence. There was no time to dig in, and though the Keldons were numerous, the League army was confident they could be beaten. The crabs went forth with supporting squads of infantry. A few launchers discharged, and rockets flew into the oncoming lines of men and hollow warriors. The Keldons once more had smoking embers and sticks of incense burning in their armor. The ants advanced at a trot, held back to keep the line steady. The mantises in their bright colors anchored the right side of the League line. It was growing harder to see the action as the lines closed, but Barrin could just make out Mageta at the front. The old mage waved for Yarbo to take them up as he jumped into the ornithopter.

The Keldons were closer, and a roar of thousands shook the battlefield as they charged. The League responded with its own roar. The crabs fired not rockets but oversized net rounds. The opposing Keldons and their machines were transformed into cursing, roiling barricades that continued to trap warriors. The enemy troops trampled their more unfortunate fellows as they crested the barrier, but each crab had three weapons modules and another wave of Keldons fell entangled. The infantry with the crabs settled into a sustained barrage of light rockets at the webbed forces.

The ants were not as impressive, but almost as many Keldons died when they first met. The ants discharged their single rockets, and the sheer number of launchers overwhelmed the front ranks of the Keldons. The supporting infantry was armed with only swords and bolt launchers. The ants, when they did not dismember the enemy, held them long enough to be killed by the men supporting the machines.

The mantises stayed well back to deal with any breakthroughs or to lead a new attack. The main weapons pod was loaded with a heavy rocket to bust barges, but their high heads held a single light launcher, and the rockets shot out over the League forces to kill targets of opportunity.

The crabs advanced now, and their heavy arms crushed the helpless foe. The Keldons were held in place, and Alexi called to Barrin.

"I'm in position, and you're well out of the weapons' path," she said.

"Fire on the barges!" Barrin ordered, and he sent two pulses to Rayne's crystal. Soon he would relay a single pulse, sending forces in to attack the Keldons from the rear. Victory tasted so sweet.

* * * * *

Rayne was separated from the rest of scouts. Shalanda and Jolreal had prepared a device for detecting concentrations of the blight and disease. Rayne had insisted that she be able to identify concentrations when separated from the other two. Back along the Keldons' path she had identified a trace. Like a lodestone to iron, she could feel the needle pulling her forward away from the other scouts. The trail of dead bodies behind the Keldon army showed traces, but the strongest concentration beckoned her farther and farther on. She slowed as she neared the parked barges. She wouldn't follow the trace any farther. In fact, she began a slow retreat, for the battle was too close. She needed to return to the scouts off to her right. The barge guards looked toward her, and she turned her machine. A warrior surprised her from behind, and he swung his sword, missing her by inches as she jumped her machine to the side.

"A wonderful dodge, lady!" the warrior yelled, and rushed forward, a wide grin lighting up his face. Rayne triggered her wings and opened his abdomen as she maneuvered her runner. Something like intestines poured from the wound, but the warrior did not buckle, he laughed. Huge guffaws burst from his gaping mouth as Rayne stared. The warrior hugged his sides but from the force of his laughter, not the pain of his wound. She still gripped the needle on the string. It was pointed toward the warrior, pulling at her hand.

"You're thick with the disease," she said under her breath as she unleashed her bolts at the enemy.

The warrior dodged too fast, and her shots buried themselves in the ground. He stumbled as he came at her, and she triggered her wings once more before retreating a few yards back. She ducked down as a thrown knife came at her head. It clipped her temple as she dodged, and she was stunned for the moment. Blood poured down the side of her face and then dripped down her chin, spattering on the runner controls as she tried to stay conscious.

"My name is Greel, pet," the monster said. Another knife was in his hands, but instead of throwing it, he used it to cut the tubes of flesh still hanging from his body. "First you cut me with blades then you cut me with words. You really can't expect me to ignore that bad behavior."

He stalked toward her, and she shook her head, hoping the pain would burn through the fog in her brain. She needed to live through this. Her hand grasped the stock of her launcher as she backed and turned her machine. If she ran, the bestial creature in front of her would put a knife in her back. End this now and get back to your friends, she thought. Then she felt the crystal in her pocket vibrate twice. Barrin was ordering Alexi to attack. The blimps would drop their bombs any second and she might still be in the path of destruction. More barge crew guards were coming, and time was running out. Then Barrin's crystal pulsed once more.

"It appears playtime is almost over, darling," Greel said. "If I don't kill you now you might say something embarrassing about me. My feelings are far too tender for that." He looked quickly to see how close the Keldons were, and in that instant Rayne charged.

Every bolt she had left snapped through the air as the runner closed. Two caught Greel's legs, and he fell as his limbs gave way. Rayne drew her launcher, determined to put a rocket into the monster. Then there was a great explosion, and her runner seemed to fall away underneath her. Rayne flew from the saddle as her mount lost all control. At high speed Rayne approached the ground, turning in midair. She came down on her side. Her arm and ribs shattered as they contacted the soil, and her body flipped over and hit once more. Her pelvis and legs broke as she slid to a stop. The pain hit her like a sledgehammer, and she gasped. She was facing Greel, and the monster was still smiling, his flesh remolding itself on his legs.

"I do believe I am going to win the race to get up first," Greel said in a jolly tone. "I think broken toys are the most fun, but don't worry. With an audience I am always quick."

Rayne couldn't move. She felt cold and knew shock was killing her. Her opponent vanished from her thoughts as she tried to move. Nothing seemed to work, and the enemy was closing too fast. She was going to die. She thought of her daughter and the decades she had been with Barrin. So many years of happiness and love.

"It was a good life," she whispered, and closed her eyes.

* * * * *

The discharge of the Keldon weapon was sudden and without warning. Barrin watched for signs of the fire swallows, but he never detected Latulla's weapon. She had developed it on Keld after gaining access to captured League machines.

A wave of disruption spread in all directions from the Keldon barges. It battered artifacts and power drained from crystals in a sudden surge. Barrin was deaf and blind as energy flared all around him and drowned his senses.

Yarbo cursed as the ornithopter lost power but managed to coax the machine into a glide. On the ground, the power discharge was far more deadly. The League machines stopped. The crabs stopped swinging their arms, the ants fell in heaps, and the mantises teetered in place. Alexi had begun her attack run with bloodthirsty anticipation, but her bombs fell straight to the ground instead of gliding toward the land barges. They impacted with dull thuds, breaking into pieces, unnoticed by anyone except the incredulous crews that had hoped to win a battle.

As war machines lost power on the battlefield, the Keldons fell on the League forces, but these were not the same soldiers who had routed before at turns of fortune.

"Fire and close!" screamed Mageta as warriors tried to cut him down. The soldiers emptied launchers, and the front ranks swarmed over their opponents with short swords and knives. The war manikins were slow as the magical attack affected them. Soldiers trampled them to reach the warriors powering the Keldon artifacts. A bloody line of battle swayed back and forth as Mageta continued to cut down the enemy, favoring his injured arm but still gutting the warriors who closed with him.

Yarbo regained power in a sudden rush. The more advanced Tolarian technology recovered faster, and they were farther from the generator. He climbed as other machines on the plain below twitched. Barrin remembered that Rayne was to attack just before power was lost, and he pushed Yarbo aside from the controls. He sent the machine into a steep dive over the battlefield.

He spotted her runner as he flared over the mass of men and machines. The land barge crews had charged toward the main battle, but several dozen were still behind the main battle. Barrin saw Rayne's machine sprawled from a fall.

Barrin flew the ornithopter into the ground. Yarbo was knocked unconscious, but Barrin ignored him as he kicked his way free of the cabin. The Keldons ran at him yelling. Barrin raised his hands but not in surrender. Like a scythe, lightning poured from the wizard's hands, spearing into the helmets of the enemy. The continuous flare of power waved from side to side. Heads exploded, sundering flash-heated helmets. Warriors ducked but still charged forward. Barrin had aimed high to avoid hitting his wife, but now slow arcs of flame fluttered through the air and settled on the charging warriors. They turned to fiery pillars as Barrin hurried toward his wife's machine, still hoping to be in time. The warriors between him and the runner were piles of ash. He reached the fallen machine and saw Rayne's body. It was deformed, nearly crushed. Barrin slowed to a crawl. His eyes took in her broken legs and the pool of blood from her torso—her headless torso. He dropped to his knees and screamed. They had taken his beloved's head. They had destroyed her body.

"They're dead," he hissed through gritted teeth. "They'll all burn."

"There isn't enough rage and hate in the world to burn me," someone chortled.

Behind Barrin, Greel was getting to his feet. Barrin's fires had burned into its body, but the flesh was healing as Barrin looked on.

"I killed her, and now I get to kill you."

"There's always enough hate," Barrin rasped, stretching his senses deep into the bowels of the creature. It was disease and death made manifest. Like a pool of quicksand, it tried to suck his spirit into oblivion. Greel picked up a sword and closed with the kneeling wizard. The energy that flew from Barrin's fingers was not a mighty bolt of lightning but a cascade of sparks. Greel laughed as it soaked into him, but this energy attacked and disrupted the very cells and fluids of the monster's body. The blood and flesh separated into wildly different parts. The monster gasped and stumbled closer, raising the sword to kill but unable to travel forward on disassembled legs. Bones and a spray of liquid landed in front of Barrin, searing into the old wizard's legs. He ignored the pain.

The guards from the barges were closing on him, believing him spent. Once more he sent forth a blade of lightning, but now it moved at knee level and severed legs. The screams of agony were a salve to Barrin's pain. He rose to his feet and looked over the field of cripples. It wasn't enough. He looked toward the sky, and his mind raced higher and higher. Then high over the ground he found what he was looking for—a river of air that circled Dominaria. Like a man filling a bucket, he dipped into the jet stream and brought it toward the earth. His mind fell with the wind, pushing it faster and faster. The blast of air scooped the wounded men into the sky, their screams drowned out by the wind. They dribbled out of the sky, icy corpses as Barrin returned the power to the heavens.

It still wasn't enough. The Keldons near the barges were frozen numb as they stared at Barrin. Perhaps these would ease his rage. The wizard began advancing, and the warriors ran toward the battle. Better to fight men and metal machines than Barrin.

"Craven scum!" Barrin yelled. "Come and die!" He sent a wave of nightmarish illusion to turn them back, driving the warriors where he could see their faces as he killed them. Monsters appeared in the Keldon lines and fell on the enemy. Mageta looked at a huge dragon dripping slime. It loomed over the Keldons and struck at them, spreading fear. Warriors killed each other as they fought the Tolarian wizard's deceit, but few ran back toward the barges, preferring monsters to wizard.

Barrin was aware of the battlefield now. Mageta was closing with the last of the reserves, and the machines had reactivated. Barrin's attack spread panic among the Keldons, and more warriors were cut down trying to flee.

The charging of the fire swallows in the barges was a shout across his mind. The Keldon commanders were going to unleash a wave of destruction that might finish the League even if it savaged their own army. He lacked the power to stop the attack, but they had killed his wife. He could not rest as long as a single one of them lived.

Barrin stumbled toward the barges, his mind and powers preceding his body. Only a few of the barges were ready to launch, and Barrin could feel the instructions trickling down to the reanimated birds. It was his voice—his will—that filled the tiny weapons. His mind followed the links already established between the barges.

"Fly here, roost here." It was a cajoling cry that silenced the cold instructions delivered by a Keldon artificer. Whether it was the intensity of Barrin's will or the hatred he channeled he did not know, but the birds responded, and on release they rose into the air and fell upon the Keldons and their barges. Wooden shells burned, and Barrin enjoyed it. The smell of burning flesh was a cloud over the battlefield, assaulting his brain. This scent had always sickened him, but now he sought it, craved it. He walked among the barges, weak and wavering.

The enraged wizard stooped and plucked a sword from a dead warrior's hand. A few still lived and fled from the battle. He fell upon them, striking weakly at warriors but ignoring the slaves. An easy target, the Keldons fled from him in mindless fear. At last he reached a collapsed barge. The legs were blown free, and it had fallen on its side. It had crushed the Keldon commanders and been abandoned by everyone. A thick layer of soot was covering everything, and Barrin wiped his eyes. Someone was trapped by the barge. He moved forward and saw that it was a Keldon woman, her face rigid with pain and a cane clutched in her hand.

"Dig me free!" ordered Latulla, blinking rapidly to clear her tearing eyes. "Hurry, slave, or I'll have you beaten." The symmetry of it was so perfect, and Barrin came forward without hesitation.

* * * * *

It was almost an hour before General Mageta and a platoon of marines finally reached him. The Keldons were routed and still running from pursuing groups of cavalry and steel ants. Mageta was wounded again, three fingers showing on a bandaged hand and his chest bare and wrapped in bloody cotton. Barrin leaned against a smoking barge shell, a headless Keldon at his feet. Mageta rushed to express his grief, for he knew how Rayne had died.

"Barrin," Mageta said. "We've won the battle and shattered Keldon power on Jamuraa. The enemy is running, and Teferi's forces march to cut off their escape." Barrin said not a word at the news but continued to stare at Latulla's broken body.

"What should we do now?" Mageta said, trying to jar Barrin out of his silence. "There are still warriors on the plains and small detachments across Jamuraa. What are your orders?"

Barrin leaned against the side of a burning barge with his eyes closed. Decades of loving memories tried to fill the gap Rayne left when she died.

His voice was as cold as ice. "No quarter."

* * * * *

Haddad lay at the rear of the battlefield. Despite his fears, he was never noticed during the fighting, his pain and suffering lost against the backdrop of others dying. He witnessed parts of the battle, but every explosion and scream was muffled by his own agony. How long he lay there, he couldn't say. Finally a voice penetrated his mind.

"Where are you wounded?"

It was a handsome woman speaking with kindness and concern. He was so close to home that the pain seemed almost gone.

"I am Haddad. A soldier of the League." He had to pause and muster strength before he could continue. "I was captured months ago and made a slave. I have important information."

Latulla's bracelet sent even more pain into Haddad's body as he tried to betray her. He hammered his head into the ground as his bones seemed to twist and grate.

"What's wrong?" Shalanda had come searching for wounded and maybe information. This former slave appeared to be both, but he might die before he could tell her anything.

"It's the bracelet. It's killing me. Please destroy it. Please!" The need was overwhelming in Haddad's voice, and at last she agreed.

Shalanda breathed and focused on Haddad's pain. The bright core of it nearly blinded her. She lay her hands on the bracelet and could feel the tension barely restrained. Just a gentle nudge should dislodge it.

The bracelet unwound itself in a spray of blood and twisting wire. The device had sent wires up and down Haddad's side, and they were expelled violently in response to Shalanda's ministrations. The shock reverberated in her mind, and she could feel herself falling toward the ground. If she hit, her mind and spirit would break, and she prayed to fall forever.

Haddad could only see the sky and the end of pain. At last, a free man. He closed his eyes and the world went away.

EPILOGUE

Teferi sat in his palace on his island. He retreated here to be alone after the destruction of the Keldon colony. Almost all the Keldon's warriors had been on the plains meeting Barrin in battle. Teferi and his marines had rescued thousands of slaves as the last die-hard Keldons had been rooted out. The fighting was over when he finally viewed the interior battlefield.

Rayne was dead. A friend and wife of a friend. Immortality became more bitter each time someone close died and bitterest of all when an old friend died. Barrin had won but cared nothing for his victory. He only demanded a cargo dirigible be sent from Tolaria to pick up his wife and her volunteers. Shalanda, Rayne's aide, was in a coma and no one was certain why, though Teferi feared it had something to do with the disease sweeping the continent. Perhaps it would burn out, but the planeswalker knew that was too optimistic.

More people were dying from this mysterious plague, and Teferi considered the old rantings of his one-time teacher, Urza Planeswalker. If what Urza had been preparing for all these years actually came to pass, there would be even more death in the coming months. Teferi looked into the darkness and swore an oath.

"I will guard my lands and the people who look to me, but I will never follow Urza. I will make my own way."

Tales of Dominaria

LEGIONS

Onslaught Cycle, Book II
J. Robert King

In the blood and sand of the arena, two foes clash in a titanic battle.

EMPEROR'S FIST

Magic Legends Cycle Two, Book II
Scott McGough

War looms above the Edemi Islands, casting the deep and dread shadow of the Emperor's Fist.

SCOURGE

Onslaught Cycle, Book III
J. Robert King

From the fiery battles of the Cabal, a new god has arisen, one whose presence drives her worshipers to madness.

THE MONSTERS OF MAGIC

An anthology edited by J. Robert King

From Dominaria to Phyrexia, monsters fill the multiverse, and tales of the most popular ones fill these pages.

CHAMPION'S TRIAL

Magic Legends Cycle Two, Book III
Scott McGough

To restore his honor, the onetime champion of Madara must battle his own corrupt empire and the monster on the throne.

The Four Winds Saga

Only one can claim the Throne of Rokugan.

WIND OF JUSTICE

Third Scroll
Rich Wulf

Naseru, the most cold-hearted and scheming of the royal heirs, will stop at nothing to sit upon the Throne of Rokugan. But when dark forces in the City of Night threaten his beloved Empire, Naseru must learn to wield the most unlikely weapon of all — justice.

WIND OF TRUTH

Fourth Scroll
Ree Soesbee

Sezaru, one of the most powerful wielders of magic in all Rokugan, has never desired his father's throne, but destiny calls to the son of Toturi. Here, in the final volume of the Four Winds Saga, all will be decided.

Now available:

THE STEEL THRONE

Prelude
Edward Bolme

WIND OF HONOR

First Scroll
Ree Soesbee

WIND OF WAR

Second Scroll
Jess Lebow

R.A. Salvatore's War of the Spider Queen

Chaos has come to the Underdark like never before.

New York Times best-seller!

CONDEMNATION, Book III
Richard Baker

The search for answers to Lolth's silence uncovers only more complex questions. Doubt and frustration test the boundaries of already tenuous relationships as members of the drow expedition begin to turn on each other. Sensing the holes in the armor of Menzoberranzan, a new, dangerous threat steps in to test the resolve of the Jewel of the Underdark, and finds it lacking.

Now in paperback!

DISSOLUTION, Book I
Richard Lee Byers

When the Queen of the Demonweb Pits stops answering the prayers of her faithful, the delicate balance of power that sustains drow civilization crumbles. As the great Houses scramble for answers, Menzoberranzan herself begins to burn.

INSURRECTION, Book II
Thomas M. Reid

The effects of Lolth's silence ripple through the Underdark and shake the drow city of Ched Nasad to its very foundations. Trapped in a city on the edge of oblivion, a small group of drow finds unlikely allies and a thousand new enemies.